An enjoyable read, where love grows strong while hardships aim to chip away at what Sallie and Manfred hold dear.

—CINDY WOODSMALL
NEW YORK TIMES BEST-SELLING AUTHOR

A beautiful story about the tender tenacity of love and the sweet stubbornness of faith-drenched hope.

—TAMERA ALEXANDER
USA TODAY BEST-SELLING AUTHOR OF *TO WHISPER HER NAME* AND *A LASTING IMPRESSION*

A heart-wrenching story of sacrificial love set in the post–Civil War turmoil that plagued our nation.

—DIANN MILLS
CHRISTY AWARD–WINNER AND AUTHOR OF *THE CHASE* AND *THE SURVIVOR*

Love Stays True

THE HOMEWARD JOURNEY
BOOK ONE

Love Stays True

THE HOMEWARD JOURNEY

BOOK ONE

MARTHA ROGERS

REALMS

Most CHARISMA HOUSE BOOK GROUP products are available at special quantity discounts for bulk purchase for sales promotions, premiums, fund-raising, and educational needs. For details, write Charisma House Book Group, 600 Rinehart Road, Lake Mary, Florida 32746, or telephone (407) 333-0600.

LOVE STAYS TRUE by Martha Rogers
Published by Realms
Charisma Media/Charisma House Book Group
600 Rinehart Road
Lake Mary, Florida 32746
www.charismahouse.com

Scripture quotations are from the King James Version of the Bible.

This is a work of fiction. The characters in this book are fictitious unless they are historical figures explicitly named. Otherwise, any resemblance to actual people, whether living or dead, is coincidental.

Cover design by Bill Johnson

Visit the author's website at www.marthawrogers.com.

Library of Congress Cataloging-in-Publication Data:
Rogers, Martha, 1936-
Love stays true / Martha Rogers. -- First edition.
   pages cm. -- (The Homeward Journey ; Book One)
   ISBN 978-1-62136-236-4 (trade paper) -- ISBN 978-1-
62136-237-1 (ebook)
  1. Homecoming--Fiction. I. Title.
  PS3618.O4655L68 2013
  813'.6--dc23

                                              2013003596

First edition

13 14 15 16 17 — 9 8 7 6 5 4 3 2 1
Printed in the United States of America

To my Whiteman cousins—Milton, Patty,
Kay, Susan, Julia, Sarah, Jolly, Linda,
Timmie, Holly, and Tom—and my sister,
Betty, and my brother, John, who continue
the legacy begun by Manfred and Sallie

ACKNOWLEDGMENTS

Thank you to:

- The wonderful people at the courthouse, Grace Church, and the historical society in St. Francisville, Louisiana, who answered my questions and showed me where to find the documents I needed to put together the story of Manfred and Sallie.

- My writing buddies DiAnn Mills, Janice Thompson, and Kathleen Y'Barbo Turner, who were the first readers of this story and gave me great suggestions.

- My Serendipity Life Bible Studies Class at First Baptist Church in Houston for their love and continual prayer support when I'm on a deadline. You ladies are the greatest prayer warriors I know.

- My extended family of cousins and now deceased aunts with whom I had great fun tracking down leads, listening to stories from the past, and putting together the information we found on our excursions.

- My editors Lori Vanden Bosch and Deborah Moss, who give such wonderful advice and help my stories to be stronger and tighter. You ladies rock.

- My agent Tamela Hancock Murray and Steve Laube for having faith in me and taking care of me.

- My husband, Rex, who chauffeurs me all over for speaking engagements and book signings and puts up with my being "holed" up in my office for long periods of time.

- My Lord and Savior, who gives me the words to write and a long life to fulfill my dreams. To Him be all glory and praise.

Who went in the way before you, to search you out a place to pitch your tents in, in fire by night, to shew you by what way ye should go, and in a cloud by day.

—Deuteronomy 1:33

PROLOGUE

THE GLOW FROM the lantern cast an eerie light into the darkness. Huddled in the root cellar with her mother, sister, and two servants, Sallie clutched the cold metal of the pistol in one hand and cradled a musket in the crook of her other arm. Shouts, gunshots, and screams permeated the walls of their sanctuary, sending fear into her heart and onto the faces of the others. *Lord, keep us safe!* Sallie prayed over and over.

The Union soldiers had appeared so suddenly from around the curve from town that Sallie's father only had time to shove the guns into her hands and push them all down under the kitchen into the root cellar. Then he'd left with her brothers Will and Tom to fight.

Her sister, Hannah, sat wrapped in Mama's arms as she rocked back and forth with quiet words of assurance. Their servants Lettie and her mother, Flora, sat hunched together with encircling arms, fear etched across their dark faces. All of them looked to Sallie for their safety and survival.

How could she save them when she'd never shot a gun at anyone? Although Papa had taught her to handle firearms, she'd never shot at much but a jar or two out in the back pasture. Aiming at a man meant something else entirely.

She prayed for Papa, Will, and Tom to be all right as they defended their home against the invaders. George, Flora's husband, and Moses, another servant, had also stayed with Papa to do battle. Others from the area would join in with

Papa to ward off the enemy, but were they enough to save the homes and people living here?

The war had raged for four years, and now it had come to their yard. What had only been stories from young men returning from battle now became very real, and it shook Sallie to the very core of her being. Would she have the courage to do what must be done if the enemy found them here in the cellar? That was one question she didn't care to have answered.

After what seemed like an eternity, but had to have been less than an hour, Sallie could stand the suspense no longer. Against her mother's wild look of warning and shaking of her head, Sallie ascended the stairs with Lettie right behind her. Two young women, one white and one black, ready to face whatever lay upstairs. The cellar opened into the house just beyond the kitchen into a coatroom of sorts, and Sallie pushed up the door just enough to see around the room. All was quiet, so she opened the door fully and climbed out.

Still clutching guns in both hands, she tiptoed around the corner to the kitchen. A figure loomed before her. Sallie yelped and dropped the shotgun, which clattered onto the wood floor. The figure turned with something in his hand, and Sallie closed her eyes, raised the pistol with two hands, and pulled the trigger. *Blam!*

Lettie screamed. Sallie opened her eyes to find a boy clutching his side, his eyes wide open. Blood streamed between his fingers before he fell forward and landed only a few feet from Sallie.

She raced to his side and turned him over to find eyes empty of life. Frantic, her eyes darted around. Then settled. A loaf of bread, one bite taken out, lay near the body.

Her throat closed to the scream lodged there. She reached out a shaking hand, and Lettie took it. "Lettie, it was only a loaf of bread. He's just a boy. What have I done? What have I done?"

Tears poured from her eyes, but noise from outside sent fear racing through her blood again, and she grabbed up the musket. Papa had loaded it for her, but she prayed she wouldn't have to use it. Then another soldier burst through the door. This one held a gun and yanked his arm up to aim it, but Sallie fired her gun first. The shot hit the arm that held his weapon.

The soldier clutched his wound and ran from the building. Sallie sat down hard on the floor, her hands trembling. She thrust the gun away from her and began to sob.

A gasp from behind her sent Sallie scrambling for the gun, but it was just her mother. Mama surveyed the downed soldier, a hand over her mouth. Flora followed close behind, saw what had happened, and quickly turned to shield Hannah from the sight. For a moment they all stood in stunned silence, unsure what to do next.

Just then Papa shouted from the yard. "Amanda, Sallie, hurry! I have a carriage for you."

As if a spell had been broken, Sallie got up slowly, keeping her eyes resolutely away from the downed soldier. Flora kept Hannah's head buried in her shoulder, with Mama too shielding her from the sight of the soldier. Without speaking, Sallie followed the others out the door to find Tom in the driver's seat of the family carriage. The women scrambled up behind him.

Papa had time only to quickly clasp Mama's hand. "Tom will take you to Grandma Woodruff's while Will and I stay to fight. We will join you as soon as we think it's safe." He pointed away from the house. "Tom, go that way and then swing back around. Run the horses fast as you can. Sallie, keep an eye out for soldiers."

Sallie could only nod as Papa slapped the horses and sent them racing away. But no matter how far they went, the image of the bloody soldier left behind on that kitchen floor would forever haunt her.

CHAPTER 1

COLD AIR CHILLED his arms, and a sharp object poked at his cheek. Manfred Whiteman reached down to pull a ragged blanket up over his arms and brushed away the straw scratching his face. A few moments later a sudden brightness aroused him again. His lids opened to a slit. Slivers of sunlight peeked through the tiny windows and dispersed the shadows of the night.

He shut his eyes against the sun's rays, but sleep would not return. He lay still in the quiet of the new morning and sensed a difference in the air that settled over him like a cloak of peace. Raising his head, he glanced around the room. The same familiar stench of wounds, dirty hay, unwashed bodies, and death permeated the air, but in it all the difference vibrated. Something had happened, he could sense it, but nothing unusual appeared in the confines of the prison barracks.

After being captured in the Battle of Nashville in December, he, his younger brother Edwin, and other prisoners had made the long march from Nashville to Louisville, Kentucky. From there they were transferred to Camp Chase in Ohio. Then, in the first week of February, they had been loaded onto trains like cattle and sent to Point Lookout, Maryland, a prison housing nearly fifty thousand men. Upon their arrival the captured soldiers had been stripped of everything personal, and as the days progressed, hundreds of men died. Manfred mourned the loss of friends but thanked the Lord every day for sparing his life, as well as the life of his brother.

Edwin lay sleeping on the pallet next to him, curled on his side as usual. Others still slept, their snores filling the air with sound. No use in trying to sleep now. Manfred's stomach rumbled with hunger, but most likely the only breakfast would be hard tack or biscuit.

Several weeks ago an officer with the rank of general had visited. For some reason the general had asked Manfred about the one thing he would most like to have. When Manfred answered he wanted his Bible, the man had been somewhat taken aback. Still, he'd managed to find the Bible and Manfred's journal, which he returned.

Manfred now pulled that worn journal from beneath his dirty mat. The almost ragged book, his lifeline for the past three years, fell open. Manfred wrote.

April 10, 1865

> *Three more died the night before last.*
> *The nearly full moon shining through the*
> *windows gave me light to see. I took one*
> *man's shoes and left him with my holey worn-*
> *out ones. He won't need shoes, but I will.*
> *Took his socks and another man's for me*
> *and Edwin. God, I never dreamed I would*
> *do such a thing, but we are desperately in*
> *need. Please forgive me. Help Edwin and me*
> *to get out of here and get home safely. I so*
> *desperately need to see Sallie and my family.*

The scrape of wood against wood echoed in the room. Union soldiers, making their usual morning inspection, checked for any who may have died during the night. Manfred shoved the journal under his mat just before the door thudded against the wall and the guards' shoes clomped on the wooden floors. He turned on his side once again to feign sleep. The blunt toe of the sergeant's boot kicked Manfred's hip and sent a sharp pain through his leg. He grunted in response and raised his head to let the sergeant know he was alive. When the man passed, Manfred sat up on his mat and stretched his legs out in front of him to relieve the usual early-morning stiffness.

Others awakened, and their groans filled the air as they rose to sit on their bedding. Manfred waited for breakfast, not knowing if he would even get rations this morning. The guards exited carrying the bodies of the souls who didn't make it through the night.

Manfred voiced a silent prayer for the boys and their families who would receive the news of the death of their loved ones. He bit his lip. He and Edwin had to survive. They had too much life to live, but then so had the ones just taken away. What if God chose not to spare him or Edwin? No, he wouldn't think of that. Instead he filled his mind with Scripture verses memorized as a child. God's Word stored in his heart gave him the comfort and hope he needed to survive each day.

A little later the guards returned and ordered them to the part of the cookhouse where they would eat what the cooks passed off as food. Manfred accepted the cup of what the men called "slop water" coffee and a hard biscuit that would have to suffice until they brought a lunch of greasy water soup. Weeks ago the putrid smells of death, the filth in the camp, and the lousy food sickened him, but now he barely noticed.

Manfred managed to eat half his biscuit and drink a few sips from his cup then leaned toward the man on his right. "Here, James. You take the rest of mine. You need it more than I do."

The man clasped a trembling hand around the cup and reached for the biscuit with his other. A few drops sloshed over the rim. "Thank you, Manfred. You're a true friend." He stuffed the biscuit into his mouth and lifted the cup to his lips to gulp down the last dregs of liquid. With a nod to Manfred, the young soldier returned the cup.

After they were sent back to their quarters, Manfred breathed deeply and almost choked on the rancid air. What he wouldn't give for a bath, shave, and haircut. A good meal wouldn't hurt anything either. His nose had mostly numbed itself to his body odor, but dirt and scum became more visible every day. When he had tried to wash his shirt, the brackish water left stains he couldn't remove.

When would this nightmare come to an end? A question unanswered for these four long months of marching, fighting, and incarceration. Too many lay ill and dying. The end had to come soon.

He glanced once again at his brother, who cushioned his head on his crossed palms with his eyes closed. Manfred reached over to touch the boy's shoulder. "You all right, little brother?"

Edwin didn't open his eyes. "Yeah, I'm okay. Just hungry. I dreamed of home last night and Bessie's cooking. When I close my eyes, I can see her and Momma in the kitchen, Bessie up to her elbows in flour making biscuits and Momma stirring the fire and making grits."

"Shh, brother, you're making me hungry too." Manfred pulled what was left of his jacket tighter about his thin body. "We've been captive four months, but it seems a lifetime. Home, our parents, and Sallie may as well be a million miles away."

Edwin sat up and pounded his fist into the straw. "Yeah, and sometimes I think we'll never get back there." He stretched his legs out on his mat, hugging what passed for a pillow. "I sure pray I'll get to see Peggy again soon."

Manfred positioned his body to sit squarely on his mat. "Soon as we're home, I'm asking Mr. Dyer for Sallie's hand in marriage, that is, if she still wants me. No telling who she's met since I've been gone."

"I wouldn't worry about that if I were you, big brother. Sallie loves you." He smacked his fist into the open palm of his other hand. "I just want to be out of here and out there where the action is, fighting with Lee. They told us the Yanks are fighting Lee in Virginny, and that's just across the river. Lee has to beat them Yanks. We'll be hearing about it any day now. I just know it."

Manfred simply nodded. He didn't agree with his brother, but Edwin cared more about the war than Manfred. At this point Manfred had resigned himself to waiting out the war.

If only he could somehow communicate with Sallie and let her know he was alive. Almost a year had passed since he'd seen her last summer and six months since he'd been able to send a letter to her or received one. From his Bible he removed her last letter and opened it, being careful to handle it as little as possible. Already small holes appeared in the creases from his folding it so often. She had written from her grandfather's home last fall before he'd gone to Nashville. He prayed her family was safe there in St. Francisville, Louisiana. He'd been at Port Hudson, Louisiana, two years ago and would have been involved in that skirmish in May, but he'd been among the ones in the brigade deployed elsewhere in March. Major General had been sure he had enough soldiers to turn back the siege, but that had not been the case, and Port Hudson fell into Union hands in early July.

That battle took place too close to his hometown of Bayou Sara and had even damaged Grace Church up at St.

Francisville. He'd seen the damage on his furlough home. His two older brothers had been captured at Port Hudson, and Manfred had no idea where they were now.

St. Francisville may have been spared, but it had been a close call for Sallie's grandparents and the other citizens of the small town. He held the worn paper to his lips. With God's help he'd get home and claim Sallie for his bride.

The hair on the back of his neck bristled, and goose bumps popped out on his arms. The foreboding feeling from earlier wouldn't leave and swept over him now even stronger, as though he sat on the edge of something powerful looming in the day ahead.

St. Francisville, Louisiana

Sallie Dyer sat at her dressing table running a brush through her mass of tangled curls. Tears blurred her image in the mirror, and she grimaced as the bristles caught in another snarl. She dropped the brush onto her lap.

"Lettie, what am I to do? Not knowing about Manfred is too painful to bear." She scrunched a handful of auburn hair against her head. "Nothing's going right. I can't even brush my hair. I hate the war and…" Her voice trailed off, and she dropped her gaze to the floor then turned toward Lettie. "What am I to do?"

The housemaid clucked her tongue and fluffed the pillows on the walnut four-poster bed. "I don't know, Miss Sallie. I hate the war too. Too many are dyin' out there."

Lettie's skirt swished as she crossed the room. She picked up the discarded brush and began smoothing out the mass of curls. "You know, Miss Sallie, you have the prettiest red hair in all of Louisiana."

Sallie lifted her tear-stained eyes and found Lettie's reflection in the mirror staring back.

"You got to have courage. God is takin' care of Mr. Manfred."

"Oh, but the waiting is so hard." Sallie swiped her fingers across her wet cheeks. In a letter last fall Manfred had written that he was headed to Nashville. Stories coming back from that area spoke of the volumes of soldiers killed at Franklin and then up at Nashville in December. Reports said the surviving young men had been taken prisoner, but no one knew to which prison.

"Lettie, do you truly believe Manfred will come home?"

"Yes, Miss Sallie, I do, and when he comes, you'll be ready and waitin'." In a few minutes Lettie's skilled fingers had tamed the unruly ringlets and secured them with a silver clasp at Sallie's neck.

"Thank you. I'm all out of sorts this morning. Here it is April, and I haven't heard a word since November." Her fears tumbled back into her mind. "Too many have died, and I don't want Manfred…" She couldn't utter the words. Saying them might make them true.

She pressed her lips together and pushed a few stray tendrils from her face. She had to get her fears under control. She once believed God would give her the peace He promised, but no matter how hard she prayed, no answers came. God had abandoned her on that awful day last week when she had killed that young man. He hadn't protected her that afternoon, and now her prayers fell on deaf ears.

Lettie secured the wayward strands with the others under the clips. "Now, Miss Sallie, I done told you we got to believe they're alive and comin' home. We can't do nothin' about the war. Your mama and grandma need you to be strong. When Mr. Manfred gets home, he'll be courtin' you right proper like. You'll see."

Lettie must be more concerned than she let on. She only slipped back to the dialect of her family when worried. Sallie turned and wrapped her arms around the dark-skinned girl's thin waist. "I want to believe you, I really do, but it's almost more than I can bear."

After blinking her eyes to clear them, Sallie stared into the dark brown eyes of her friend. Lettie had been with Sallie since childhood, and they shared so much life with each other. If it had not been for Lettie and her mother, Sallie might never have regained her sanity after the incident in Mississippi that brought them all to St. Francisville.

A chill passed through her body at the memory of the day they had fled from their home. Sallie's last act of defense would be one that would stay with her the rest of her life. Even now she could see the young soldier with the red oozing from his chest. It was the first time she'd ever seen a dead person, and now, only a week later, the image would not leave her, fresh as the day it happened.

The young servant's brow furrowed, and she pursed her lips. "Are you thinking about what happened back home?"

How well Lettie knew her. Sallie sniffed and blinked away the tears.

"Then you best stop it. What you did had to be done, and we both know it. You saved all our lives."

It didn't matter that Lettie spoke true. The images of war could not be erased from Sallie's mind. "I just want this war to end."

"Well now, I want that too, but it's all in God's hands. But think how Mr. Charles and Mr. Henry got back from the war only a few weeks ago. Theo's back home too, so you have to believe the other two will come home before long."

True. Of the five Whiteman brothers, only Edwin and Manfred remained unaccounted for. Charles and Henry Whiteman had been taken prisoner at Port Hudson but exchanged and sent home. Even Theo now sat safe at home after his last escapade revealed him too young to be in the army. She must have hope for Manfred and Edwin.

Lettie lifted the edge of her white apron and patted Sallie's cheeks dry. "There now, Miss Sallie. It's all goin' to be fine. It'll all be over soon. I just know it. I feel it in my bones. Besides, Easter's a comin', and that means a new season, new life, and new hope."

"You and Mama, the eternal optimists, but I love you for it. You always know how to make me feel better." Sallie breathed deeply and reached for a green ribbon to secure in her hair.

She would get through this day just as she had all the ones since Manfred left. Then the memory of what she overheard between her father and mother last night drained away her determination. She peered up at Lettie. "I need to tell you something." Sallie squeezed the hand now clasped in hers.

At Lettie's solemn nod Sallie took a deep breath and revealed her worry. "Last night I couldn't sleep, and I heard Papa come in from his trip back to Woodville. I sneaked downstairs to see him, but he was in the parlor talking to Grandpa."

Sallie's lips trembled. "Our house in Woodville is ruined. The Yanks ransacked the place and took all kinds of things from our home. Papa said they'd left it in shambles. Mama's beautiful things. Oh, Lettie, it's just terrible." After Sallie and the other women had fled the land, Papa and her brothers stayed behind until the next day, then joined the rest of the family in St. Francisville. He'd gone back to Woodville a few days ago, a twenty-five mile journey, when he heard the Yankees had moved on north.

Lettie pressed her hand against her cheek, her eyes open wide. "Oh, I'm sorry. Your poor mama. It's so sad. No wonder you're feelin' blue this morning."

Sallie squeezed Lettie's hand again and for the next few moments sat in silence. Lettie understood her better than anyone else. The servant girl knew her deepest secrets and could be trusted to keep them.

"You are such a comfort. I don't know how I'd get through these days without you to share my worries."

Lettie patted Sallie's hand. "We've been together too long and been through too much for me not to be with you." She stepped back. "Come, now, let's get you dressed. Your family will be waitin', and you know your grandpa doesn't like cold eggs or tardy children, even if you are his favorite."

That statement brought a bit of smile. She did love Grandpa Woodruff, but he could be gruff when the occasion arose. She hastened over to a bench by the bed and picked up a green and white print cotton dress. Lettie grasped it and slipped her arms up inside it, and Sallie held up her arms.

"I believe Mama invited the Whiteman family for supper one night soon. I'm anxious to speak to Manfred's mother. Perhaps she's heard from him."

The dress billowed about her as Lettie placed it over Sallie's shoulders. She pulled the bodice up over arms and let the full skirt fall down over her hips and the myriad number of petticoats. At least Mama and Grandma didn't require her to wear a corset or hoops with her day dresses. Lettie's nimble fingers went to work on the buttons lined up the back.

"I think you lost more weight, missy. This dress is looser than it was last week. You sure don't even need your corset.

You have to eat more." She peered over Sallie's shoulder into the mirror and shook her head.

Looking over her shoulder, Sallie smoothed the dress around her waist. She gathered the wrinkles from the excess fabric. "It is big, but I'm just not hungry." At Lettie's stern gaze she added, "But I'll try to eat more."

Lettie sniffed the air. "If that aroma coming from the kitchen is what I think it is, my mammy's ham and eggs should do the trick. She'll have biscuits and gravy too."

Sallie nodded. "I promise I'll eat some of everything this morning." A promise she would try to keep, especially with her grandmother's and Flora's cooking being so delicious.

The two girls locked arms and walked down the stairs together. At the bottom Lettie headed for the kitchen to help her mother. Sallie forced a smile to her lips and went into the dining room to join her family for breakfast.

CHAPTER 2

Point Lookout, Maryland

THE PRISON CAMP offered nothing much to do most days except to sleep or just sit and talk. Most were too weak and ill to do anything else. Walking up and down the main aisle and a few stretching exercises helped keep Manfred more fit than some of the others, but it still wasn't enough to keep him as physically strong as he had been. Still, he'd stayed strong enough to fight off the typhoid and dysentery that took so many of the men.

"Morning, Manfred. How's it going?" Luke Grayson, one of the other prisoners, knelt beside Manfred and twiddled a piece of straw in his hands.

"Same as usual." Manfred moved over and made room for the fair-haired young man to sit on the mat. Although like him Luke had only been here a little less than two months, his body told the same tale of lack of food as those who had been here longer.

Manfred gazed around at the damp, filthy structure that had served as both prison and home for the past few months since his transfer from that horrible place in Ohio. Clumps of straw covered with moth-eaten blankets and rag sheets served as beds. None of them had any more than the clothes on their backs and a few personal items in knapsacks or small packets that had been returned to them.

His gaze shifted from Luke to Edwin. Both were too young to be away from home fighting a war. Luke's blue eyes were as sunken into his face as Edwin's brown ones. Their dirty hair needed a good washing and cutting. But at least they were alive.

Luke reached across to touch Edwin's arm. "And how is your healing coming along?"

Edwin flipped back to face them and rubbed his shoulder. "I'm getting better. The pain's almost gone. How about you?"

"I'm fine. But I want to get home. It's so close—just across the river there in Virginia. About a day or so walk from the Rappahannock River to the Grayson farm. If I could get out of here, I'd be home in a couple or three days. That is, if there's anything left. No telling what those Yanks have done." Luke's hands dropped into his lap, and his chin sagged to rest on his chest.

Edwin sat up and crossed his legs with his fists clenched and resting on his thighs. "We have to believe we'll get home. I hate sitting around here all day rotting with nothing to do."

Manfred shook his head. "So do I, but we can plan, hope, and dream about the future. I believe God will see us through this." He reached over to grasp his brother's arm. "At least we're still alive."

Manfred stood and stretched. The stiffness in his knees reminded him once again of his lack of real exercise the past months. How he longed to run free. "After Port Hudson was captured, we lost contact with our brothers. Ma's last letter said Pa was getting his shipping business started again with the one boat they salvaged. I still worry about them."

Manfred sat back down. He wiggled a toe peeking through a hole in his sock and reached over for the pair he had picked up the night before. "Don't suppose we'll find much of the South the same. It's all been touched in some way by the looting and burning of property. But something's up. I can feel it." He removed the tattered sock and pulled the better one up over his foot.

Edwin unwound his legs then rolled over on his stomach and rested his forehead on his hands. "Can't come too soon for me." He closed his eyes.

Luke squatted with his elbows resting on his knees. "Saw you reading a while ago. What was it?"

"Just my journal, and a letter." Manfred patted the straw where he had stowed the book. "It helps me keep my sanity."

"I wish I had my Bible, but it got lost in the battle." He nodded toward Edwin, now asleep. "Looks like Edwin has the right idea. Think I'll get on back to my little space." He shuffled down the narrow aisle to his blanket.

Manfred's gaze rested on his younger brother. Edwin had joined the Fourth Louisiana unit a few weeks after his seventeenth birthday. Now nineteen, he had served with Manfred while their two older brothers fought in other areas.

Images of home brought a smile to Manfred's lips as he remembered Sallie, his sweetheart. The Dyer family lived in Woodville, a little over half a day's ride up the road from his home and over the Louisiana line into Mississippi, but Sallie's family made frequent trips to her grandparent's home near where Manfred and his family lived, and that's where they had met and courted.

He reached into his pocket and removed Sallie's letter once again. No need to open it, he'd memorized every word. As long as he believed his dreams and held on to them, he'd get home and see Sallie and fulfill his desire to become a doctor. He wanted to heal people, not hurt them.

St. Francisville, Louisiana

Amanda Dyer found her husband in the barn. She wrinkled her nose at the odor of hay and horseflesh. "Thomas, why must you muck out the stalls yourself? Papa has plenty of men who can do that."

"I need to work off my anger. Besides, only Moses and George stayed after the others were given their freedom. Remember?" Thomas leaned on his shovel.

"Yes, but couldn't George do it?" Her gaze swept around the stalls where horses whinnied and bobbed their heads. At least they still had the horses that had provided their escape a week ago. Amanda shuddered at the memory of their flight.

Thomas swiped his brow with a kerchief. "What brings you out here?"

"I must speak with you about our house in Woodville."

Thomas laid down the shovel and grasped the crook of Amanda's arm. "Let's go outside and talk there."

She walked beside him to the yard and left the unpleasant odors of the barn behind. They sat on a bench under a large oak tree surrounded by azaleas at the end of their season.

"Now, what more do you need to know than what I've already told you?"

Amanda plucked a leaf from a bush beside her and twisted it between her fingers. "I must know if you told me everything. It sounded bad, but I'm wondering if was really worse."

Thomas wrapped his arm around her shoulders. "My dear, I told you all of it. The house itself is stable, and we can repair it without too much trouble if I can get the supplies. Only the inside sustained much damage, just like I said. I might even be able to scrounge around and find some of our belongings spread over the land."

She blinked back tears. "I don't care about things. It's you and the boys I'm worried about. You're sure it's safe to take the boys with you? With Will's eagerness to fight this war, he might do something foolish. Next fall he'll turn seventeen and will be of age to run off and join the Louisiana regiment if he takes a mind to, even though he knows I disapprove. What if he gets up there and decides to go off on his own?"

"He won't. There's too much work to be done, and I believe the Yanks have moved far enough away to keep us from harm. I promise you I'll keep Will and Tom close by and busy."

"You said that this morning, and I do want to believe you, but my heart fears the unknown."

"Trust me, Amanda, I won't let anything happen to our sons." He placed his fingers on her chin and turned her face toward his. "My dear, we will be all right, but if you have such worries for our safety, I can delay the repairs. The supplies haven't arrived as yet, so a few more days after they do won't make a big difference."

She shook her head. How she loved this man who had come into her life over twenty years ago and persuaded her to go to Mississippi to live. He proved his love now by his willingness to stay here and keep their sons at home. How could she not trust the Lord to take care of him and the boys?

"No, as soon as the things we ordered arrive, you must go, Thomas. The Lord will watch over you and calm my fears. I must remember that when I cast my cares on Him, I should not try to take them back."

"That's why I love you. You let the Lord be your guide." His lips brushed hers then settled in a kiss that transported her back to their first one under this very tree.

She leaned back and smiled. "I love you, Thomas, and whatever you do, I *will* support you." Amanda stood. "I'll get Flora to help me pack sacks of supplies for you and the boys when you leave. You surely won't go hungry with her help."

She left him sitting in the shade and hurried back to the house and her duties to prepare the midday meal.

The family gathered around the dining table for the noon meal prepared by Flora. Sallie gazed at those around her, her heart full of love for her family. They were all here in one place, safe. Sallie glanced toward her grandmother. The elderly lady smiled and nodded toward her husband. "I believe it's time for grace."

The tall, silver-haired man held out his hands to the ones on either side of him. The rest of the family joined to complete the circle while Grandpa Woodruff returned thanks with his deep bass voice.

At the "amen," Sallie's two younger brothers reached across to fill their plates. Sallie smothered a chuckle when her father's stern look stopped the boys' forks in midair. Will and Tom sat back and waited for the platters of ham and potatoes to be passed to them.

Grandpa Woodruff cleared his throat and addressed Papa. "When will you be going back up to Woodville to repair your home?"

Papa reached across for Mama's hand. "As soon as I have what I need to get started." He peered around the table at each of his children.

At the sight of Mama's red-rimmed eyes Sallie's heart filled with love and sorrow for the two people who meant so much to her.

Papa's slate gray eyes flashed with determination. "It'll take work, but I think we can restore the house by mid-summer. We won't be able to live in it until then."

Grandpa Woodruff cleared his throat. "It appears to me you'll have to stay here with us a while longer. We'll enjoy that. Won't we, Mary Catherine?" He peered over his glasses at his wife.

"Of course we will. These past days have been pleasant, but don't you think it may be dangerous to go back up there with the boys? What if the Yanks come back?" Grandma wrinkled her brow and leaned toward Papa.

Papa buttered a chunk of cornbread. "No need to worry, Mother Woodruff. I don't think they will. When I went back yesterday, all was peaceful and quiet. The railroad is still intact, and the town fared well. Rosemont suffered some damage, as did a few other homes, but they too can be repaired. Seems it was just a renegade group of Union soldiers on their way north. Most others moved on out weeks ago. From what I've heard, they plan to march on across Mississippi and join the troops with Grant in Georgia. I don't believe there'll be much more fighting around these parts."

Grandma Woodruff shook her head. "I don't care. Look at poor Bayou Sara. Why, if the men down at the landing hadn't fought back so hard, they just might have come on up here to St. Francisville."

Grandpa reached over and patted her arm. "Now, don't fret yourself over that. It's been a few years since then, and I haven't heard anything about other Yankee troops anywhere near except in New Orleans."

"And that's too close for me."

Her father and grandfather spoke of the fierce fighting only a few miles down the road at the river landing in 1863 during the battle for Port Hudson. The gunfire had been loud, and Grandma and Grandpa had hidden in the root cellar when shells hit Grace Church less than a mile away.

Talk of that battle reminded Sallie again of the day she too had hid in a cellar to escape Yankee gunfire. The firm set of Grandma's mouth revealed her fears of the Yankees' return that matched Sallie's personal ones. Listening to their talk elevated her fears over what she had done. Those two battles had been too close to home.

Her body quivered with the memory, and then a hand squeezed her arm. She glanced up to lock gazes with Mama. From the sadness seen there, her mother remembered too.

Grandma tapped on her glass. "Enough of this war talk." Her voice took on a more cheerful note. "It'll be good having all of you here. We have plenty of room, and until the river trade is back up to what it was before the siege of Port Hudson, we have enough fresh vegetables growing, meat in the smokehouse, and preserved foods to last through summer."

Papa folded his napkin on the table. "Thank you, Mother Woodruff. Like I said, the railroad is running and what cotton can be harvested will be brought down to Whiteman's for shipment north, so supplies should be coming too." Papa turned his gaze to the two teenage boys across the table. "I plan on taking you two with me to Woodville. You're young and strong and able to do man's work. With this warmer weather we can sleep on the grounds."

Sallie's two younger brothers puffed with pride and sat up straighter. They missed their home in Mississippi just as much as she did, but she wasn't as anxious to return as they seemed to be.

Hannah, Sallie's younger sister, spoke up. "What can I do to help, Papa?" Her strawberry blonde curls bounced on her shoulders as she wriggled in her chair.

Papa stroked his chin. "Well, now, missy. Let me see. Mother, what do you think our Hannah can do to help?"

Mama adjusted the lace cap on her head. "I think we'll have plenty to do around here to help your grandmother. Besides, you have your lessons."

Hannah protested, "Tom and Will have lessons too. It's not fair. I want to go to Woodville." She slumped back in her chair and pursed her mouth in a full pout.

Sallie smothered a giggle. Her twelve-year-old sister's love of the outdoors amused her, but with her shortened right leg and special shoe, she wouldn't be much help with the repair work.

Papa put his arm around his younger daughter and kissed the top of her head. "I know you want to go with us, but you'll be more useful to your mother and grandmother. I'll help the boys with their lessons in the evening, and when we come back on a Friday or Saturday, you can show me all you've learned during the week. Perhaps you'll play that piano piece you've been working on for me."

Hannah beamed at her father. "I'll practice every day, Papa. It'll be perfect for you."

Sallie grinned and picked up her fork to stab a piece of tender pork. With Hannah, the piano piece would be more than perfect. Her young sister played the piano far better than Sallie, but no jealousy arose because Sallie much preferred reading and writing to practicing scales and such.

After the meal, dishes clinked on the tray as Lettie carried it out to the kitchen. Sallie followed with a stack of her own. "Let's get this done in a hurry. I want to get on with writing in my journal and reading my book."

"I'm grateful to your mama for helping me learn to read."

"She enjoyed teaching you." Sallie set the dishes on a table beside her mother. Mama stood over a bucket and scraped the remains of food on the plates into it. Sallie and Lettie then arranged the dishes in a wooden tub on the floor. When it was filled, they lifted it between them and carried it out to the summer kitchen. Mama followed behind with the linens and headed for the shed where they did laundry.

Sallie set the load down outside the little building used for food preparation and cleaning. She planted her hands on her hips. "I heard Mama telling Papa she's glad to have a farmhouse kitchen in our house in Woodville. Sure is easier for serving and cleaning."

Lettie wiped her hands on her apron. "That it would be, but it was hot in the house during summertime. Let's get the water for Mammy."

They each picked up a bucket and raced to the pump near the barn. Sallie tumbled to the dirt with Lettie falling on top of her. They both giggled, and Sallie reached up to touch the ebony braids on Lettie's head. "I just love the way your braids are so even and straight."

Lettie grinned and pushed herself from the ground. "I love the way yours curls all over your head."

Sallie giggled again. By all standards she may be a woman of marrying age, but that didn't matter today. Today she could be a young girl like her sister and simply enjoy life. She had plenty of tomorrows ahead to be a grown woman with wifely duties pressed on her.

Sallie stood and brushed the dust from her gown. She lifted her skirt and petticoat, and the toes of her black slippers peeked out. "Look at this. Mama's going to be furious." She bent down and licked her fingers then rubbed them across the toe of her scuffed and dusty shoes.

Lettie laughed. "I'll clean them for you this afternoon. They'll be good as new."

Sallie wrapped her arm around the shoulders of the

servant girl and laughed. "I'll help you since I messed them up."

When they passed through the pantry area by the dining room, Lettie headed for the back stairway. "I'll meet you in the parlor later after my chores. I look forward to finishing that story we started."

"Me too. I'll practice on the piano and write in my journal until you can join me." Sallie strolled into the parlor and over to the piano. Each day Mama taught Hannah reading, writing, French, sewing, and piano just as she had done with Sallie and Lettie. Papa taught the boys arithmetic, reading, writing, and science.

Even now Sallie wished she had been allowed to learn arithmetic and science too, but Papa didn't think it necessary for girls to know about such things. He'd always told her, "Young ladies needn't bother to fill their heads with numbers and experiments. They are better being busy with household matters."

Sallie sat down and let her fingers run through the scales on the ivory keys. Lettie had no desire to learn the piano, but she loved the reading and writing time they had together. Sallie silently thanked her mother for including the young Negro girl in their lessons the past few years.

Now that she sat on the eve of her nineteenth year, school had been left behind, but Sallie hoped to never lose the desire to learn. The music she'd studied gave her such comfort in times of distress. Her fingers now moved with grace across the keys. She might not be as accomplished at the piano as her sister, but she still played quite well.

As she played, images of Manfred in his uniform danced through her mind. He'd looked so gallant when she'd seen him just after he enlisted back in 1861. She'd been fifteen at the time and quite taken with his handsome good looks in his uniform. How proud they all were of him and his brothers. A chilling tingle raised bumps on her arms. Had something happened to Manfred?

She bit her lip and clasped her hands in her lap. *Manfred, please be all right and come home soon. I miss you so.* Tears dropped from her cheeks to stain the front of her dress.

CHAPTER 3

Point Lookout, Maryland

MANFRED DOZED AS the day wore on. So far nothing major had happened, but still the feeling persisted that something was about to happen. He sighed then blew out his breath. Just another day in the life of a prisoner.

After the noon meal of the greasy liquid that passed for soup, he opened his journal again and began writing. He extracted Sallie's last letter from his pocket. If only he had the means to send a letter, he'd tear out a sheet of paper from his journal and send word that he was alive. How worried she and his family must be about him and Edwin and their whereabouts.

At the end of the letter she'd written a verse. He spoke the words of David from 2 Samuel just under his breath. "The Lord is my rock, and my fortress, and my deliverer; the God of my rock; in him will I trust: he is my shield, and the horn of my salvation, my high tower, and my refuge, my saviour; thou savest me from violence." The declaration of the beleaguered warrior still brought comfort to his soul.

Manfred glanced up from the words before him to gaze around the barracks that served as his home. One thing gave him hope for the future of the country. After Manfred had been allowed to keep his Bible, every man who had carried a Bible had been allowed to keep it. At least the enemy had respect and reverence for God. The Scriptures had served all of them well through these terrible months.

The sudden banging of the door caused him to jump. Four

guards marched in. Strange, they usually didn't return until time for the evening meal, and they carried no weapons. Manfred's hair prickled at the nape of his neck again. Something had happened. He folded the letter from Sallie and stuffed it into his pocket then stood along with those who were able to do so.

The four men in dark blue Union uniforms rested at ease, smirking and gazing around the room. They turned to salute as the provost marshall, Major Brady, entered the small building. Dressed in his blue and gold officer's uniform, the major planted his feet apart and crossed his arms behind his back as the officer's dark eyes peered at them. A chill went through Manfred. Something mighty big must have taken place for Brady to pay them a personal visit.

The officer spoke, and his words echoed through the barracks like a cannonball. "We have an announcement that will impact all of you." He paused with a smirk on his face as the injured and ill sat up and turned their faces toward the officer.

Manfred glanced at those around him. The thirty remaining men in the barracks all peered at the general with fear, curiosity, and even indifference written across their faces. Edwin's countenance displayed great anger, and Manfred reached out a hand to calm his brother.

The general's voice thundered across the room. "This past Sunday, April 9, Lee surrendered to Grant at the courthouse in Appomattox. The southern rebellion has been defeated by the armies of the United States."

Complete silence lasted only a moment before Edwin jumped to his feet. "Lee surrender? Never! This must be a joke." He grabbed at one of the soldiers. "You're lying."

The man in blue grabbed Edwin, hit him in the face,

then shoved him to the ground. Manfred leapt forward and caught his brother.

"Wait, Edwin, listen to what he has to say." Manfred turned to the others murmuring behind him. "All of you, be quiet and listen."

Edwin shook off Manfred's hold and glared at the general. The officer stood firm, waiting for their voices to cease murmuring. Manfred stumbled his way back to his mat, tugging Edwin behind him. Finally the confused men stopped their mumbling and turned listening ears to the commander.

"The war is over, and we have been ordered to begin releasing you by your units. We'll begin with those from the far southern states first." Major General Butler paused for a moment. Silence greeted the announcement, and men gazed at each other with mixed emotions flooding their faces. Once again they whispered among themselves. Manfred's heart beat wildly. They had lost the war, but they were leaving their prison.

He turned and grabbed Edwin in a bear hug. "We're going home, little brother. We're going home." Tears streamed from his eyes.

The officer bellowed, "Attention!" All sound stopped again, and the imprisoned soldiers waited for him to speak.

"You will be carried across the Potomac River to Virginia where you will be exchanged. The sick and wounded will be given transportation as far as it can take them. The rest will be given a canteen of water, a few rations, and a blanket to start you on your homeward journey. The first group of men will be from the Fourth Louisiana regiment. As soon as arrangements are completed for the exchange, we'll move you out. Gather your belongings and be ready to depart when we are notified, which may be later today or several days from now." He turned on his heel and strode through the door with his men following.

Stunned silence enveloped the quarters. The enormity of the announcement sank in; the complaints of only minutes ago became shouts of joy that rang through the building.

Manfred dropped to his knees and began sorting his few meager belongings. Next to him Edwin sat on his mat with arms crossed and anger burning in his eyes. Manfred leaned across to him. "If Lee has surrendered, it's all over. The South has lost, but we're going home."

Edwin shook his head. "No! It's just a hoax to get our hopes up. You'll see. Lee would never surrender. He'd fight to his death to save the South. They're just telling us this to see if we will really try to leave so they can shoot us down."

"I don't think this is a hoax. Come on, might as well get your things together." Manfred patted Edwin's shoulder then turned back to his task.

Manfred rolled up the extra pair of socks he had taken from his dead comrade and put them in his small knapsack with his Bible and journal. He pulled on the boots that had seen better days but would have to suffice for the journey home. He glanced again at his brother, the bitterness evident in the set of the young man's mouth.

Edwin sat up straighter and locked eyes with Manfred. "I want to go home, but I don't want to lose the war. Too many died for us to just give up."

"C'mon, little brother. The war is over, and there's nothing we can do about it but go back to help rebuild our home and our lives. I'm planning to marry Sallie, and you want to court Peggy. We'll have a good life. You'll see." Manfred bent over to squeeze his brother's shoulder then began gathering a few of Edwin's possessions.

Edwin pushed him away and stacked his things on a ragged blanket as he continued to mutter and complain.

Manfred returned to his own business, but his gaze turned to his younger brother. They were headed for home, but what would they find? He frowned and lifted a prayer that his two older brothers would be there too and that his father's business hadn't been destroyed.

A shadow darkened the mat. He glanced up to see Luke once again standing beside the mat. "Hello, Luke, what can I do for you?"

The young soldier rubbed his hand across his forehead. "Since your group will be leaving first, I have a favor to ask."

Manfred stood and clasped his shoulder. "Of course, I'll do my best."

Worry etched Luke's brow, and his eyes glistened. "My ma and pa don't know if I'm dead or alive. I won't be leaving here until the last of us is let go. That might be a week. If you could stop over at our place and let them know I'm coming home, they'd be mighty proud to give you a good meal and a bed if they have it."

Manfred's arm went around his friend's shoulders. "We'd be happy to do that. How do we find your folks?"

"Grayson farm is just a little south of St. Stephens Church about forty miles across the Rappahannock River towards Lynchburg. I'd like for you to give this letter to my mother. There's a rough map of how to get to our farm with it."

"I'll see she gets the letter." He tucked the paper into his shirt pocket. "They'll be happy to know you're coming home soon."

With a nod of thanks Luke turned and trudged back to his own mat. Luke's family would receive good news, but Manfred mourned for the thousands of others who wouldn't.

St. Francisville, Louisiana

After a while Sallie left the piano and gathered up her cross-stitch sampler with her threads and needle. The desire to write had left her, so she headed for the coolness of the front porch. The laughter of her brothers rang in the air as they entered the stables to take care of the horses. Hannah's voice reciting her French lesson with Mama drifted from the parlor through the open window.

Sallie breathed deeply then let her breath out with a puff. What good would it do to try to rebuild the house in Woodville? She didn't want to return to Mississippi or her old home, ever. The memories now associated with that place erased all the happy times. If she returned, she'd remember what had happened there every day for the rest of her life.

A tear dropped on her cheek. She was a grown woman now and could choose to stay here if she so desired. Her gaze swept across the beauty of the well-kept lawn of her grandparents' home. Living here would not be bad at all. They had managed to escape with only a few personal belongings, but Mama, in her wisdom, had brought clothes in the past to have here in case of an emergency. This certainly qualified as an emergency in anyone's estimation.

Mama said God would help her through these days, but He'd turned His back on her. Praying hadn't made the memories go away, so why waste time on God? She needed Manfred, but even he might turn away from her when he learned what she had done. Why did life have to be so complicated? She'd much rather be the young girl of fourteen before the war when her only worry had been what to wear and what party to attend.

The door opened, and Hannah stepped onto the porch. "I've finished my lessons." She plopped down into the chair next to Sallie.

Although she was twelve, Hannah still enjoyed playing with her dolls. She had managed to grab one to bring with her when they had fled their home, and she held it in her arms along with two Grandma had saved from Mama's childhood. Her calm expression and smile as she sat up straighter gave evidence of the girl's spirit. Despite her handicap, Hannah seemed to find joy in everything she did, and she could make the simplest tea party with dolls into a grand affair. Oh, to be that innocent and unbothered by the war.

While her sister arranged the dolls in a semicircle on the wicker table between them, Sallie stitched and let memories of Manfred play through her mind. Those memories drifted back to the first time the two had seen each other. She had traveled down to St. Francisville to visit her grandparents during the summer when she was ten years old. Closing her eyes, she let it unfold now as though it happened yesterday instead of eight years ago.

⁀ᘒ

The aromas of peppermint, coffee, spices, and lamp oil filled the general store. Sallie stood on tiptoe and eyed the shiny jars of multicolored candies. She clutched a penny in her hand and licked her lips in anticipation of the sweet taste of peppermint.

"I like the cinnamon ones best."

She jumped at the voice so close to her, and she turned to see a boy taller than she standing beside her. He had to be at least thirteen to be so tall. Her gaze took in his sandy-colored hair, gold-flecked brown eyes, and neatly tucked-in shirt. She didn't remember ever seeing such a handsome boy in town before today. He stared back with an even look that sent heat to her cheeks. Sallie reached toward the containers of sweets and shrugged to cover her embarrassment. "Peppermint sticks are my favorite. Cinnamon's too hot."

The boy shoved his hands into his pockets and rocked on the balls of his feet. "No, they're not. But I like peppermint too."

Mr. Brady leaned over the counter. "Now what can I be doing for you two young 'uns today?" His blues eyes twinkled as he smiled at them.

The boy plopped two coins on the counter. "Two peppermints for her, and two cinnamons for me."

Sallie gasped. She quickly plunked her penny beside his. "I have my own money, thank you."

The boy pushed her money back. "Don't be getting all huffy. I want to buy the peppermints. My name's Manfred Whiteman. What's yours?"

Sallie's head bowed, and she shuffled her feet. "Sallie Dyer." No boy had ever bought her candy before, nor had one ever been so bold. Even though he was nice looking and polite, he had been quite forward in shoving her pennies aside. Besides, she wasn't supposed to take things from others without permission. She raised her head slightly and peeked up at Mr. Brady.

The pink-faced storekeeper leaned over the counter and crossed his arms. "Now that you two have met, here's an extra peppermint and an extra cinnamon for you both. Go on and enjoy them."

She glanced over to her grandmother, who gave a nod of approval. Sallie picked up the sweet treats. "Thank you, Manfred. It's nice of you to buy them for me."

Manfred grabbed his treat and swung his hands behind his

back. Bright red splotches rose in cheeks as he moistened his lips. "I…I think you're the prettiest girl I've ever seen." As soon as the last word left his mouth, he bolted out the door as if the law chased after him.

The heat rose again in her cheeks, and she stared at his fleeing back. Mr. Brady chuckled behind her. "I think you have an admirer there, Miss Sallie."

Hannah's voice brought her back to the present. "What is it, Hannah?"

A frown wrinkled the girl's brow. She now sat on the floor with her dolls around her. "Do you think I could ever be a nurse like that Clara Barton lady who is helping take care of wounded soldiers?"

"Hannah Grace Dyer, I think you can be anything you want to be."

She pushed her feet out from under her dress. "Even if my legs don't match?"

Sallie scrambled from her seat to kneel beside her sister. "Honey, that won't keep you from learning all you want to learn and being a nurse if that's what you want to do. Your personality and sweet nature make you the person you are, not your legs or feet."

Besides, as Sallie noted inwardly, Hannah loomed on the edge of becoming a beautiful young woman. Her flawless skin and golden-red hair along with eyes as blue as the sky on a summer day created a smidgeon of envy in Sallie, whose own unruly locks wanted to curl and fly in every direction and whose eyes couldn't decide if they wanted to be blue or green.

Hannah sighed and leaned against Sallie's chest. "I just

wish God had given me two good legs. It's hard to run and play, even with the special shoe Papa had made. I always feel so awkward and clumsy."

So despite her outward sunny disposition, Hannah did worry about her leg. Sallie hugged her sister and placed her cheek against Hannah's head. So many times she'd seen Hannah stumble and fall when she got in too big a hurry and ran for something. Life could be most unfair at times, especially when it hurt her sister.

"Hannah, when this war is over, we'll be able to make plans for our futures. Papa will let you go to school to learn whatever you want. We've already learned a great deal from Mama and Papa here at home, and with your head for details, I think you'd make a wonderful nurse."

Hannah lifted her gaze to Sallie, and a smile played about her lips. "You really think so?"

At Sallie's nod of affirmation, Hannah sat back and held her head high. "Then I'm going to study extra hard and be a good student."

Laughter pealed forth from Sallie. As if Hannah wasn't already the smartest of the four Dyer siblings, except maybe for their brother Will's arithmetic skills. "Oh, Hannah, I love you so much."

Lettie stepped out onto the porch. "My mam has refreshments prepared. She sent me to fetch you."

Sallie hopped up and helped Hannah beside her. "We'll be right in."

Hannah steadied herself and frowned. "I hope Papa can repair our house. I want to go back to Woodville as soon as we can. I miss being there."

Sallie said nothing as she walked with Hannah into the house. Woodville held only bad memories, but if she had to, Sallie would return to that house. If only Manfred would come and ask her to marry him, she could forget Woodville and settle here as his wife. How much more exciting that would be. Someday, somehow, her love had to come home.

CHAPTER 4

THICK COILS OF rope secured a barge at the dock on the Potomac River below. Manfred and more than fifty men followed a Union officer along with several blue-clad guards to the water's edge. Sand slowed his steps, but at least he had shoes. He glanced around him. Most trudged the path on their own steam, but a few lay on makeshift litters pulled by a comrade.

At the landing the group halted. Manfred stood next to Edwin and watched the officer as he strolled through the ranks deciding if a man's injuries were sufficient enough to give him special treatment and transportation home.

A sergeant tapped Manfred then Edwin. "You two go there." He pointed to the group boarding the boat on foot.

Edwin stumbled, and Manfred grabbed his arm to steady his brother. The boy leaned his weight against Manfred. When they reached the plank set up to board the vessel, he cautioned Edwin and assisted him up the ramp. "Careful, little brother, you're still weak."

The two young men stepped gingerly over several others already lying or sitting in exhaustion amidst the crates and barrels on the deck of the barge. Manfred picked his way among the soldiers to find a clear spot near the back of the boat.

"Here, Edwin, by the rail." Manfred tossed his bundle to the space then helped Edwin with his belongings. He sank onto the wooden planks beside his brother. "We're going home, little brother. We're on our way."

Edwin shrugged. "Who knows what we'll find. The Union Army is in control."

"It'll be all right. Look at the river. Isn't it beautiful? Breathe the fresh air. Look at the sunshine. We're free men, and we'll soon be away from Maryland and on the Virginia shore." Manfred took a deep breath, savoring the warm sun and gentle April breeze. He lifted his eyes toward heaven.

"Thank You, Lord, for taking care of us these past months. We have a long journey home, and I pray Your light will guide us, protect us, and provide for us as we go."

Edwin hung his head and didn't respond to the prayer.

Manfred ran his hand over his brother's thick brown hair and spoke softly. "I figure we can be home by early June even if we have to make a few stops along the way. We can most likely travel eight or nine hours a day. Do you think you're strong enough to go that long?"

The slender boy only nodded and hugged his knees to his chest. When he finally raised his head, his cheeks held rivers of tears. "Now that it's all over, I'll walk until my legs drop off. I just wanna get home."

"So do I. So do I." Manfred leaned back and closed his eyes, basking in the warm sun. The vessel shuddered, and Manfred listened to the slap of the water against the hull. All around the murmur of voices spoke of freedom and home.

After a bumpy trip across the river that emptied into Chesapeake Bay, the boat hit the pier with a jolt. Manfred stood and reached down to pull Edwin to his feet.

"Come on, boy. We're in Virginia, and I see gray jackets coming to meet us."

A shout of greeting rang from the men on the boat. The gray-uniformed men on shore waved, whistled, and hollered back. The stoic expressions of the Union soldiers now changed to frowns. Those men would rather see their prisoners dead than going back to their homes. Even now the hatred on both sides sent chills racing through Manfred.

An older soldier wearing the gray of the Confederates stood at the bottom of the plank on shore. Manfred greeted him with a salute. Although Manfred was no longer the eager young man who'd joined Confederate forces four years ago, being back on Southern soil renewed his hope and energy. "It's good to be back with ya'll. We may have lost, but we're not beaten."

The soldier gripped his hand. "We're glad you survived. We've heard of the harsh conditions of the prison."

"It was bad, but now we're free, and home beckons." Harsh barely began to describe what he and Edwin endured for those few months. Starvation, disease, and cruelty had taken their toll on too many men, but that was behind him now. He faced his future with high hopes and complete trust that God would see him home safely.

Manfred then glanced beyond the man and grinned at the number of gray uniformed soldiers who welcomed the freed men with open arms and shouts of greeting. Younger men picked up the litters of the wounded and toted them to the field surgery, no more than a tent with rows of cots and a few medical supplies. Manfred observed the scene and breathed a sigh of relief to be on Southern soil again.

Those not headed for medical help remained near the shore and huddled to wait for someone in authority to join them and give further instructions. In a few minutes the others seemed to fully realize their freedom. Young men and old milled around talking and laughing. Even with his heart heavy over the defeat and worry about what might await him at home, Manfred wanted to join in and shout, sing, and dance all at one time. The days of pain, hunger, and bloody battles lay behind him. He hoped he would never again have to lift a weapon to fire at another man. The death and destruction of the past year would stay branded in his memory forever, but someday he'd be the doctor he'd dreamed of being since childhood and give life and hope to men rather than destroying them.

The sharp clang of the bell on the ferry rang out as it shoved away from the shore and headed back across the river for more young men to bring to freedom. It was not much to look at as far as boats went, but to Manfred it represented an end to all he'd endured the past months.

When they left the pier, Manfred relaxed as others around him sighed and dropped their gear on dry ground. Out of the corner of his eye he spotted his brother, who finally smiled, and that brought more hope to Manfred's heart than being on Virginia soil. If Edwin quit fretting over the South's defeat, the journey home would be much more pleasant.

An officer in a gray uniform trimmed in gold approached the group. "I am Captain Parker. We don't have much, but our cook has managed to set aside a meal for you. You need that and a good night's sleep before beginning your journey. Wash up or take a bath in the river if you like. We're glad you're here." His black eyes looked stern, but a hint of smile played at his mouth. Then he grinned broadly and announced, "Troops dismissed. Go fill your bellies."

A whoop went up from Manfred and the others as they all scattered to the mess area. Several tables stood filled with piles of sourdough biscuits, kettles of steaming potato soup, and pots of hot coffee. Manfred marveled at the orderly way the men lined themselves up to be served after so many days of dreaming of food like this. The cook ladled the warm grub with a warning. "Careful how much and how fast you eat. It's been a long time since solid food warmed your stomachs."

Manfred listened, but he still filled his plate with

sourdough biscuits and potatoes swimming in thick gravy. He and Edwin joined a small group sitting under a tree. He ate in silence for a few moments, enjoying the taste of tender potatoes and sweet carrots, almost forgotten in the months past. The laughter and talk soothed his soul as he sat back and enjoyed his meal, savoring each morsel as it slid down his throat. Remembering the cook's warning, he ate slowly as he drank in all the details of the scene around him.

Captain Parker wove his way among the groups before reaching Manfred. He stopped at the grove of trees where several had joined Manfred. "I'm glad you're enjoying the rations. I only wish we had more to offer you."

Manfred swept his arm toward the tent barracks behind them. "How did all this come about?"

"Part of the exchange agreement included treatment of the wounded and provisions for all prisoners released to our regiment, or what's left of it." The captain knelt to talk to the group.

He placed an arm across his knee and leveled his gaze to fix on their faces. "Our boys fought valiantly, but the Yanks were too much for us. We had to evacuate St. Petersburg and Richmond. Lee wanted to retreat to the west and join Johnson, but Grant barred his way."

A few murmurs of protest scattered through the men. When silence again fell, the captain continued. "Lee figured more fighting would mean useless sacrifice of lives, so he wrote to Grant and asked for a meeting. The end came at a courthouse in Appomattox on Sunday. That's a sight I won't soon forget." He paused and peered around the group.

No one spoke. They all needed time to allow the words to sink in. No more fighting, no more killing, no more injuries. Peace had finally come, but at what price? He'd probably see more death in his days ahead as a doctor, but it wouldn't be the same as it had been on a battlefield.

Edwin asked, "Has all the fighting stopped?"

The captain stroked his chin. "Don't know if Johnson's got the word yet, and there's probably fighting in Mississippi and farther south, but it won't be long before the news is spread and the war will be over for good." He let the words settle over the men. "You found out so quickly because you're just across the river. You're the first group to be exchanged."

Edwin's eye's burned with excitement in the wake of Captain Parker's announcement. The smile of joy at being free a few minutes ago disappeared.

Somehow Manfred would have to help Edwin accept their defeat so that they could put their full strength toward the trip back to Louisiana. Their journey home would not be easy. Weather could be unpredictable and fickle in the spring in the South. He'd have to make sure they had provisions, which meant stopping in some towns to seek work. And they would have to watch out for thieves and renegades. Manfred picked up his spoon and finished his soup. They were almost sure to get home, but how many more trials would they face before the journey ended?

Later in the evening, at twilight, a group gathered around a campfire and sang songs of home, the South, and God. Manfred leaned against a tree and listened to the soft strains of a mouth harp blended with the deep voices of the men.

Edwin sank to the ground beside Manfred. "Sounds good, doesn't it?" The words to "When I Survey the Wondrous Cross" echoed around them.

Manfred shifted his position and pulled his knees to his chest. "Yes, but I still think of those we left behind in prison and on the battlefields. Some were friends and neighbors, others strangers, but we were all brothers for our cause."

"I think of them too. Why did it have to end this way?" Edwin leaned his head against the tree and closed his eyes.

"It had to end sometime. I wish it could have been different, but now it's time to join together and restore our country to its former unity." But if men continued to talk like his brother and refused to accept the defeat, no telling how long the restoration would take.

Edwin shook his head. "I know, but it's hard for me to digest. I want to keep our cause alive."

Manfred peered at him in the waning light of day. "And just what is our cause?"

Edwin chewed his lip a moment. "I guess it's just to be sure we maintain our freedoms of choice in making laws for our state."

"I think that will be the case when the dust settles and we get back to the basics of democracy." Manfred stretched. For the first time in a while, his belly was full, and he could relax without fear. What a day this had been. The music wafting through the cool April air filled him with the eagerness to return home. There a young woman lived, and if all went according to his dreams, Sallie would be his bride before the summer drew to a close.

The words of "A Mighty Fortress Is Our God" floated to his ears. Yes, God was their fortress, and He had not failed them. The war may have been lost, but God still reigned and would unite the country again under His sovereign power. Manfred believed this with all his heart.

He gazed toward the heavens, and the silver orb of the moon rose in the darkened sky. Tiny pinpoints of light peeked among the clouds floating across the dark skies. Not many more moons would rise before he'd see his beloved Sallie. He prayed for her to feel his love tonight and know he was coming home to her.

How he longed for the simple life before the war when he'd helped his father load the big boats at the docks beside the family shipping company. He could only hope the docks would still be there and that goods and merchandise would be available for shipping. One thing would change, though. Instead of working the docks, he'd be practicing medicine with Dr. Andrews and curing whatever ailed the people of St. Francisville.

A question from Edwin broke his reverie.

"What was that you said?"

Edwin echoed Manfred's thoughts. "I wonder what life is going to be like when we get home. Do you think the shipping company's still there?"

"I was just wondering the same thing. I don't know, but Father and Mr. Felton would do whatever it took to save it."

After a few moments of listening to the music, Manfred stood and brushed leaves and grass from his pants. "I figure if we walk at a good pace tomorrow, we can make it to Grayson farm by the next day. Gotta let Luke's folks know he's alive and coming home."

Edwin rested his chin on his drawn-up knees. "Do you really think we can be home by June?"

Manfred shook his head. "I don't know. I guess it all depends on whether or not we can find means to ride part of the way. We might need to find an odd job or two to make money, and that would delay us a bit too."

He'd spent some time after their meal figuring how far they could go in a day. With good weather and food to eat, they could set a pace of three miles or so an hour. That'd be less than thirty miles a day, but it would get them there.

"Wonder what the Graysons will be like? Hope they will take us in."

Manfred laughed and poked him on the arm. "Now

little brother, you know they'll treat us with great kindness. Virginia is a part of the South, you know."

"Yeah, I know. Sure would be good to have a taste of a good old Virginia smoked ham. I remember the ones we had at Christmas a few times when Pa had them shipped in." Edwin raised his hands behind his head and leaned against the tree and stretched out his legs.

Manfred leaned back and rested the sole of his shoe against the tree. Again his thoughts filled with home and his parents. He prayed his three other brothers made it home safe and sound.

The rolling strains of "Dixie" filled the air. Edwin jumped to his feet and pulled Manfred to follow him to the campfire. "Come on, they're singing our song."

Manfred laughed and joined heartily in singing "I wish I was in the land o' cotton." The laughter and camaraderie of the men contrasted sharply with the previous months of silence and suffering. No matter what lay ahead, just being free to sing and enjoy fellowship tonight brought joy and peace to his soul.

Tonight he'd sleep in the great outdoors, surrounded by trees and fresh air. No odors of sweat or dying men. Dreams of home drew close to fulfillment. Their long journey home had begun.

CHAPTER 5

THURSDAY MORNING LETTIE joined Sallie and Hannah in the bedroom. She laughed at Sallie's awkward attempts to tie a yellow bow in Hannah's hair and took over the task.

"Miss Hannah, I do believe you've grown taller this year. Look at you, almost as tall as Miss Sallie." Lettie fluffed the younger girl's golden red curls.

Hannah grinned with pleasure. "Thank you, Lettie. I think I'm taller too." Then she stuck out the foot wearing the special shoe. "If only I didn't have to wear this. I'm going to need a new one soon."

Sallie wrapped her arms around Hannah. "I know, but you've probably stopped growing like I did and Papa can request several pairs of nice shoes for different occasions."

"You really think so? The only ones I've seen are these ugly laced-up kind."

"Yes, I do think so, and we'll probably be the same height from now on since you are about even with me now." Being tall ran more to the boys in the family. She and Hannah resembled Mama.

"So I am, but then you're not so tall yourself." With a grin at Sallie, Hannah clumped from the room, her special shoe thumping on the floor.

"That child is a growing into a pretty girl and a lively one." Lettie smiled, shaking her head before attending to the linens and quilt on the bed.

"I'm glad she's not aware of what the war has meant to all

of us. I'm not sure she even understands what really happened that last day in our home." Mama had protected her youngest daughter from the horrors of the war on that day, but Sallie had seen it all.

"I think she knows more than we believe she does." Lettie gave the covers one last swipe. "Breakfast is waiting."

Mama and Papa and the rest of the family had already gathered at the table. Sallie stopped beside her mother's chair. "I'm sorry to be late, Mama."

"Just by a minute or so. Your brothers arrived only seconds before you did."

Sallie headed for her chair but caught the wink Will sent in her direction. He'd tease her later about arriving before she did. She'd scolded him often enough for his tardiness.

After the blessing she ate and listened to her father tell of his plans for the day and the rest of the week.

"Mr. Whiteman sent up word that some of the supplies have arrived from upriver. I'll go down to the pier at Bayou Sara this morning and load them onto the wagon. Then the boys and I will head up to Mississippi later this morning. We'll be back on Saturday evening. We can get in a good day and a half of work, maybe two if we get there early this afternoon. With all the debris cleaned from the house, we can have it ready for when the remainder of the building supplies arrive."

"Mother and I will prepare food for you to take with you to last until Saturday noon." Mama reached out and grasped Papa's hand. "I will pray for your safety every moment you're gone."

"Thank you, my dear. I'm sure we'll be plenty safe with your prayers going up." He then peered at Will and Tom. "I'll expect you to have everything ready to go by the time I return with the supplies. We'll load up the rest from here and get on our way." He paused then added, "I also expect your school books to be part of the supplies you ready."

That elicited groans from her brothers and a giggle from Hannah. No matter what else went on, Papa would make sure his boys studied and prepared for the future, especially since the war made the future so uncertain.

Later, after clearing the table, Sallie, Hannah, and Lettie helped Flora, Mama, and Grandma with preparing sacks of food and supplies for the men to take with them. Her mother went into the pantry and removed jars of canned peaches and peas, and Sallie stood beside her scooping out cornmeal. Sallie peered at her mother and noticed the gray salting her chestnut locks. Mama's hands, though still smooth as silk, bore the signs of the hardships of the past year. Sallie wished she could be as brave and full of faith as her mother always was. No matter what had happened in the past, Mama believed only good would come in the future. Sallie shrugged and dug her scoop into the bin of meal before her. Mama's optimism did not change anything.

In no time Sallie and her mother finished filling saddle packs with provisions for the next two days. Will led one of their horses to the kitchen door and came in to tote a few bags outside to be loaded onto their packhorse. Mama stood by to oversee the job.

"Now you be careful with those utensils. You'll have to use them the whole time you're there. No sense in toting them back and forth every week."

"Yes, ma'am, I know." Will nodded and continued tightening ropes and straps.

Sallie secured a bag to the horse's pack. "I'm going to miss you and Tom." Even a few days without her brothers would be lonely. They provided distraction that she sorely needed these days.

Will didn't respond, but he offered a smile before he took the reins and led the horse to the side yard where Moses and George waited with the two horses Will and Tom would ride. The men doubled-checked everything while Mama checked her list.

The creak of wagon wheels came up the drive. Papa had returned with supplies. He stepped down from the wagon and inspected the packhorse. "Good job, Will. You're learning well." He tied the reins to the back of the wagon then turned to Mama.

Sallie blinked back tears when Papa wrapped his arms around Mama and kissed her. Papa made no bones about his love for his wife and didn't always save kisses for the privacy of their quarters. Sallie admired that in him and loved him even more. That's the kind of love she hoped to have one day.

Sallie hugged her father then stepped back to stand with her arm about her mother's waist to watch the three men head off down the road. Just before they rounded the curve that would take them out of sight, the three of them turned back and waved one more time. A minute or so later all that remained was a settling dust cloud.

Mama clapped her hands together. "Now let's not dilly-dally. We have our own work to do." She turned to the two colored men. "Thank you for your help. George, I know you would have liked to go with them, but I'm grateful you stayed behind. I feel safer with you and Moses around."

Sallie followed her mother to the house and headed for the parlor. She picked up her book of literature and sank onto the sofa. She'd no sooner opened the book than Hannah came in.

She held up a tablet and pen. "I have a writing assignment Mama gave me to do. I have to write about my favorite stories and why I like them."

"That sounds like a nice project. If you need any help, just let me know." Writing had always been a favorite activity of Sallie's when she had lessons. Even now, writing in her journal brought her a satisfaction that sewing and even playing the piano didn't.

Without the noise of her brothers around, the afternoon stretched quiet and peaceful. She picked up her journal and pen to write about the day. She almost wrote her once favorite verse of Scripture at the top but stopped before the first letter appeared. The Lord was supposed to be her shepherd and protect her from the evil things of life, but He had failed her. And she had failed Him by breaking one of His commandments. *Thou shalt not kill.*

Virginia

Manfred stood in line with the others who had been exchanged. After a hot breakfast of biscuits and gravy at sunup, urgency to be on his way filled him. Since he didn't know the exact way he should go to reach the Grayson farm, he headed for the captain's tent quarters.

A soldier stopped him and handed Manfred a blanket and canteen of water along with a pouch filled with biscuits and hard tack. "This is enough for a day or two. After that you'll be on your own. Wish it could be more, but our own supplies are limited."

No one said how they came to have decent rations and supplies for the men, but the why and how didn't matter to Manfred, only the fact it was there. It must have been part of the treaty, but supplies had been scarce in his unit, so where had these come from?

He accepted the offering, thankful for whatever they could give him for provision while they traveled. They'd have to depend a lot on the goodness and mercy of others. In Philippians Paul had reminded the people that God would supply their needs. He'd hold on to that promise in the days ahead.

Instead of going to the officer's tent right away, Manfred went to an empty spot by a tree and knelt down. "My Father, we are depending on Your promises to sustain us and see us through the next days and weeks until we're home. You promised to provide for us, and I promise that I will return the provision where people need me. I pray Edwin will agree to my vow to You." The trip may be long and hard, but with God's help, they'd make it.

Manfred made his way to Captain Parker's tent. The officer spotted Manfred and beckoned him to enter. "At ease. What can I do for you, son?"

"If you have a map I might consult before we head out, I'd appreciate it. I'm looking for a Grayson farm and St. Stephens Church." Without more explicit directions Manfred had no idea where they were going except south.

Captain Parker consulted some papers before him then picked one out. "I believe this is what you need." He handed the map to Manfred then a pen and a sheet of blank paper. "Here, copy the information you need from this. It shows the areas you're headed for. If you'll head southwest from here to the Rappahannock River, you can cross over the river to Tappahannock. The ferry should be running to take you across. St. Stephens Church is about fifteen maybe twenty miles or so farther. Miller's Tavern is a small town on the way. I say it should take you a half a day or so on foot after you cross the river to reach the town, and then the rest of the day to go on to St. Stephens."

Manfred studied the map carefully and laid the smaller map Luke had given him beside the larger map and wrote further directions and landmarks to make the smaller one match the larger. When he finished, he tucked it into his journal.

The captain leaned forward. "Is that a diary you have there?"

Manfred laid the pen back on the table and pushed the book into his pack. "Yes, sir. It's a journal of all we've been through."

"Keep it close to you. Records like that will be important someday." He lifted his hand to his cap in salute. "I wish you Godspeed. May the rain and winds always be at your back."

Manfred snapped to attention and saluted. "Thank you, sir." He turned on his heel and marched from the tent. A few yards outside and he broke into a full run, waving his arms to signal Edwin.

"I got us a map, and we're leaving now." Manfred hefted his belongings to his shoulder then turned to several others standing nearby. "This is it, brothers. We're heading home, but we're making a stop by St. Stephens first."

One of the soldiers scratched his chin. "We'll be leaving soon too, but I hear we should steer clear of Richmond and keep south down to Petersburg before going west."

"Don't know about that, but we're bringing word to a fellow soldier's family. They'll be able to give us more information." At least that was Manfred's hope. They'd have to cross the mountains either in Virginia or the Carolinas, but he had no idea about direction except to go south and west. The sun and stars and kind folks would be their guide.

He and Edwin marched away from the group. Edwin stretched his legs forward in a long, quick pace.

"Whoa, little brother, don't want to use up all your energy at the beginning. You'll need it at the end of the day."

Edwin grinned but slowed his steps. Manfred slapped his brother's shoulder. Edwin's healing took a huge leap when they met freedom and good fresh air. Manfred had gained renewed strength himself. He gazed up into the sky, dotted with lazy clouds. God was still in His heaven, and all was right with the world once again. Their journey had begun.

CHAPTER 6

Virginia, Friday, April 14, 1865

ARLY MORNING SUN dappled the ground beneath the oak tree when Manfred awakened and stretched his arms above his head. He sat up and reached to retrieve his journal from his knapsack. How good it was to be free and in the open air. Might as well write a few words before Edwin wakened.

He wet the stub of pencil with his tongue and began writing.

> *We traveled to Haynesville before stopping for lunch then made our way here to the Rappahannock River to camp for the night. The sun during the day is warm, almost too warm for our wool jackets, but the nights are still cool. Then the jackets provide warmth against the chill. Edwin seems to be gaining strength much faster now. After our stop at Grayson's farm, we can make better time. I plan to ask Mr. Grayson if he knows the best way through the mountains.*

His brother stirred and turned over. Manfred stowed the journal and unwrapped a packet of biscuits. He fanned the flames of the campfire built the night before.

Edwin opened his eyes and sat up. "Hey, it's late. Why didn't you wake me?"

"You needed the sleep." Manfred handed two biscuits to his brother and took two for himself. "Sorry they're not hot and buttery like yesterday morning."

"Don't matter none, but I sure could use a cup of that coffee we had then." Edwin stuffed a portion of biscuit in his mouth.

Manfred chuckled. "You put those away too fast, and you'll be hungry within the hour." He checked the sky and the position of the sun. It was early enough to get a march in before noon. He had set a goal of at least ten hours a day of walking, no matter how tired he became. They wouldn't have anything to do after dark but to sleep. He'd get his rest then.

A few minutes later Edwin ate the last morsel of his meal, and Manfred rolled up his blanket. He patted his brother's back. "Time to hit the road."

Edwin nodded and in a few minutes tossed his bedroll over his shoulder. "How far do you think it might be to the Grayson place?"

"Luke said the farm is a few miles south of St. Stephens Church, and according to this map I drew from the big one, it's about fifteen, maybe twenty miles after we cross the river. I'd say we should be there by late afternoon or dinnertime." Manfred scraped the sole of his boot across the ashes of the campfire, making sure no sparks remained. He hitched up his pack and motioned for Edwin to follow him.

They trekked down to the river, boarded the ferry, and sat down near the edge to watch the water. Several others sat or stood as they made their way across. Two of the men commented on the uniforms. The older of the two said, "We had a few skirmishes around these parts, but nothing like what we've heard from around Richmond. Where are you headed?"

"We're stopping by the Grayson farm first to relay some news about their son. After that we'll head for Louisiana and home."

"Ah, yes, I know the place. Right friendly folks. You have news of their son, you say?"

"Yes, sir. Luke Grayson was with us in the prison at Point Lookout. We want to let them know he'll be coming home soon."

The old man nodded and leaned on his cane. "Good, good. News like that will do them well." He shuffled on over to stand closer to the front of the ferry where his horse was tied.

Minutes later the ferry bumped against the shoreline, and passengers disembarked to walk or mount horses to continue their journeys.

Manfred perused his map and checked the directions. He stopped one of the men who had been on the ferry. "Is this the way to St. Stephen's Church?"

The man nodded. "Yep. Keep going on this here road. It's about fifteen miles or so. Miller's Tavern is nine, and St. Stephen's beyond that."

"Thank you." Manfred folded the map and stuffed it in his pocket then picked up his pack.

The sun served as their guide, and they marched at a brisk pace, the younger boy matching him step for step. Manfred smiled. Edwin was determined to prove his strength or die trying.

After a while Manfred slowed his gait. Edwin wiped his brow and turned to peer at his brother. "I'm glad you finally remembered my legs aren't as long as yours."

Manfred glanced sideways at his brother. "You didn't seem to be having any trouble keeping up."

"I was beginning to." Edwin shifted the load on his back. "I hope Luke's momma is as good a cook as he said. I'll be ready for a good meal."

"You and me both. I'm sure they'll be happy to share whatever they have with us in good old-fashioned Southern style. Imagine Luke's ma and pa will be mighty glad to know he's alive and coming home soon."

They walked a bit in companionable silence until Edwin puckered up and whistled "Dixie." Manfred joined in, and they spent the next few miles singing and whistling. Edwin expressed the same exhilaration of freedom as Manfred. Blue skies, fresh air, and warm sun filled them both with the joy of being alive.

A few miles past Miller's Tavern they came upon a small stream. Manfred removed his hat, knelt, and swished a handful of the cool water over his face. He tested the water for purity then scooped it with his cupped palms and drank. He wiped his mouth with the back of his hand. Edwin dropped his pack and fell to his knees beside Manfred.

"From the looks of the sun, it's about time for the last of our rations. We've made good time today. If we can keep up the pace and have a good rest each night, we'll make it home by June."

After eating the last of the biscuits, Manfred refilled his canteen with Edwin beside him. Having clean, fresh water helped to bear the warmth of the afternoon sun. Manfred stood and settled his hat securely on his head. "Let's go."

As they walked, Manfred shared his plans for their journey with Edwin. "We don't have any money, so we'll have to seek work along the way wherever we can. We'll go on down Virginia and into Tennessee then down to Alabama and across to Mississippi. I figure we can get to Woodville and see if Sallie's family is there. I fear the battle at Natchez may have wandered far enough south to hit their home." That route may take a little longer, but it wouldn't come near Nashville. He'd seen more of that place than he cared to in his lifetime.

"I hadn't considered that. With the fighting so close, no telling what we'll find." Edwin stopped and pulled a canteen from his pack. He took a swig of water and glanced toward the sky. "Wish some clouds would come along to cover the sun."

Manfred paused alongside Edwin, winced at the sun, and drew the sleeve of his shirt across his sweat-beaded brow. "Does get warm this time of day. I see a town up ahead. It must be St. Stephens Church since we passed Miller's Tavern already. We can't be more'n half an hour from the Grayson place."

"Good. A nice shady porch and a cool glass of lemonade sounds mighty fine." Edwin returned the canteen to his pack and headed for the town ahead.

St. Francisville, Louisiana

Meals today had been quiet with the men folk not there except for Grandpa. Now Hannah had gone upstairs to get her books to study, so Sallie wandered into the parlor where she sat down at the piano. Her fingers swept deftly across the keys to play her favorite, Beethoven's *Moonlight Sonata*. At the end of the music she sat with hands limp on the keyboard.

"I've always loved that piece." Mama slipped in behind her and rested her hands on Sallie's shoulders. "But it always makes me sad."

"I guess I'm feeling a little sad. I want to know Manfred is alive and well." Sallie sighed and eased the piano lid down to cover the keys.

Her mother placed an arm around her shoulders. "I think I have something to cheer you up. Your grandmother and I spoke with Grandpa today. We think it's time to have some happiness around here, so we're going to give you a party for your nineteenth birthday."

Sallie turned and wrapped her arms around her mother's slim waist. "Oh, Mama. What a wonderful idea, but do you think it's all right? With the war and all?"

Mama held Sallie's chin with the palm of her hand and stroked her cheek with a gentle touch. "We thought of the war, but we decided a party would be fine. It won't be a lavish ball like we would have had at home, and it won't be a grand dinner, but we do have eggs, staples, and some fruit, so we will serve beautiful desserts and have coffee and tea. Besides, it will give you a chance to get together with your friends."

"Not many young men left around here, but it will be good for those who have come home." Sallie sat back and clasped her hands to her chest. "I wish Manfred could be here. It won't be as much fun without him."

"I know, but we want to do this for you. I'm hoping it will cheer you to be around others your age." Mama stood and held out a hand to Sallie. "Why don't we go to Mr. Brady's store and select the fabric for your party dress?"

"All right. Let's get our bonnets." She hugged her mother.

Sallie didn't want to dampen her mother's enthusiasm and efforts. Even though a party would be good for everyone's spirits, it wouldn't be the same without Manfred to help her celebrate. Even with her birthday, Sallie's heart would not rejoice as it would when Manfred came home. She may have much for which to be thankful, but God had let her down and given her an afternoon of terror she could not forget. A still voice in her heart reminded her that God had protected them. If that was so, then why did that boy have to die? Why hadn't God protected *him*? Most likely she'd never know the answers to such questions.

The bell jingling on the door to Mr. Brady's store brought

her back to the present. Sallie breathed deeply to savor the scent of peppermint.

Mr. Brady looked up from his writing a receipt for a customer to greet them, a broad smile creasing his ruddy face. "Be with you in a few minutes, Mrs. Dyer." He turned back to helping the lady standing at the counter.

Sallie peered around the store until she found the bolts of piece goods stacked on a shelf. She strolled over to the area and lifted several to inspect them. Mama joined her and picked up a bolt of pale yellow lawn with a tiny green leaf pattern.

"Sallie, this will look lovely with your hair. It will bring out the golden highlights and complement the green in your eyes." She held the swath in one hand and spread out a corner of the cloth.

Sallie fingered the delicate fabric. "Oh, I like that one, Mama. And here's solid yellow cotton to go under it." She held up the yellow sample in her arms.

Mama took the bolt from Sallie. "I'll take these to the counter while you look for a pattern. You'll need lace and ribbon too."

Sallie nodded and headed for the table stacked with several issues of *Godey's Lady's Book*. She flipped through page after page of one then discarded it for another. The book fell open to an illustrated page of party dresses. One featured a full skirt over crinolines and a slightly rounded neckline trimmed with lace. The same lace adorned the short sleeves and front of the bodice with ribbon bows at the edge of each sleeve.

"Mama, I found one I like," she called to the front of the store. She carried the book to the counter and pointed a finger to the design. "This one will look pretty with the edge of the neck and sleeves trimmed in lace."

Mr. Brady leaned over to see the picture. He nodded his approval. "That's a good choice, Miss Dyer. It's in my newest book."

"Then that's the one we'll use. Mrs. Tenney should have no problem with it." Mama unrolled the dry goods for a better look. "Yes, I think this fabric will do nicely. We'll take both of these." She stepped back from the counter.

Sallie reached over to the display of ribbon spools and selected a dark green satin to complement the green design. She also chose the lace to adorn the collar. Tingles of excitement shot through her, and she hugged her mother. "Thank you so much for the new dress. It's going to be beautiful."

Much of their clothing had been left behind in Woodville, and looting and pilfering had made short work of those, so having the new dress now lifted her spirits and shoved the darker memories to the recesses of her mind.

Mr. Brady cut the ribbon and lace and smiled at Sallie. "Been a while since you were in to see us, Miss Sallie. I know your grandmother and grandfather are happy to have you here even though it's not under the best of circumstances."

"Being with them is a blessing, Mr. Brady. God has provided a safe haven for us."

He raised his eyebrows then folded the fabric just cut. "Must be a special occasion coming up for you."

Heat rose in Sallie's cheeks. "Yes, sir. It's my birthday."

He shook his head. "Ah, me. You're all grown-up. Still like peppermints?"

Sallie ducked her head. "You remembered."

He tied the bundle of merchandise with twine. "Well, now. Let's see what I can do about that." He handed the package to Mama and then reached into the candy jar with the red and white candies. He scooped out a handful and poured then into a brown bag. "Here's an early birthday gift." Mr. Brady handed her the bag. "Have you heard from Manfred Whiteman since his furlough last summer? He sure seemed smitten with you."

Sallie's heart skipped a beat. "No, Mr. Brady. I haven't heard from him since before the fighting at Nashville last fall." She held the bag of sweets tightly to her chest. Somehow, doing so brought Manfred closer to her.

Mama hooked her hand onto Sallie's elbow. "When the war is over, we expect he'll be back soon after. Come, Sallie, we must make a stop at Mrs. Tenney's. Thank you, Mr. Brady, for your help." She guided Sallie to the door.

Sallie turned and waved to Mr. Brady. "Good-bye, and thank you for the peppermints." He smiled and nodded his head. Why in the world had her mother been so short with him? Sallie detected the hint of anger that had pierced the words. Mama didn't like to talk about the war, and neither did Sallie, but that was no cause for Mama to be rude to Mr. Brady.

They stepped out into the bright sunshine, and Amanda released Sallie's arm. Amanda's mouth set in a firm line. Her shortness with Mr. Brady bothered her, but she didn't want to talk about the war. Perhaps she should go back and apologize. No, he would understand without her saying a word.

"He was just being nice, Mama. Why did we have to leave so quick?"

Amanda blinked. Of course Sallie would notice and comment on the rude words. "We have too much to do to stand around and visit and talk about the war. It's drawing close to suppertime, and we must finish our business in order not to be late."

The confusion and pain in Sallie's eyes brought more guilt into Amanda's heart. Her words were true, but Amanda found no pleasure in her explanation to Sallie. Time to change the subject and tell Sallie about the surprise for this evening.

"My dear, Mr. and Mrs. Whiteman are coming for supper tonight. We wanted it to be a surprise, but I might as well tell you now, so you'll be prepared."

Sallie stopped short. "Mr. and Mrs. Whiteman are coming tonight?" She clasped her hands to her chest. "You said they'd come sometime this week, but I didn't expect it to be so soon. Perhaps they've had news of Manfred."

"I don't know about that, but it will be nice to visit with them. Harriet has been a good friend all the times we've visited in the past." She stopped in front of the dressmakers. "Here we are. We'll give Mrs. Tenney the fabric and show her the pattern we want." Amanda doubted Harriett had any news, but she didn't want to dampen Sallie's hope. Her child needed to be distracted as much as possible so as not to dwell on the past few weeks.

Sallie opened the door and stepped inside. Amanda followed her, and Helen Tenney rushed out from the back room to greet them. "Why if it isn't Mrs. Dyer and Miss Sallie. What can I help you with this fine day?"

Amanda handed her the package of fabric. "We need a dress for Sallie's birthday. There's no real hurry as the occasion isn't until May, but we did want to get it to you now."

"Then we have plenty of time." She laid the bundle on her table, but before she could open it, Sallie asked, "Mrs. Tenney, is Miriam here?" Miriam was Mrs. Tenney's daughter, and like Sallie, she was waiting for her young man to return from the war.

The seamstress unwrapped the fabric. "No, I'm sorry, my dear. She's at home taking care of her brother, who was feeling poorly this morning. Why don't you stop by the house and visit with her? I'm sure she'd love to see you."

"Thank you. I might do that. We only arrived a few days ago, so I haven't had a chance for a visit."

"Yes, your grandmother said you had arrived when I saw her at church last Sunday." Mrs. Tenney spread the green-sprigged cloth across a large cutting table. "Oh, my, this is lovely." She peered at Sallie. "What a perfect choice for your coloring, Miss Sallie. Do you have a pattern in mind?"

Amanda handed her a piece of paper. "Here's a description of the pattern from the book at Mr. Brady's. He didn't think it could be ordered in time. Can you adapt one of yours?" It would take more than three weeks to get the pattern, and if Mrs. Tenney couldn't duplicate it, then they may have to decide on a different style. Helen Tenney had talent with needle and thread, but did it run to design as well?

The dressmaker studied the information then turned to a counter along the wall. She pulled out a book similar to that at the store and motioned for Amanda to come over. "I think this is like the one you describe."

Sallie peered over the woman's shoulder. "Yes, that's it. Can you design a dress like it without the pattern?"

Mrs. Tenney smoothed the black cotton fabric of her skirt and smiled. "I can do better than that. I have a pattern already here that I did for Judge Clarion's wife before the war. With a few adaptations and alterations, I think it will be exactly like the one you chose." She headed for another cabinet and opened it. After searching through a drawer, she returned with the pattern in hand.

Amanda's relief spilled over in a hug for Sallie. "Oh, that will be perfect." With the uncertainty of transportation and mail service, having a pattern on hand would solve many problems. She determined to give Sallie the best celebration of her life even if it couldn't be like the lavish galas before the war. They would keep things simple but as elegant as their resources and circumstances would allow.

Satisfied with Mrs. Tenney's suggestion, Amanda sat down and waited for the seamstress to measure Sallie. She made a mental note of what would be needed to help her mother and Flora when they arrived home. With the food mostly prepared after the noon meal, all she and her mother had left to do was to decorate and set the table. They planned to use the best china and crystal and flowers gathered from the spring blooms in the garden.

This evening would be a nice break in their usual routine. The only thing to mar the occasion would be the absence of Thomas and their sons. The purpose of their journey clouded the good feelings Amanda had built in her heart. Even if the house was fully restored, could they ask Sallie to return? But if Manfred returned, he could court Sallie properly, and then she wouldn't have to return to Woodville.

Amanda smiled with satisfaction. Yes, everything would work out in perfect order once Manfred came home.

On the way home they passed the Tenney house. "Mama, do you need me to help before supper?" Sallie asked.

"No, we can take care of everything. Why?"

"I want to stop in at Miriam's and speak with her. I haven't had a chance to visit with her since we've come here, and I also want to see if she's heard from Stuart. You know he and Manfred enlisted at the same time." They'd joined up at Camp Moore in the Fourth Louisiana Infantry the summer of 1861. Both had been eighteen, the same age she was now.

"Of course, my dear; have a nice visit." She kissed Sallie's cheek then proceeded down the street toward home.

Miriam answered Sallie's knock on the door, and a smile lit up her eyes. "What a delightful surprise. I was thinking about you just yesterday. Come in. Jeremy wasn't feeling well, so I stayed home with him." She hugged Sallie then led her into the parlor.

"We just came from your mother's shop, and she told me you were here with your brother. She's making me a new dress to wear to my birthday party next month."

"Mama is so talented. She'll sew up a beautiful dress for you. I'm sorry we haven't had a chance to visit since your coming here."

"I am too, but we'll have to change that. I also want you to be at my party. It's not going to be anything really fancy, what with the war and all. I think Mama just wants to keep my mind off all of it and Manfred, but that's difficult to do."

"I know. I keep thinking about Stuart." She jumped up. "I have his last letter. Let me get it."

Sallie's heart quickened while she waited for Miriam's return. If Stuart was all right, then that meant Manfred could be too.

The two had been home on furlough once last summer. Manfred had all but declared his love for her then, but with the uncertainty of the times, he didn't speak with her father. His correspondence in late November arrived just before his unit engaged in another battle, but nothing had come since then. How she longed to see him. Any news Miriam could share from Stuart would help. She twisted a fold of her skirt between her fingers.

Miriam reappeared. "Here's what I received a few weeks ago just after he returned to his regiment."

"Does he make any mention of Manfred?" One word, that's all she needed.

Miriam scanned the letter again. "No, he doesn't, but then he said that most of their regiment had been lost or captured at Nashville. Stuart is in Mississippi now, but I don't know exactly where, and he doesn't say that Manfred is with them."

Could Manfred have been killed or captured? It couldn't be. Tears welled, and Sallie fought to control them. Perhaps he hadn't written because he'd lost interest in her during the war.

Miriam dropped the letter. "I'm so sorry, Sallie. I didn't even think." She reached across and wrapped her arms around Sallie. "Stuart would have told me if Manfred or Edwin had been killed. That means they may have been captured and taken north."

Sallie swallowed hard, but no sound came when she tried to speak. She rested her head against Miriam's shoulder. Captured and sent to one of those prisons that could possibly kill him, according to stories she'd heard. Then she'd never know if he loved her and wanted to marry her. Hearing words of endearment from him last year was far different from hearing words of true love and commitment now that she had become a more mature young woman.

Miriam patted Sallie's back. "Manfred's brothers came home safe from a prison camp in New York. We must believe Manfred and Edwin will too."

"Yes, but Charles and Henry were in poor health, and, according to Grandma, refused to talk about what they'd endured." Still, she must hold on to hope. This war had gone on too long. The time had come to end it, but men didn't see things that way. They'd keep fighting to defend what they believed no matter what the odds. *Please, Lord, let this war be over soon.*

CHAPTER 7

Grayson Farm, Virginia

J UST AS MANFRED predicted, when the sun began to dip
in the western sky, they topped a hill and spotted a two-
story, white clapboard house rising from among a few
trees. A barn needing paint stood behind the main house
along with a fenced area holding a few horses. Freshly plowed
fields stretched beyond the outbuildings.

From the description given him, the house must belong
to Luke's family. As they approached, a man in the shadows
of the porch called to someone in the house. A few moments
later other family members joined him. The older man ran
down the steps and trotted up the hill to meet them.

Manfred called to him. "Are you Mr. Grayson?" At the
man's nod he said, "We bring you news from your son, Luke."
He extended his hand to grasp that of the gray-haired farmer.

Tears glistened in the man's pale blue eyes. "Is he alive?
Is he well? Where did you see him?" Then before Manfred
could answer, Mr. Grayson turned to the house and called,
"They have news of Luke."

A woman on the porch gathered up her skirts and hurried to greet them. "What do you know about our son? Is he
alive and well?" Her lined face reflected her worry, and her
mouth trembled.

Manfred hastened to reassure them. "We were in the
same prison at Point Lookout, Maryland. He's well and will
be released soon and should be home shortly. I'm Manfred
Whiteman, and this is my brother, Edwin. We're from
Louisiana." He handed Luke's letter to Mrs. Grayson.

Mrs. Grayson clasped the letter to her chest and raised her eyes heavenward. "Thank You, Lord. Thank You."

Manfred waited as she read the paper. Still holding the letter, she threw her arms around her husband's neck and cried. "He's coming home. Luke's coming home." Tears streamed down her cheeks. She handed her husband the letter then backed away and turned to Manfred, using a corner of her apron to pat her eyes.

"Forgive my manners. You boys are worn out. Come on to the house. We were about to sit down to supper." She locked arms with Manfred and Edwin and led the way.

Two young men waited at the bottom of the porch steps, and Mrs. Grayson called a greeting. "Mark, John, your brother Luke is alive and will be home soon. These young men are Manfred and Edwin Whiteman, and they were in prison with him."

When they drew near, one of the men reached for Manfred's hand. "I'm Mark Grayson." A red slash of a scar on his neck and the cane on which he balanced spoke of his participation in the war.

Before Manfred could comment, the young man said, "I fought at Lynchburg. They sent me home to heal."

Manfred swallowed a lump in his throat and gripped Mark's hand. He stared deep into the young man's eyes, and he needed no words to express the feelings each had for what they had seen and experienced in the past months.

Next to them Edwin and John stood engrossed in conversation, their heads close. As they climbed the stairs to the porch, Mrs. Grayson introduced the others gathered there. An attractive young woman held a small child in her arms. Her brown eyes reflected a sadness Manfred had never seen in one so young.

Mrs. Grayson wrapped her arm around the young

woman's shoulders. "This is Rachel. She was married to our son Matthew." She blinked away tears. "He didn't come home from the last battle."

Another young woman with long brown hair tied back with a ribbon introduced herself as Ruth, the Grayson's daughter.

Mrs. Grayson herded them all into the house and to the kitchen. Manfred savored the simplicity and comfort of the home while the aroma of home cooking tantalized his nose and caused a low rumble in his belly.

A long table in the dining area held bowls of steaming vegetables and platters of homemade bread. Ruth and Mrs. Grayson bustled about setting two extra places on the table. Mr. Grayson and the others stood behind the chairs. At Mr. Grayson's nod everyone seated themselves then joined hands for a prayer.

Manfred's heart pounded at the familiar ritual. He pictured his own family at home doing the same thing and squeezed Edwin's hand. Edwin returned the squeeze and glanced sideways at Manfred.

Mr. Grayson's simple prayer filled Manfred with a sense of peace. The first leg of their journey had drawn to a close in a place of comfort, safety, and welcome.

St. Francisville, Louisiana

Sallie had looked forward to the evening with the Whiteman family, but Miriam's news dampened her spirits. Her desire to learn even more about Manfred grew stronger, despite the anxiety of her heart.

When the rumble of carriage wheels drew her to the

window, her heart leaped with anticipation. She gathered up her dress above her ankles and raced down the stairs. Halfway down she caught her mother's disapproving look. Sallie stopped abruptly, let her skirts fall to the floor, and ran her hands over her hair to capture any loose strands that may have strayed in her haste. Lettie helped Mrs. Whiteman with her cloak and bonnet but managed a playful wink at Sallie. Grandma hid a smile behind her fan.

Sallie joined her mother and Mrs. Whiteman in the foyer. The murmur of male voices drifted in from the parlor where the men gathered. The women strolled into the sitting room.

"Sallie, please entertain us with one of your new pieces." Her mother nodded toward the piano then settled herself on the settee.

Mrs. Whiteman sat and adjusted her skirt. "Please do, Sallie. Manfred always comments about your playing."

Sallie smiled. "Thank you, Mrs. Whiteman." She perched on the bench, arched her fingers over the keys, and struck the opening notes of a Beethoven melody. At the moment, playing didn't fit her agenda. She wanted to hear about Manfred and when he was a little boy. How he worked on the docks with his father and brother would be much more interesting than Beethoven.

Her fingers flowed easily over the keys as the strains of the music filled the air. At the conclusion of the piece, the clapping of hands behind her gave her a start. She whirled around to find her grandfather, Mr. Whiteman, and Charles Whiteman applauding.

"Bravo. Bravo." Her grandfather ambled over and kissed her cheek. "You play more beautifully every day, my dear."

Heat rose in Sallie's face. She turned away from the admiring glances of Mr. Whiteman and Manfred's oldest brother, Charles. "Thank you, Grandpa, but after dinner we must ask Hannah to play for us. She is learning so well."

Hannah's cheeks turned pink, but the pleased expression on her face warmed Sallie's heart. Encouraging her younger sister had become one of Sallie's main goals now that they lived in St. Francisville.

Lettie stepped into the room and announced dinner. The men and ladies joined arms with Grandpa and Grandma, leading the group to the dining room. Charles grasped Sallie's hand and tucked it under his arm. "I know I'm no substitute for Manfred, but I'm honored to escort you to dinner. Henry didn't come with us, for he's not feeling well."

"Oh, I'm sorry to hear that. I understand he suffered a few injuries." Rumors had it that Manfred's next older brother, Henry, had not fared well since coming home from war. His hair had turned snow white, and he had become a recluse, but Sallie didn't want to ask and appear too nosy. Things that had gone on in this war may well turn a young person into an old one.

Charles only nodded before they seated themselves at the table. After Grandpa said grace, Flora and Lettie served the meal. During the dinner Sallie listened for any word or mention of Manfred, but none came. Her parents and Mr. and Mrs. Whiteman discussed the weather, happenings at the church, and everything else but Manfred.

Charles sat between Sallie and Hannah, and he divided his attention between them. While he and her sister discussed her activities, Sallie picked up a few words from Mama's conversation with Mrs. Whiteman. Although Mama didn't discuss the war itself, she did tell Mrs. Whiteman about their home in Woodville and the repairs going on there. Sallie missed the banter her brothers usually brought to the table, but they wouldn't be home until Saturday and would even miss the Good Friday service at the Methodist church later this evening.

Her mother reached over to grasp Sallie's arm and squeezed it as though she read Sallie's thoughts.

"My dear, I was telling Mrs. Whiteman about the fabric we purchased for your birthday dress."

Her smile encouraged Sallie to take on a more pleasant manner, and she dismissed the memory to pay more attention to Mrs. Whiteman.

Mrs. Whiteman touched the corners of her lips with an ivory damask napkin. "It sounds lovely, my dear. And yellow with green is perfect with your hair and eyes. I'm sure you will be beautiful in it."

"Thank you, Mrs. Whiteman. I do hope Charles and Henry will be able to attend as well as Teddy, I mean, Theo." She remembered how he hated to be called by his childhood name now that he had fought in the war. Of course, Charles had discovered him at camp and sent the boy home when the officers learned he was only fifteen at the time. Apparently that few weeks had cured him of the desire to go off and fight.

Mrs. Whiteman chuckled. "Ah, yes. Theo. He's calling on Lucy Simpson this evening for dinner and afterward to attend services with her family. All three will look forward to your celebration. I heard just today from Mrs. Elliot that her son, Benjamin, will be home this week. He'd make a handsome addition to your party."

Mama nodded. "I must be sure to see an invitation is sent. If I remember, he's the tall, dark-haired one."

Sallie searched her memory trying to recall his face, but no one came to mind. On all their previous trips to St. Francisville, she had paid little attention to the young men in town. Only Manfred filled her free time. It didn't really matter whether she remembered him or not, he'd still be welcome as a guest.

After dinner the group returned to the parlor, where Hannah entertained with her playing. True to Sallie's word, the young girl played with complete abandon that made the melodies soar and fill the room with the beauty of the music. Yes, Hannah had a tremendous talent and would be an accomplished musician if she continued with her studies.

Then Lettie appeared and announced that Moses had the carriages around front for the short ride to the church.

Mrs. Whiteman invited Sallie to ride in the Whiteman carriage, and she climbed up beside Mrs. Whiteman with delight. "Thank you so much. I haven't had many chances to visit with you for very long, and I have so many questions to ask about Manfred." She grasped the older woman's hand.

Manfred's mother smiled and patted Sallie's arm. Her brown eyes shone with warmth and love. "I know you must miss him as much as I do. I'm thankful for the three at home, but I won't rest easy until my other two are safe back in the fold. Manfred has great plans to be a doctor."

Although she relished the idea of being a doctor's wife, Sallie had so many questions about the young man who had come into her life when she had been ten years old and he thirteen. "I haven't seen him but that one weekend in four years. I don't really know much about him as a younger boy, only what I saw when we came for summer visits until the war started."

"Well, with five boys, we always had things happening, but one thing in particular occurred when he was about four years old. His brothers took to calling him Manny, and he didn't like it. Finally he stomped his foot, crossed his arms over his chest, and announced, 'My name is Manfred, not Manny. Manny is for babies, and I'm not a baby.' After that we never called him Manny again. He's a stubborn one, that middle son of mine. I think Manfred's the reason Theo abandoned the name of Teddy when he grew older."

Sallie grinned. She could picture the young Manfred in his determined stance. Perhaps they would have a stubborn little boy one day. Of course, Manfred hadn't asked to marry her as yet or even truly declared his love, but as soon as the war was over, he'd be home and they could court properly.

Mrs. Whiteman squeezed Sallie's hand. "I also remember the tenderness with which he cared for his animals. He used to bring home every stray dog, cat, rabbit, goat, or whatever he found. A stubborn will but a tender heart. Just what a doctor needs."

Sallie had observed Manfred's tenderness with Hannah and with Lettie when he'd been around them. Remembering only made her wish even more for his presence now. When Mrs. Whiteman related the story of his and Edwin's chasing a goat around the yard and falling in the mud when they were seven and five years old, Sallie laughed out loud with the picture that scene produced in her mind.

Then Mrs. Whiteman's eyes clouded, and her expression became somber. "My precious Manfred celebrated his twenty-second birthday somewhere on the battlefield. The next time he comes home, he will be a more mature young man than the young man who signed up with Charles and Henry."

Sallie said nothing. Her heart ached for the mother who hadn't heard from her sons. A lot could have happened in four years. Manfred may be a completely different man than he was when she last saw him right before he left to rejoin his regiment.

They arrived at the church, and Mr. Whiteman assisted her and Mrs. Whiteman from the carriage. She joined her mother and Hannah to sit with her family for the services. Even though their own Grace Church still could not be used for services, the solemn atmosphere of this church for remembering Christ's suffering on the cross filled her heart with gratitude for the sacrifice of His life.

After Communion the minister led the parishioners in prayer then dismissed them. Mama had invited the Whiteman family for a stop on the way home for coffee and dessert Flora had prepared.

As much as Sallie wanted to hear more about Manfred and his childhood, fatigue had set in, but good manners required her to play hostess with her mother and grandmother. When they arrived home, Hannah went up to bed. Sallie remained in the parlor with Mama, Grandma, and Mrs. Whiteman for a wonderful pastry layered with chocolate and cream.

When her mother turned the talk to household matters, Sallie stood and addressed their guest. "Mrs. Whiteman, I'm so glad you were here tonight. If you'll excuse me, I'm going to retire to my room." She kissed her mother's cheek then gave Grandma a hug.

The murmur of the women's voices and the low hum of the men's discussion followed her upstairs. Hannah lay sprawled on the four-poster bed, already sound asleep. Sallie marveled at how quickly the child could fall into slumber. She pulled the covers gently around her sister and kissed her forehead.

She undressed quietly then sat in her white cotton gown and chemise at her desk. The middle drawer held Manfred's letters. She drew the pink-ribbon-tied packet to her cheek and breathed in the sweet scent of the lilac sachet she had placed with it earlier. Seeing his letters brought the shadow of another memory to mind. A chill skittered down her spine. She shook her head and fingered the satin ribbon.

Someday soon he would be home. He'd work with Dr.

Andrews and learn what he needed to know to have his own practice someday. What a fine doctor he would make. He'd be the best one in town. She placed the letters back in the drawer, electing not to read them tonight. Doing so brought more sadness than happiness into her heart.

Hannah murmured in her sleep, and Sallie pulled the covers back over her slender form. So much had happened in the past four years. She'd been a girl of fifteen when Manfred first left, and now she had grown into womanhood. Although they had been apart for so long, somehow love had grown in Sallie's heart.

Although he hadn't come right out and declared his love the last time they'd been together, his letters since spoke of how much he cared for her and how he prayed she'd be waiting for him when he returned. Only then would he be able to declare his intentions and speak with Papa. That's what she'd cling to in the days ahead.

Then the shadow of what happened in Woodville crossed over her heart. A tear trickled down her cheek as she slid between the sheets next to Hannah. She had never intended to kill a person, but would Manfred understand?

CHAPTER 8

Grayson Farm, Virginia, Saturday, April 15, 1865

MANFRED AWAKENED AND gazed about the strange room, letting his eyes become adjusted to the dim light from the windows. Then memory kicked in. They slept in the Grayson farm home. He shoved back the covers and reached over to shake Edwin. "I hear stirring downstairs. We best be getting ourselves down there." He washed his face in the basin and urged Edwin to do the same.

Delightful aromas of bacon wafted up the stairs and accentuated his hunger. Yesterday's meal had proved that Mrs. Grayson was an excellent cook, and Manfred looked forward to the breakfast this morning.

When he and Edwin entered the kitchen ten minutes later, Mrs. Grayson motioned for them to sit where the other family members now gathered.

She placed a plate of biscuits on the table then sat down by her husband. After Mr. Grayson returned thanks, she passed a bowl of scrambled eggs to Manfred. "We have chickens to give us eggs and slaughtered a pig last fall, so we have more than many people around these parts."

Manfred helped himself to the eggs. "Did you have much fighting here?" The land around the house looked much better than some they'd passed through on their way north as prisoners.

Mr. Grayson frowned. "Not much, but enough for us to know the war was much closer than we'd like. Of course, after what General Lee gave up in his home at Arlington, we have nothing to complain about. I was sorry to hear he surrendered to Grant, but at least the fighting will stop around here and we can get on with our lives."

From the corner of his vision Manfred noticed the grim set of Rachel's mouth. This talk must be hard on her. "Your little boy is a handsome fellow. How old is he?"

Her eyes brightened as Manfred had hoped. "He's just a year now, and trying his best to walk."

Mrs. Grayson smiled and reached over to pat the child's head. "He's our pride and joy." Then she turned her gaze to Manfred. "Now tell me exactly where Bayou Sara is and about your family. You mentioned three other brothers."

Manfred nodded and swallowed a bite of biscuit. "Yes, ma'am. We have five boys, no girls, in the family. Bayou Sara is the landing down the hill from St. Francisville, and that's about fifty or so miles north of New Orleans. Father runs a shipping company."

"My, my. Five sons. Did all of you join the army?"

Edwin stabbed another slice of bacon. "Yes, ma'am, I'm the next to the youngest. Theo joined up too, but he got sent home 'cause he was too young. We don't know where the other two are now except that they were taken as prisoners at Port Hudson because they were officers. They let the enlisted men go back to their regiment."

Mrs. Grayson nodded sadly. "Your poor mother. How worried she must be about you."

Mr. Grayson placed his napkin on the table and leaned back in his chair. "The South lost some mighty fine men. She'll never be able to replace them. After we learned of Matthew's death, Mark here came home with his leg busted."

He rose and stood behind his two sons. With a hand on each boy's shoulder, Mr. Grayson said, "We thank the Lord for bringing home these two and rejoice in knowing Luke will be here soon. John here is like your Theo. He joined at sixteen but didn't get to see much fighting. His regiment stayed close by."

Manfred searched his brain for another topic to get away from the talk of war that so upset Rachel. "Did you say last night you have a vegetable garden?"

Mr. Grayson returned to his seat. "Yes, we do. Several farms were destroyed, but ours survived. We praise God for that. As long as we have ground to grow food, we'll never go hungry."

Rachel jumped up and threw her napkin on the table. "Well, I don't feel grateful. I'm sick of this war and talking of death and prisons. Nothing can bring Matt back to me, and I just wish you all would hush. I don't like little Matt hearing all this neither." She grabbed up her young son and fled from the room.

"She's right. Talk about something else. I'll go to her." Mrs. Grayson shoved back her chair and hurried to console her daughter-in-law.

Manfred sympathized with the young woman. He didn't want to talk about the war, but it was what interested those not actually involved in the battles.

He pushed back his plate. A good meal to start the day filled him with satisfaction. Too many months had passed since the last hearty breakfast he had enjoyed. A few more meals like this, and he and Edwin would be healthier for the long journey home.

He must think of a way to repay the Grayson family for their kindness. With the meal ended, he followed the men out to the front porch where a gentle breeze wafted through the trees.

The elder Grayson puffed on his pipe and gazed into the morning sky. The leaves danced a jig in the soft wind, and the smell of lilacs filled the air.

Mark Grayson broke the silence. "How long will it take you to get home?"

"I'm hoping we'll be home by early June." Manfred leaned back against the railing and rested his arm on it.

Mr. Grayson tapped his pipe in the palm of his hand. "We're finishing up the spring planting. Looks like we'll have good weather for a few days to get it done."

Manfred glanced at Edwin. The boy sat with his head bowed. He raised his eyes to Manfred and nodded. Manfred breathed deeply. "Mr. Grayson, I think we can spare a few days or so to help. We want to repay your kindness."

The farmer shook his head. "You boys don't need to do that. You want to get on home."

Manfred stood and leaned toward the older man. "But a few days won't make that much difference. It's the least we can do for food and shelter."

"He's right, Mr. Grayson. We'd be hungry and worn out without your help," Edwin said.

"If you really mean it, we'll get started early Monday morning. With tomorrow being Easter Sunday, we'll go to church and worship and rest up for the week ahead. We can work all day Monday and Tuesday. With your help we should get it all done by then. Of course we'll be happy to have you join us for Easter services tomorrow." Mr. Grayson stood and stretched.

Easter Sunday? Manfred had lost track of the days in prison. How nice it would be to worship in an actual church after so many months without. Easter Sunday would be the perfect way to acknowledge their freedom by worshipping and celebrating the resurrection of Jesus.

"What can we do today to help out, Mr. Grayson?" Manfred gazed about the well-kept lawn and outbuildings.

"I'll be working in the barn making sure all the equipment

is ready for Monday. You two can help load the wagon with the seed and equipment. That way it'll be all ready for our trek to the fields."

"Sounds good to me, Mr. Grayson. Edwin and I are more than happy to help in any way we can." He stepped down from the porch and followed Mr. Grayson to the barn.

Mark walked beside him. "We had a fine crop last fall, and we put up a nice supply of vegetables. The smokehouse has a few things left in it, and we had a new batch of chicks last fall, so the farm is doing better than some others in the area. Pa likes to share as much as he can with those not so fortunate."

Manfred had noticed the same giving nature in Luke during their days of imprisonment. He had been ready to give up a blanket or a cup of soup if it would make someone else more comfortable. "We can't thank you enough for your hospitality."

Edwin stretched his arms to the sky. "I don't know about Manfred, here, but I slept like a log. Luke sure has a comfortable bed."

"I did sleep well. In fact, I can't remember the last time I slept so sound unless it was when we were home last year." His heart swelled with gratitude to this family who had sacrificed for the war. From this day on he would do whatever he could to help those who needed it. His journey home may take longer, but the reward of helping others would outweigh the delay.

St. Francisville, Louisiana

Sallie hurried downstairs to the kitchen. This day would be busy with preparations for Easter Sunday dinner. Grandma and Flora had worked on the menu all week. Although only limited supplies were getting through to Bayou Sara, the Yankees had settled down toward New Orleans and left this corner of Louisiana to itself. The Whiteman shipping company had survived the Port Hudson attack and now received and shipped some supplies from upriver. Mama and Grandma would be able to take the provisions available and turn them into a feast that would satisfy all of the family.

Sallie found Mama standing in the pantry with a list in her hand. She peered up at the shelves and removed jars of preserved vegetables and fruit. "There you are, dear. Would you take these out to the kitchen for me?"

"Yes, ma'am." Sallie grasped the jars and positioned them in her arms and hands. She stepped carefully down the steps and across the yard to the kitchen out back. Grandma glanced up from her work and nodded her head toward the table.

"Put them there by those pots, then help Lettie peel those sweet potatoes."

Sallie set the jars down and sniffed the air. Yeast, cinnamon, and apples filled the space with an aroma that caused her mouth to water in anticipation for the meal tomorrow. "Oh, Flora, I smell those cinnamon buns rising. Breakfast will be wonderful with them in the morning."

"That it will, Miss Sallie. Along with some of dat bacon from the smokehouse and eggs from de hens, we be having a breakfast fit fer a king."

Sallie laughed at the cook's enthusiasm and sat on a stool across from Lettie. "Are these for a pie or for that concoction your mam makes with syrup, sugar, and butter?"

"I'm not sure. Either one will be good." She halted her knife and peered at Sallie. "You didn't look too happy yesterday when you came home. Your mam said you were at Miss Miriam's. Did she have bad news?"

Breath caught in Sallie's throat, and she could only nod.

"Was it Mr. Manfred or Mr. Stuart?" Lettie reached across and grasped Sallie's hand.

"Stu... Stuart's fine. Last time he saw Manfred was at Nashville last December. A lot of men died and many more captured and taken to prison camps up north. Stuart was with a small band that escaped." Sallie swallowed hard to keep a sob from choking her.

"I'm so sorry, Miss Sallie. We'll have to pray real hard for Mr. Manfred to come home."

Sallie could only nod again and pick up a potato. Praying hadn't done any good in the past, so praying would make no difference now. Maybe Mama, Grandma, and Lettie would have more influence.

While her mother and grandma worked in the background, Sallie's thoughts jumped back to the last time she spent time with Manfred. His last furlough had been the past summer. How she wished they could have spent more time together. What with Mama being sick and the danger of travel in Mississippi, she had missed the opportunity. He had come up for a few hours one day, and what a wonderful time they'd had.

She now remembered that afternoon as though it had happened yesterday. They had walked in the garden back home and held hands. So much had run through her thoughts that day, but her voice could not utter the words she so wanted to say. They'd stood only inches apart with hands entwined.

Her hand went to her mouth. How she'd wanted him to kiss her then, but being the gentleman he was, he had refrained. She'd never forget his words as he said good-bye.

"Sallie, I spoke with your father and asked permission to

write to you in the coming months until this war is over. When it is and I return, we can speak more about our future. With so much uncertainty in our lives now, it is best this way. I care a great deal about you and pray you return those feelings."

"I do care, Manfred, and I'll wait for you."

"You've made my heart glad today, and when I do return, we will have a proper courtship." With those words he had kissed the back of her hands then mounted his horse and rode back to Louisiana.

Even after all these months the memory of that afternoon filled her with a longing she didn't quite understand. All she wanted at the moment was for him to return safe. With a heavy sigh she picked up another potato.

A shadow fell across the floor, and a cheery voice called out a greeting. "Hello, everyone. I thought I'd find all of you out here getting ready for tomorrow."

Sallie jumped from her stool to embrace the woman standing near. "Aunt Abigail, what a wonderful surprise. Is Peggy with you?"

Mama and Grandma both hurried over and embraced Aunt Abigail. Mama brushed a hair from her sister's forehead. "Why didn't you let us know you were coming home?"

Aunt Abigail laughed with a light ringing of sound that had always fascinated Sallie. Her aunt pulled off her gloves and glanced about the room. "With the uncertainty of mail service these days it was quicker to just come. I couldn't stay away any longer. Magnolia Hall repairs are not quite finished, but the man in charge said we could live there while they are working." She glanced at Sallie. "Peggy had things to do at home, so I didn't bring her with me."

Sallie's heart fell. Spending time with her cousin would be much more fun than peeling potatoes, but the news about the house repairs helped relieve the disappointment. "I'm so happy to hear about your home. I love your great house and its beautiful trees." So many times Sallie had visited there as a child and been quite taken by the enormous white blossoms on their waxy leaf stems that gave the home its name.

Abigail turned to Mama and Grandma. "I came through town and stopped at Mrs. Tenney's to place an order for several dresses, and she told me about your birthday party. I want to offer Magnolia Hall as the place to have it."

Sallie squealed and wrapped her arms around her aunt. "Oh, that would be wonderful." She stepped back and glanced at her mother. "Oh, Mama, please say yes. It's such a grand place to have a party."

"We'll have to discuss it with your father first, Sallie." Mama stepped over to her sister's side and grasped her elbow. "Let's go into the house where we can talk further." She inclined her head toward Sallie. "You stay here with Lettie and finish helping Flora. Your grandmother and I will be back shortly."

Sallie gazed at their backs as the three women disappeared into the house. Grandma Woodruff's house was nice and had lots of room, but in comparison Magnolia Hall was magnificent. That and the Rosedown Plantation a few miles farther up the road were the most beautiful homes around. Another home nearer town, The Myrtles, was pretty and well known about these parts, but it wasn't near as grand as Rosedown or Magnolia Hall.

If Papa said no to the party being at Aunt Abigail's, it would be disappointing, but there'd be no argument from her or Mama. She plopped back on her stool and picked up the sweet potato dropped a few minutes earlier. "I do hope Papa will accept Aunt Abigail's invitation. A party there would be grand." He'd be home tonight, so perhaps Mama could ask him then.

Too bad Manfred wouldn't be here, but for him to come home, the war would have to be over, and that wasn't likely to happen anytime soon.

CHAPTER 9

Grayson Farm, Virginia, Easter Sunday, April 16, 1865

MANFRED AWAKENED EASTER Sunday morning to bright sunshine flooding the room. He poked Edwin in the ribs. "Wake up, little brother. It's Easter, and we're going to church."

Edwin rubbed his eyes and sat up. "Easter and we're free! What a day to celebrate." He hopped from the bed and hurried to the washstand. He splashed water on his face and groped for the towel.

Manfred stretched then padded over to his brother. He picked up a straight razor. "Look, Mr. Grayson must have put this here for us." He rubbed his hand across the beard on his chin. "Well, it'll feel good to get this off and be clean shaven again."

"Oh, I don't know. I might look better with a beard." He fingered the sandy growth on his own chin.

Clean shirts and trousers caught Manfred's eye. He picked up a shirt and held it to his chest. "Must be one of Luke's. The Graysons are being really kind to us. I'm glad we volunteered to stay and help them tomorrow. Finish your washing up and try this on." He tossed the shirt in Edwin's direction.

Edwin sniffed the air. "I smell breakfast cooking, and it's calling my name." He pulled the shirt over his head and smoothed it around his waist. "A perfect fit. Must be Mark's 'cause Luke's more your size."

Manfred slipped on the other shirt. Edwin had been right. This one had to be Luke's. His friend wouldn't mind since they'd shared too much over the past two months. A few pieces of clothing shared between friends made the bond even closer, especially in times like these. The crisp, clean cotton hugged his chest and smelled like the sun and fresh outdoors, an aroma Manfred had doubted he'd ever have the pleasure to smell again.

In a few minutes both men were dressed, and Manfred led the way downstairs to the kitchen where the Grayson family gathered around the table and greeted them with smiles and hearty handshakes.

Mr. Grayson grasped Manfred's hand. "I can't thank you boys enough for staying to help us finish planting. It's late, but we'll have a crop. With what we did yesterday to prepare, we can be out in the field a little after sunup."

Manfred returned the man's firm grip. "Glad to do it, and working will help build up muscle lost these past months."

"And thank you for the razor and the clothes. Be nice to wear something besides our uniforms to church this morning." Edwin grinned and rubbed his clean-shaven face.

"Just our way of thanking you. Mother has your things in the basket to wash tomorrow morning. You'll have clean clothes when you're ready to leave." Mr. Grayson took his seat at the head of the table. The others found their places and sat down to breakfast. Mr. Grayson stretched out his hands and the circle completed itself. "Let's thank the Lord for His bounty."

Manfred echoed his host's feelings in the deep places of his heart. In the short time in their presence he had come to appreciate even more the sacrifices families all over the South as well as the North had made for their country. Many families like this one would never be complete again.

After breakfast Mr. Grayson brought around the buckboard for the ladies and little Matt. The young men saddled horses and mounted them to follow the buckboard to the church.

A large crowd had gathered on the steps of the white building. As the Grayson family arrived, several of the men hurried over to greet Manfred and Edwin.

Manfred dismounted and answered questions as best he could. "Luke's the only one I know about for sure. I think some of the other boys from around here may have been with us, but I didn't know all their names." He glanced over and spied Edwin answering questions too.

They finally broke away and entered the small building. The service began with prayer then hymns of praise. After welcoming Manfred and Edwin to the congregation, the pastor began his sermon on the Resurrection.

Manfred reflected on his family's church in St. Francisville and imagined the service there today. His family would occupy a pew near the front as was Pa's usual custom. Sallie and her family would probably be visiting her grandparents and attending church with them. How he longed to sit in the familiar pews of the church of his childhood. Then he remembered the damage done during the siege at Port Hudson and prayed the repairs had been made to bring the building back to full use.

Halfway through the service the back door banged open, and the minister stopped in mid-sentence. The congregation turned, and a familiar figure ran down the aisle. Mrs. Grayson jumped up and met her son, tears streaming down her cheeks. "Luke! Luke! Thank You, God, thank You!" Luke held his arms open, and his mother flew into them and wrapped her arms around her son.

Behind him four other soldiers raced through the door hunting for their families. Children cried, women wiped their eyes, and the men beamed as mothers and sons and wives and husbands reunited.

Mr. Grayson stepped up to the platform. He cleared his throat and called for attention. "This is a day for which we all have hoped and prayed. The ladies planned a homecoming celebration for the day after the return of our men. Looks like that'll be tomorrow. Everyone is invited to meet back here for dinner on the grounds at six in the evening."

Men and women laughed and chatted. The minister joined Mr. Grayson at the altar. "I can think of no better ending for Easter Sunday than to have these men with us. Let's thank God for them and pray for those still out there and for those families whose sons and husbands and brothers won't be back."

After the prayer the families dispersed. Joyful calls and greetings crossed from buggy to wagon to those on horseback. Manfred's heart swelled with longing for such a reunion. Only a few more days, and he and Edwin would be on their way to such a welcome home.

He noticed Rachel sitting quietly in the back of the wagon and strolled over to her. He stopped beside her, his hat in his hands, fingering the brim. "Pardon me, Rachel. I don't mean to intrude, but I know you're thinking of Matthew." At her nod he continued. "I'm really sorry he's not here with us. You're one of the many brave women who've had to say good-bye, and your courage is to be admired. God will bless you in a special way."

The young woman raised her tear-stained eyes to his. "Thank you, Manfred. Nothing's going to bring him back, but little Matt will always know how brave his Papa and all the other young men were."

"Yes, ma'am. He can be proud of his pa." Manfred mounted his horse and swiped at his damp eyes with his sleeve. His gaze took in the families rejoicing with their loved ones come home. He turned his horse and trotted over to join Edwin. Lord willing, he and his brother would reunite with their own family in a few short months.

The atrocities and horrors of war would be left behind, and the South would once again become part of this great nation. The South may have lost the war, but her men had been brave. He prayed the people of the South could put this all behind them and work toward a better future.

St. Francisville, Louisiana

Sallie climbed into the buggy and adjusted the folds of her peach-hued skirt. Hannah sat beside her and beat her shoes against the seat support. "Hannah, do sit still. You're making me nervous with that banging."

Hannah glanced sideways at her sister and pouted, but she stilled her feet. Papa hefted himself up beside Mama and clicked the reins. The horse clip-clopped down the old brick road to the Methodist Church where they would join with the members to celebrate Easter.

Sallie missed going to Grace Church for Easter, but church officials said the building wasn't safe with one wall leaning so. During the fighting the Reverend Mr. Lewis had made a name for himself when he ran down the hill with his coat-tails flying in the wind and waving a white flag. Grandma said he hollered all the way, "Quit firing at the church! Quit firing at the church!" They did, but not before shells hit one side and all but knocked it down. He promised the church would be rebuilt and stronger than ever as soon as the bricks, stone, and wood became available, but he'd left for another parish and wasn't around to make sure it happened.

Papa halted the buggy before the building, and the boys assisted Sallie and Hannah from the carriage. Papa helped Mama then secured the reins at the hitching post. The family paraded down the aisle and took a pew behind Aunt Abigail and Uncle Clark with their family. Peggy Bradford turned and mouthed "I want to talk this afternoon." Sallie smiled and nodded at her cousin.

The service this morning included special prayers for the men still away from home. The reverend prayed, "Father God, Almighty. We lift up our men to Thee today. Keep them safe as they continue to defend our rights and land. We look forward to the joyful time of the end of this war and their return. Until then, hold them in Thy hands."

Sallie gazed around the church. Where had they found so many white flowers to fill the space along the altar rail? The fresh scent of them wafted her way, giving hope of new life after all the death they'd witnessed in the last four years.

The minister spoke of the sacrifice of Jesus and His willingness to lay down His life for those He sought to redeem. His glorious resurrection served as the promise of eternal life to all those who sought Jesus as Savior and repented of their sins.

Sallie pursed her lips and frowned. She'd heard these words most of her life, but they held no meaning for her this day. If God was truly merciful, none of this would have happened. No war, no killing, no lives uprooted, and no destruction. As hard as she tried to fill her mind with happy memories and forget the past, the pictures still played in the back of her mind and resurfaced at times like this.

After the service Sallie joined Mama and Papa on the church grounds. Members gathered in small groups greeting one another. Easter Sunday brought with it a promise of a new season, new growth, and new life. That's what she had to grasp and hold for the future. Hope didn't come easy, but she had to practice it now.

Grandpa stood near his buggy talking with Colonel Bradford. Her uncle wore his uniform with such pride. His white hair and elegant mustache completed the picture of an officer of the Confederate Army. His regiment had come home on furlough for a few days of rest before resuming their duties.

Peggy peeked around her father's back and waved to Sallie. She said something to her father then hurried over to grab Sallie's hand. "Come ride with us back to Grandma and Grandpa's. It's been so long since we visited."

Sallie called out to her mother, "Mama, I'm going with Peggy if it's all right with you and Papa." The ride would give them time to talk without Hannah's ears picking up every word. Not that she really minded her sister listening, but some things she and Peggy said were for their ears only and not those of little sisters.

Mama hugged Sallie. "Of course, dear. Run along. Have a nice chat with your cousin."

Sallie and Peggy hooked arms and rejoined the Bradford family. Her uncle assisted her up onto the carriage seat. She settled herself beside her cousin in the back.

Peggy giggled and grabbed Sallie's hand. "Oh, Sallie, I'm so excited Mama wants to have your party at our home." Then her expression sobered. "If only Manfred and Edwin could be here with us."

"Yes, that would so wonderful, but…" She stopped and peered at her cousin. The color rose in Peggy's cheeks, and Sallie grinned. "Margaret Elaine Bradford! Are you keeping secrets from me? I detect some interest in Edwin."

Peggy placed a finger against her lips. "Shush. Not so loud. He came calling on me twice before he left again last summer, and he's written me several times. Oh, Sallie, he's as wonderful as your Manfred."

Still smiling, Sallie placed her arm around Peggy's shoulders. "Well, I don't know about that, but then they are brothers, so I'll take your word for it. Although I don't see how anyone can be as nice and sweet as Manfred."

"Humph. Of course you don't." Peggy laughed and clasped her hands together. "Oh, I'm excited about having your birthday party. It'll be such fun."

Sallie merely smiled and listened to her cousin's chatter. As the daughter of a plantation owner Peggy had much more free time on her hands. Of course Uncle Clark had given most of the slaves their freedom when the house had been damaged, but a few remained. They must have decided that life with her uncle was better than the unknown they faced with freedom. Although she didn't like the idea of owning people, having servants at one's beck and call did make life easier.

The carriage halted in front of the Woodruff home, and the girls stepped down then ran up the steps and into the house. Mama halted them in the entryway. "Girls, girls. Slow down. You are young ladies now and not hoydens."

"Yes, Mama. I'm sorry." Sallie removed her bonnet but turned to wink at Peggy, who stifled a snicker.

Hannah hopped up the steps, her special shoe clomping on the boards. She grabbed her cousin by the waist. "I'm so glad to see you, Peggy. Will you come up to my room later? I want to show you some of my needlework."

Peggy tweaked one of Hannah's curls. "I'd love to. I understand you have quite the talent for needlepoint."

Hannah's cheeks grew pink at the compliment. Sallie

wrapped her arm around Hannah's shoulders. "You heard right. Her stitches are much neater than mine, and the back of her work is almost as good as the front. Mine is all knots and snarls."

"I'm sure you both would put mine to shame, but right now the aroma from the dining room is calling me. Flora's sweet potatoes are begging to be eaten. Come on." Peggy grasped Hannah's hand and ambled into the room where the remainder of the family gathered.

The table had been extended to provide room for the larger group. Grandma's best china and silver glistened and shimmered in the sunlight. Grandpa said grace and thanked God for the bounty and their safety through the past year.

Sallie enjoyed having her brothers home again. She had missed their teasing and antics over the last few days. Will had grown so tall over this past year. In church this morning she noticed his head was almost even with Papa's in height. Even Tom seemed taller than a few days ago.

Will's eyes sparkled with mischief. "I say, Peggy, you look happy today. Are you thinking about a certain young soldier named Edwin Whiteman?"

Heat filled Peggy's cheeks with a bright red glow. "Now why should that be of importance to me, Mr. Will Dyer?"

"Oh, none, except that last summer he looked at you like a fox eyeing a chicken."

Mama gasped. "Will Dyer! I will have no such talk at my table."

"Sorry, Mama." He ducked his head, but not before Sallie saw the twinkle still there. Poor Peggy. It was too bad she didn't have younger brothers, or she'd be used to such talk. Peggy's older brothers were more like protectors than anything else. They were off fighting the war with the other young men.

Papa's voice drew her attention back to the dinner table. He addressed her uncle. "I understand that you and Abigail have offered your home for our daughter's birthday."

"That's right. We'd be pleased if you will accept our invitation. The repairs are all but finished, and our home will be ready for a celebration."

"That is generous of you, Colonel." Papa's gaze landed on Sallie, and he smiled. "We will be honored to accept the offer. We'll have a grand party at Magnolia Hall."

Sallie squeezed Peggy's hand under the table as Grandma Woodruff stood and signaled the end of dinner. "With that settled, I think it's time we go the parlor. The girls will entertain us on the piano."

Peggy played a piece by Mozart, and Sallie sat near the window gazing out toward the road. She imagined Manfred walking up the drive. After the applause for Peggy's music Sallie followed with a more rousing tune, and Hannah ended the recital with the "Minute Waltz."

At the end of the selection Hannah hopped up. "I chose a short piece because I want to go upstairs and change clothes. This stiff fabric is making my skin itch."

Papa laughed. "Of course, my dear. You run along. Thank you for entertaining us."

Sallie envied Hannah's freedom in dress and wished she could be rid of her hoops and crinolines, but Mama insisted on wearing them on Sundays. A change of garments would be welcome right now.

Peggy grabbed her cousin's arm. "Let's go out to the porch and wait until Hannah calls for us."

Sallie followed her cousin. They settled in the wicker chairs there, and Sallie crossed her arms about her chest. In a week or so the weather would be much warmer, but today was pleasant with a gentle breeze cooling the air.

Peggy sighed. "Isn't it a glorious day?"

"Yes, it is. Makes me wish I was younger and could run about and enjoy the sun."

"Surely you jest, Sallie. Our mothers never allowed us to 'run about,' as you say, especially in the warm sun."

"I suppose not, but something in me now wants to run across the lawn with my hair streaming out behind, basking in the warmth of the spring sun." A sigh escaped her lips. If only she could turn back the clock to the days before she became a young woman, to the days before the war tore apart everything she held dear.

"I know, but that would be difficult with our skirts as bulky as they are. Besides, the sun isn't good for our complexions. Mama says we must protect our skin at all times against the elements."

"Yes, Grandma says the same every time we leave the house on a sunny afternoon." That explained the abundance of hats and parasols in Grandma's wardrobe.

Voices floated out from the parlor where the men enjoyed their after-dinner time. Papa spoke to the colonel about their home in Woodville.

"We were very lucky not to have had more extensive damage. The house will be ready for our return by the end of June if the rains hold back."

"I don't believe Magnolia Hall would have been so damaged had it been farther away from Port Hudson. I'm thankful I had already sent Abigail and Margaret away."

"Yes, they didn't experience the threat of battle like my womenfolk did. I'm thankful Sallie had the wherewithal to fire the gun I gave her for protection."

Sallie's heart lurched then thudded in her chest. Papa knew what she had done. Of course he must, because he had been in the house later, but why had he not said anything?

Perhaps he knew it would upset her to talk about it. He knew and understood, but how would she ever explain it to Manfred?

CHAPTER 10

Virginia, Monday, April 17, 1865

MANFRED GAZED ABOUT the churchyard where families swarmed over the grass. Seeing Luke reunited with his family caused the longing for his own family to rise to the surface. With Luke home the planting had gone even faster this morning. Manfred planned to tell Mr. Grayson that he and Edwin would be moving on tomorrow morning now that Luke had come home.

Tables filled with food stood under the shade trees, and Manfred sauntered in that direction. Boys and girls played chase and friends hailed one another. The reverend called for everyone's attention and offered a prayer of thanksgiving for the safe return of the soldiers yesterday. Then the pastor asked special blessings for the families of those who hadn't as yet come home.

After the hearty amen both young and old filled plates and mingled in circles of family and friends. Manfred loaded his with ham, beans, potatoes, and all the trimmings supplied by the wonderful ladies of the church. With plate in hand he sought out Mr. Grayson and Luke, who sat on the steps of the church.

"Mr. Grayson, Luke. This is a great day for you and your family. I thank you for all you've done for Edwin and me, but I hope you understand that we must be on our way."

Mr. Grayson nodded. "Of course I do. Your ma is expecting you just like we waited for Luke. It must have been difficult for you to delay your trip to help us today with the planting, but we do appreciate it. Because of your help we are well along the way."

Luke reached out to Manfred. "When I asked you to stop over with my family, I had no idea you'd go this far to help them. I don't know how I'll ever repay you."

Manfred shook the offered hand. "No need to. You'd do the same for me or Edwin."

Mr. Grayson set his plate on the step and wiped his hand with a napkin. He peered up at Manfred. "How far you planning to go next?"

"If we start out early, we can camp out tomorrow night then get to the next town by Wednesday afternoon. If we can get shelter there, we'll spend the night and head straight down south toward North Carolina and then on to Tennessee."

Luke expelled a deep breath. "That's a hard journey. We'll make sure Ma gives you a good supply of food."

"Thanks. Your ma's food will take us a long way. Right now I'd like to go over and speak with her. Looks like there's a lull in the food serving. Might get me a piece of that chocolate cake too." He had spied the huge cake Mrs. Grayson had baked. It stood front and center on the dessert table, and he longed for a taste of something so special.

Mr. Grayson laughed. "Don't forget the apple pie. Rachel makes the best around these parts."

"I'll be sure to get a slice." Manfred offered a mock salute and turned toward the food tables.

After surveying all the desserts spread out, Manfred chose the cake and a piece of Rachel's pie. With his loaded plate, he strolled over to where Mrs. Grayson and Rachel sat eating fried chicken. The large elm and oak trees, now sprouting new leaves for spring, provided some shade as relief from the evening sun. "Mrs. Grayson, Rachel. The food is wonderful. All the ladies outdid themselves."

Mrs. Grayson tucked a stray strand of hair under her bonnet. "This is what we love to do. Anytime we can celebrate, we have dinner on the grounds."

Rachel nodded in agreement. "I'm happy for Luke to be home and for all the other families too." She brushed a stray tear from her cheek. "Matt being here would have made it perfect, but I know God has a plan for all of this."

Edwin joined the trio. "You all sure know how to put on a feed." He patted his stomach. "At this rate I'll quickly put back all the weight I lost the past few months."

The women laughed and shook their heads. Manfred wanted to hug his brother for providing the exact light touch they needed to cheer up Rachel. Her laughter sounded like music to his ears.

He finished off the dessert and set his plate on a nearby table. He could use some extra pounds himself, but they wouldn't have many meals like this along their way the next few weeks.

"I just told Mr. Grayson we'll be leaving tomorrow morning after breakfast. It's time for us to get back on the road. The weather looks good today. Maybe it'll hold out for us." With good weather they could make better time. With the weather this time of year so unpredictable, judging how far they might travel each day became more difficult.

Mrs. Grayson stood and wrapped her arms around Manfred's waist. "We'll be sorry to see you go, but I know your momma is waiting for you just like I waited for Luke."

"Yes'm, I imagine she will be." He stepped back and held the plump woman's hands. "Is there any way to get a letter out from here?"

The elderly lady furrowed her brow. "I think your best opportunity will be in the next town. We don't have a place to post mail regularly here."

"If you have paper, I could write the letters tonight and—" Manfred stopped in mid-sentence as a rider on horseback galloped into the yard then reined to a halt.

A crowd quickly gathered around the young man wearing the familiar Confederate gray pants and cap. His somber countenance brought a pall of silence over the group.

The soldier's gaze swept over the group of farmers and their families. He announced, "President Lincoln is dead."

Manfred gasped in shock, as did many around him. Someone asked how it happened.

The boy shook his head. "Shot Friday night at Ford's Theater in Washington. He died early Saturday morning. Don't know any other details."

Mrs. Grayson peered up at the soldier. "Wouldn't you like a glass of lemonade or a piece of fried chicken? You look worn out."

The rider removed his cap and ran a sleeve across his sweating brow. "Don't have time to stop and eat, but a glass of lemonade would sure help in this heat."

Mrs. Grayson scurried over to the tables to fetch a glass of refreshment.

Mr. Grayson asked, "Where are you headed from here?"

"Gotta get the message to the camp about fifteen miles south. I wouldn't have stopped here except I saw the crowd gathered and figured I should tell y'all."

Mrs. Grayson returned with the cold drink and handed it to the young man. He drank quickly, wiped his mouth, and returned the glass. "Thank you, ma'am. Now I must be gone." He gazed around the crowd for a moment then stopped at two young soldiers. "I take it a few of you just returned home. Good luck to ya. I hope to be heading home soon too." The young man donned his cap and galloped off on his mission.

Manfred had a difficult time wrapping his mind around

the fact that the president had been killed. How could anyone be so angry at the man? True, many didn't like Lincoln's views, but they had to admire his courage and resolve.

All around Manfred heard conflicting opinions about Lincoln's death. Some seemed not to care, others openly wept, and several bemoaned the surrender of Lee. Not sure of his own emotions, Manfred considered the man who had declared the emancipation of the slaves. No matter his beliefs, Lincoln had been the president of the United States, an office worthy of respect.

The crowd dispersed, and Manfred listened to their words and remembered all the devastation, fighting, and turmoil of the past several years. He spotted Luke and Mark in deep conversation with their father and strolled toward them. He felt a tug on his arm and turned to find Rachel clinging to his shirtsleeve.

"Manfred, I want to thank you for being here these past few days. Your helping Pa Grayson means a great deal to all of us." She slipped a folded piece of paper into his hand.

"I might not have time to give you this tomorrow. It's a note to your Sallie from me. I want her to know how wonderfully kind you've been and how lucky she is to have you."

Manfred fingered the folded square. "Thank you, Rachel. It's women like you and Ma Grayson who are going to help us rebuild. Your strength and courage are admirable." He hesitated a moment then took her hand into his. "I know this may sound trite, but something tells me everything is going to be all right."

Neither spoke, and Rachel slipped her hand from his. She smiled and turned to hurry back and retrieve young Matt from his uncle John.

Later that evening Mr. Grayson and Luke asked Manfred and Edwin to sit with them on the porch. He tamped his pipe with his thumb and furrowed his brow. "Luke and I been talking about what we could do to help you two boys. Those two horses you boys rode while here are now yours to keep."

Edwin's mouth gaped open, and Manfred gasped. "Mr. Grayson, we can't—"

Mr. Grayson put his hand out to silence Manfred. "Don't say a word. Those horses are part of a group old Mr. Whitney gave me before he and his missus picked up and left their farm to go live with their daughter. I plan to sell the lot, but not before I give you two of them."

Luke handed Manfred a sheet of paper. "This here's a bill of sale. Makes you the rightful owner of the horses. Pa and I both signed it and dated it. Pa says you'll most likely need it because so many farms are being raided for their horses."

Manfred grasped the paper with a trembling hand. "I...I don't know what to say. I...we never expected this." He had hoped to work and buy horses later, but this was beyond his dreams. Riding would make their journey easier and faster.

Mr. Grayson lit his pipe and took a few puffs. The smoke curled upward as the old man rocked in his chair. "I thought so too. Well, you two better get a good night's sleep. I'm sure you want to get an early start."

Manfred shook the man's hand. "Thank you. Another night in a soft bed will make the hard ground easier to bear later." He turned to his brother. "Edwin, we'll be leaving early, so we'd best be getting on up to bed."

"Since we have horses now, the journey will be faster." Edwin shook Mr. Grayson's hand. "And for that we're very grateful."

God had blessed his decision to go out of his way to tell the Grayson family about Luke. Besides, helping others along their way home would be one way they could help build back what they'd destroyed in the battles they'd fought.

Up in their bedroom Manfred removed his shirt and pants. His clean uniform stood ready for the morning trip. He sat on the bed and picked up his Bible. One last night in this home, and he had much for which to be thankful. Luke had even bunked in with his brothers so Manfred and Edwin could remain in his room. Overcome with the kindness shown by the Graysons, he bowed his head.

"Lord, You've been good to us these past days, and my heart is grateful for all we've been given. Thank You for Your provision. You promised to go with us and to never forsake us, and I pray we will feel and know Your presence fully in the days ahead. Watch over and protect us as well as the hundreds of other young men making their way home."

He slid between the sheets and blew out the lamp on the side table. Soon Edwin's gentle snore sounded from the bed next to him. The days ahead were filled with uncertainty, but with God as their guide they'd be home by June.

CHAPTER 11

St. Francisville, Louisiana, Tuesday, April 18, 1865

ALLIE SCRIBBLED THE last name on her guest list then scanned it in case she had forgotten anyone. Mama wanted to get the invitations out early next week. She waved the sheet of paper to dry the ink and spoke to Hannah.

"Well, this is done. I added Jeremiah to the list. He'll make a nice escort for you."

Hannah shoved her doll's arms into a dress. "I don't need an escort. I might not even go."

Sallie raised her eyebrows. "Hannah Grace Dyer! Of course you'll be at my birthday party. You are too important to me not to be there. Besides, Mama ordered a new dress for you from Mrs. Tenney for the occasion."

Hannah's bottom lip jutted out. "I don't wanna get dressed up and have to act all ladylike for that long."

"Oh, Hannah, why don't you want to wear a new dress? It'll be fun." Sallie rose and moved to sit on the floor beside her sister. Hannah had lately become more self-conscious about her awkward boot. Sallie wrapped an arm about Hannah's shoulders. "You are so pretty with your golden red curls and blue eyes. Someday you'll enjoy getting all dressed up for parties, but for now, will you do it just for me? As a special gift?"

Hannah slid her gaze up to Sallie. A hint of a smile played at the corners of her mouth. "I suppose I could, but do I have to sit with Jeremiah Simpson all evening?"

Sallie hugged Hannah and laughed. "Not if you don't want to. I only want you there to help all of us celebrate."

Their mother's voice floated up from downstairs. "Sallie, Hannah. Come, we must go to Mrs. Tenney's for your dress fittings."

"We're coming, Mama. I have to get my crinolines." She grabbed the hoops from the bed and slipped them up under the full skirt of the dress she wore. Lettie appeared and took over making sure the ties were secure.

"Thank you so much. I'm thankful I don't need a corset to try on the dress. In fact, I don't think I'll ever wear one again. Let Peggy worry about having a tiny waist. I'd rather be able to breathe and enjoy my party."

Lettie laughed. "With the way you've been eating, your waist is small enough without the corset. You'll be the envy of all the other young women there." She stepped back. "You're going to look beautiful in your new dress."

"If you help me with my hair that night, I might look presentable." Sallie spoke in jest, but she remembered her grandmother's admonition that true beauty came from one's behavior and what was in her heart, not from how her face looked. Inner beauty, that's what she wanted.

She extended her hand to Hannah then pulled the child to her feet. "Let's go. I can't wait to see what Mrs. Tenney has done on our dresses."

Hannah sighed but followed her sister. Sallie smiled at the child's reluctance to go for her fitting. Once Hannah saw the dress Mama had ordered for her, she couldn't help but be excited.

Downstairs, Papa and Mama waited in the entry hall. Papa had decided to stay home one more day before going back to repairs on their home. Sallie bounced down the stairs holding her hoops to keep from tripping. Papa laughed, but Mama frowned.

"Sarah Louise Dyer, it's time for you to come down the

stairs like a young lady should. At your age bounding down a stairway is unacceptable." Mama always used full names when she was scolding. She handed a bonnet to Sallie and one to Hannah.

Sallie slipped hers over her curls and pushed them under the bonnet with her fingers. Someday she'd come down those stairs as a bride. That would be soon enough to walk like a lady.

When they stepped out onto the porch, a horse and rider pulled to a stop. He grabbed the reins to settle the prancing stallion then dismounted and hurried up the path to the group on the porch. His gaze went straight to Papa.

"The war's over," the young soldier proclaimed. His words hung heavy in the air. "Lee surrendered. We lost. It's all over."

Sallie's legs buckled, and she grabbed for Mama's arm. Papa's voice thundered in the air. "What happened? How do you know?"

"A courier came to our camp and told us to spread the word. Lee surrendered to Grant and signed a treaty. We've been riding for two days to let our troops know."

Sallie's heart pounded in her chest. She closed her eyes, and her hand flew to her mouth. The war was over. Oh, glory. Manfred would be coming home.

Thomas wrapped his arm around Amanda's shoulder. She shivered as her husband's eyes grew dark and he spoke to the young man. "When did this happen?"

"On Sunday, April 9. At Appomattox in Virginia. Lee surrendered to Grant. Our troops are being disbanded and sent home."

The door banged open behind her, and the boys raced

outside and slid to a stop at the top step. Lettie followed them, and Sallie grabbed her around the waist. "Oh, Lettie, the war is over! Our men are coming home."

Questions rose in Amanda's heart, but she kept silent and let her husband do the talking.

Thomas shook the man's hand. "Thank you for stopping here to let us know. We get so little war news down here."

"Now I must be on my way." The young man swung his body up onto the saddle.

Thomas grasped the horse's bridle. "Then let us pray with you before you go on." The young soldier nodded, and Thomas prayed. "Father, we thank You for Your bountiful blessings. We ask You to be with the families of those men who gave their lives for the cause of the South. Protect the husbands and sons of our family and friends, and bring them safely home to us. Grant safety to this young lad as he bears the news to others about the end of this war. May peace now reign in our land. Amen."

The soldier saluted then galloped off down the road in a cloud of dust. Amanda's heart filled with gratitude for an end to the fighting. Now young men would return to their homes, and families would once more be complete. Then sadness mingled in with the joy to darken the news. So many would never return, their bodies lost out on a battle-field somewhere and buried in a mass grave. She swallowed the lump rising in her throat, remembering the one left in the house at Woodville. His poor mama. Her son would never come home.

Once again dust stirred in the road, and Grandpa Woodruff appeared. He pulled up and jumped from his horse. "I saw a young soldier riding away. Did he tell you the news?"

Thomas nodded. "He did. I can't believe the war is actually over. And that the news traveled so fast to us down here."

"We heard it in town, and I was on my way to tell you. I imagine those in charge wanted all fighting to stop as soon as possible. I, for one, am thankful the madness has come to an end."

Young Will scowled. "Just a few months more, and I'd have been able to get into the fight."

Amanda gasped. "William Jackson Dyer, you'd do no such thing!"

Thomas reached for her hand. "Now, Amanda, don't be upset. The war's over, so Will isn't going any place except to Woodville with me tomorrow." His stern look at Will restrained the boy. The firm set of Will's jaw indicated his desire to say more, but good manners and obedience kept him quiet.

Grandmother Woodruff's voice trembled as she grasped Grandpa's arm. "Exactly what is this going to mean to all of us here in the South?"

Grandpa Woodruff wrapped his arm about her shoulder. "Well, Mary Catherine, that depends on what President Lincoln decides to do with the Confederate states. I pray we will again unite as one nation."

Thomas nodded. "Yes, we can do so much more as one nation united than as one divided. One big question will be the fate of the former slaves. I'm thankful we set our servants free to go wherever they wanted long before all this started. No man should own another."

Will fisted one hand and slapped the palm of the other with it. "Then why did we fight this war in the first place?"

Amanda grasped Will's hand. "Son, the Constitution gave the states rights to set their own laws, and that's what the South was defending. The Bible tells us to love our neighbor as we love ourselves, but when we couldn't settle our differences peaceably, war broke out."

Thomas squeezed Amanda's shoulders. "Trust your mama to put things in their true prospective."

Amanda hugged her son. Lee had been the strongest and most capable leader of the Confederate troops. Since he surrendered, the general must have realized that more fighting would be useless and only lead to more deaths.

Will mumbled something in return. Amanda heard the words *slaves* and *good for nothing*. She gasped. The young man needed a good scolding.

Thomas grabbed his son's shoulder. "I will not have that kind of talk in this family. Do you understand?"

Will said nothing but shrugged loose and headed for the house. When he reached the door, Sallie grabbed his arm and began scolding him. Trust her headstrong daughter to put her brother in his place. Will pulled loose, and his gaze shot daggers at Sallie before he turned on his heel and ran for the stables. Tom pulled away from the group and ran after him.

Thomas grasped Amanda's hand. "At least one of our children has good sense. Looks like I need to have a little more discussion with our sons in the days ahead."

So much violence and heartache in the past four years, and every family in the South had been affected whether a son or husband had gone to war or not. She had her own taste of the war at their home in Woodville, and that had been enough to last her a lifetime.

❧

Grandpa followed Grandma into the house, and Papa went after her brothers to get ready for their journey to Woodville tomorrow. Meanwhile Mama pulled on her gloves, her lips set with new determination. "Now, let's get on with our business. This news means our young men will be coming home and will make your party a greater celebration." She grasped Hannah's hand and walked toward the road.

The three of them made their way down the few blocks to Mrs. Tenney's shop. Amanda carried a parasol to shield herself from the sun's warm rays, as did Sallie. With her red hair, Sallie needed more protection for her fair complexion than some of her darker-haired friends. Hannah pulled ahead of them, and even with her uneven gait, she appeared to not have a care in the world, but that could change at any moment with the ups and downs of her age.

Sallie's own days of mood swings and self-consciousness may be past, but she still longed to be carefree and young. Of course then she wouldn't be looking forward to Manfred's return. With the war over, life would get better very soon. It had too.

She blinked the tears from her eyes and took in her surroundings. She ought to be thankful this day. The scent of lilacs and other spring flowers filled the air with the promise of new beginnings. If she could blot out that one terrible afternoon, she would, but God had forsaken her in that awful hour, and she had committed the worst of crimes. The same question haunted her over and over again. How could the Lord forgive her killing another person?

They reached the shop, and a bell tinkled to signal their entrance to the display room filled with forms wearing dresses in various stages of construction. Sallie shoved her dark thoughts to the back of her mind and pasted on a smile to please her mother.

Mrs. Tenney scurried from the sewing room. "Ah, Miss Dyer. Your dress is ready for the first fitting. Yours too,

Miss Hannah." She picked up a mound of yellow fabric and handed it to Sallie. "Go on into the fitting area while I get Hannah's."

Sallie held the soft fabric in her arms and buried her face in its folds. It had been awhile since she had a new dress, and this one was supposed to be extra special, but why make such a big fuss about her birthday when a war had been lost? Men would be coming home, but at what price? Mama followed her into the dressing area and chattered away as though it were any ordinary day and not one so full of meaning.

"I'm glad to see you wore your widest hoops and crinolines to make sure the skirt will cover it sufficiently. You may dislike wearing a corset and the hoop, but your dress will be beautiful with them."

Sallie puffed out her cheeks then blew out the air. "Mama, I don't plan to wear a corset, and that's why I don't have on one today. I simply cannot breathe with one laced up so tight." At her mother's gasp Sallie discarded the dress she'd worn into the shop, revealing only the hoop, petticoats, and a chemise as her undergarments.

"Sarah Louise Dyer, how could you? Well, it's too late now. Put on the dress."

The silky lawn fabric slipped easily over Sallie's head and shoulders then settled over the hoop petticoat.

"See, Mama, it's going to be beautiful. I don't need all that extra boning." She twirled in front of the mirror to get a better view of the back.

"I have to admit you do look quite stunning. I don't think I really realized how tiny your waist is by nature." Mama knit her brows and fussed with the folds of the skirt. Then she turned to Hannah. "Hannah, dear. You need to undress. Mrs. Tenney is bringing your new gown for a fitting too."

Mrs. Tenney entered the room with Hannah's dress and a

box of pins. She smiled at the sight of Sallie. "Now let's see how it fits." She pulled a pinch of fabric around the waist and secured a pleat with one of the pins. "You're right. You don't need boning and laces."

Sallie glanced at Mama and grinned. "We were just now discussing that very thing. I have always loathed corsets and having them laced so tight I can't breathe. I don't see how Mama and Grandma can move around in theirs, much less breathe. Such agony just to have a waistline." She held her arms out to her sides as the seamstress continued to tuck and pin.

In the mirror Sallie spotted Hannah's reflection behind her. Hannah had donned her new dress and was examining it, fussing with the skirt. "It's longer than my other skirts, so it'll hide my ugly boot. Don't you think so?"

"Yes, my dear, it does look lovely and will hide your boot." Mama drew her younger daughter to her side. "And so you won't have to wear pantaloons with this one."

"Oh, Mama, really?" She turned one way and then the other in front of the mirror. The shiny blue fabric of her skirts swirled around her ankles, making the boot barely noticeable.

Sallie raised her eyebrow. "So you won't mind dressing up in this party dress?"

Hannah's face turned red. "I guess not. It's the prettiest dress I've ever had." She brushed her hands over the fabric and fingered the lace trimming the skirt.

"Oh, my little girl is growing up." Mama beamed and hugged Hannah. Sallie noted a tear sliding down her cheek. With Hannah growing up, Mama would have no more little ones around her.

The bell tinkled again, and Mrs. Tenney rushed to check on the new customer. Amanda unfastened Sallie's garment then pushed it down over the crinoline and let it fall about her feet. Sallie carefully stepped out of it and draped the mound of fabric on a chair.

A familiar voice hailed Amanda from the display room. "Amanda, it's Abigail. I've come to see my niece in her new dress."

She entered closely followed by Peggy, who stopped short and planted her hands on her hips. "Sallie, you've already taken off your dress. I was hoping to see it on you before I try on mine."

Sallie pushed her arms into her other dress. "I'm sorry, Peggy. I didn't know you were coming too." She picked up the yellow creation and held it up for Peggy to see.

"Oh, it's beautiful. Mine is pink with a darker pink sash and trim on the bodice."

Aunt Abigail fanned herself with an ivory and green silk fan. A dark green silk dress covered her plump body and red curls peeked from her bonnet. "You're certainly looking well, my dear Amanda." She turned to finger Sallie's curls. "Your hair is so lovely. Mine once looked like that."

Sallie grinned. "That's what Mama tells me. She says I should've been your daughter."

"That I wouldn't mind. Peggy and I need another female influence in our house of men. Thank God, they're all safe. We just heard the news in town. Isn't it wonderful that our men will be coming home? We also had a letter from Joshua and Jacob. They will be home in a few weeks, in time for your party. And that's what I want to talk to you about."

Mama tilted her head. "Oh? Has here been a change in plans?"

Abigail drew her shoulders back and tilted her head. "No, of course not, but with more young men coming home, you'll have to expand your guest list. That won't be a problem as we have plenty of room for such a gala."

Mama gasped, as did Sallie. Sallie hugged her aunt. "Auntie, thank you so much."

"I know we should not be so glad since our men surrendered, but at least the fighting is over and our men will be coming home." Mama helped Hannah get out of her dress.

"Colonel Bradford and I are delighted to offer our home for such an occasion. You and I will begin making plans immediately for a larger gathering."

Mrs. Tenney brought in Peggy's dress. While Peggy tried on her dress, Sallie pictured her aunt's plantation home a little north of town. The lacy wrought-iron railings wrapping around the veranda on three sides offered a romantic setting for a dinner and dance. The large rooms and elegant furnishings would make this party the most special one Sallie could ever have.

Peggy whispered something, and Sallie jerked her head around. "What did you say?"

"I said that with the war being over, maybe Manfred and Edwin will be home soon."

"I hope so." She hugged her cousin, then stood back to admire her new dress. "You look beautiful. Wouldn't it be wonderful if they came home in time for the party? I could ask for no better birthday present."

The tinkling bell signaled another customer entering the store. "I have to run and see to our new customer." Mrs. Tenney scurried through the curtains back to the front.

Mama motioned to Sallie and Hannah. "It's time for us to go, girls. Mrs. Tenney is much too busy for us to stand around and visit."

When they entered the main room, Mrs. Tenney handed Mama her parcel. "These lace gloves will be a nice addition to your costume, Mrs. Dyer. Excuse me, I must get Mrs. Clark's dress for her." The dressmaker once again disappeared through a curtain to the back of the shop.

Aunt Abigail stepped from the dressing area and called to Mama. "Now, Amanda, be sure you have any additional invitations ready for those who come home. And remember, Sunday dinner will be at Magnolia Hall this week." She waved her hand and ducked back behind the curtain.

All the way home Mama chattered about the party. "I'm so glad all the invitations haven't been written. I must have Flora and Abigail's cook get together and work out who will do what with the menu. I have some new ideas I'd like Flora to try."

Sallie walked beside Hannah and listened in silence. Her mother's excitement warmed Sallie's heart. Mama had needed something to fill her mind and keep her busy so she didn't have time to fret about her home back in Woodville. Sallie breathed a deep sigh. If only she could blot out her fears that easily.

The future did look brighter today than it had in a long while, but the past would not go away. If she told Manfred what she had done, would he still love her? Why tell him at all? He had enough other things to think about without her worries too. Besides, her whole family seemed to act as if the killing had never happened or was of no importance at all.

Sallie chewed her lip. Mama and Papa may be able to blot out the past, but they hadn't pulled the trigger. And if she was going to marry Manfred, she wanted him to know who she was and what she had done. A secret like that could eat into her conscience and ruin the relationship.

In other times she'd be praying for Manfred right now, but lately prayer hadn't been the comfort it used to be. The gap between her and God grew larger each day she didn't communicate, and if she didn't let Him have her fears, the chasm would only grow deeper and wider.

CHAPTER 12

Virginia, Wednesday, April 19, 1865

MANFRED SAT WITH Edwin under the shade of a massive elm tree and shared the food prepared for them earlier by Mrs. Grayson. He ate the last of his cornbread and washed it down with water from his canteen.

Mrs. Grayson had shed tears as she told them good-bye the day before. The family had gathered in the yard and had prayed for their safety before the boys departed. Manfred closed his eyes, thankful again for the kindness of the Grayson family. The supplies given would last until they reached Hanover and maybe beyond, now that they had horses.

Edwin voiced his brother's thoughts. "We sure were lucky to find a family like the Graysons to take care of us." He mopped up his plate with a bit of cornbread and popped it into his mouth.

"'Twasn't luck, little brother. 'Twas the good Lord looking out for us. Proves what the Bible tells us about giving. When you do things for others without expecting anything in return, you get more than you need." He rose and began gathering the leftovers and utensils. He believed God's promises with all his heart. The past week had been proof of how the Father takes care of His children.

In a few minutes the horses were again packed with gear and ready to ride. The early spring sun continued to beam down, although clouds covered them occasionally to bring a little respite.

Neither young man said much. Manfred figured Edwin

thought about home and Peggy Bradford as much as his own thoughts were filled with Sallie.

Suddenly Edwin nudged his arm. "Look, some men are coming yonder." He pointed toward a group of men approaching on horseback from the west. They also wore Confederate uniforms.

One of them called out. "Hey, you boys from around here? I see you've been in the war too."

Manfred stopped his horse and waited until the group drew closer. "We're just out of prison at Point Lookout. We're on our way to Louisiana."

The lead man leaned on his saddle horn and peered at Manfred and Edwin. "Well, I say now. We were fighting north of here and are on our way home to Alabama. My name is Frank. These fellows are Jesse, Clem, and Al." He indicated the other three riders.

Manfred noted their scruffy clothes and scraggly beards. They looked worse than he and Edwin had a few days ago. "I'm Manfred, and this here's my brother Edwin. We're headed to Hanover for the night."

Frank laughed. "How 'bout that. So are we. Mind if we ride along with you?"

Manfred's first instinct led him to say no, but Edwin spoke up first. "Would be nice to have company. What do you say?" He turned to Manfred and cocked his head.

Manfred leaned to whisper to Edwin. "I don't like their looks. Frank's eyes are full of meanness, and their uniforms don't look right. I'm not even sure they're really soldiers."

Edwin pleaded, "Oh, come on, Manfred. We looked like that a few days ago. Remember?"

"Hey, you two. We gonna ride together or not?" Frank hollered and pulled his horse to stand sideways, blocking the path.

Frank's position gave Manfred no choice in the matter now. Clearly the man would not let them pass to go on their way alone. "Suppose so, since we're all going to the same place." Manfred gave a warning look to Edwin before trotting his horse over to the four men. He didn't like the looks of the band or the way Frank wanted to be in control.

Manfred rode beside Al and took note of how he continually glanced back at the trail. Jesse and Frank hung back from the group, and when Manfred turned, he saw them in deep conversation. He glanced at Edwin, who only shrugged and lifted his eyebrows. The hairs on Manfred's neck bristled with warning. Something wasn't right with the men. He had the same sensation last week before the news of the surrender came, only this time foreboding of disaster rather than good news permeated his bones. He made plans to separate from the group as soon as possible.

When Manfred once again turned to look back, he realized Frank had disappeared. Jesse now rode alone. Clem still manned the front of the group with Al beside Manfred and Edwin. A dust cloud appeared, and then a group of men on horseback thundered toward them.

Manfred reached over for Edwin's horse's bridle and stopped him. Clem, Al, and Jesse kicked their mounts and disappeared into the woods. Manfred didn't like the looks of the men headed their way until he saw the badges. Relief filled him. At last they could be rid of the others.

Two men pulled their horses up beside Manfred and Edwin while the remainder chased the other three.

The lawmen pulled their guns and hemmed in Manfred and Edwin. "Where you boys headed?" the older of the two asked.

Manfred swallowed hard. "We're on our way home to

Louisiana from the war." Somehow this didn't look like the rescue he'd anticipated.

"I see. And where did you get your horses?" He spat a stream of brown liquid toward the ground and peered at Manfred.

"We...they were given—" The return of the others with Clem, Al, and Jesse interrupted Manfred's explanation.

The lawmen cradled their weapons. The leader shoved his hat back on his head. "Looks like we caught ourselves a band of horse thieves."

Manfred protested. "Wait a minute. We're not horse thieves. We own our horses and have a paper to prove it." He reached toward his saddle pack, but the lawman stopped him with the barrel of his gun.

"Hold it right there. We're taking you in to the jail at Hanover. You can tell your story there. Tie 'em up." He waved his shotgun in the air.

Edwin immediately rebelled. "I've been in prison for months, and I'm not going to be tied up again." He danced his horse out of reach of the man trying to rope his hands.

Manfred called, "Calm down, Edwin. We'll be okay. This won't last long." He crossed his hands behind his back and let the rope be placed around them. As much as he hated the feel of the restraint on his wrists, he had done nothing wrong, and God would take care of him and Edwin. If only he could convince Edwin.

His brother clamped his lips tightly together and glared at Manfred, but he let his hands be tied. The three other men did the same, but an evil smirk graced Jesse's lips, and his eyes all but dared Manfred to mention Frank.

The ride into town took less than an hour. Men and women gathered on the street to watch the group trot into town. The posse pulled to a halt in front of the law office and town jail. The leader of the posse swung down from his saddle and spoke with the lawman.

Several men joined the two lawmen. Manfred overheard one of the men addressed as the mayor. After a brief conference the boys were pulled from their mounts and pushed inside the jail. Clem, Jesse, and Al sauntered into a cell and stood quietly as a deputy unbound their wrists.

The lawman then shoved Manfred and Edwin into another cell and untied the ropes. Edwin rubbed his wrists and glared at Manfred. He understood his brother's feelings. Freedom had been sweet while they had it, but when things were straightened out with the sheriff here, they'd be free again.

The cell door clanged shut, and the key scraped in the lock. Edwin slumped onto the cot and propped his head in his hands, his eyes toward the floor.

Manfred knelt beside him. "I'm sorry, Edwin. We'll get out of this because we haven't done anything wrong. Trust in the Lord and pray." If they told the truth, this problem had to work itself out in their favor.

The jailer returned. "Sheriff Dobson rode out to the Carswell farm. He'll be back with Mr. Carswell to identify his horses."

Edwin sprang from the cot and thrust his arms through the bars in an attempt to grab the jailer. He waved his arms and yelled, "We didn't steal any horses. I spent the last two months in a dirty hole of a Yankee prison, and I don't intend to spend any more time locked up. Let us out of here now!"

Manfred yanked Edwin back and held the boy's arms to his sides. "Simmer down. We'll straighten this mess out." He pushed Edwin onto the cot then turned back to the guard. Perhaps he'd be able to explain and get them out of here.

"I apologize for my brother. We've had a rough few months. We have a bill of sale for our horses signed by Zeke Grayson."

The jailer scratched his head. "Don't see as how I can do anything with that until the sheriff gets back. Maude Barnes will be over from the tavern shortly with dinner for you." He turned back to the office. At the door he turned and smiled. "I hope it all checks out. You don't look like any horse thieves to me." Then he turned to the other cell. "Sure can't say the same for you all."

The door banged shut, and a key grated in the lock. Manfred glanced over to the opposite cell. All three men sat calmly. Manfred noted the smirk again on Clem's face and figured those boys were up to no good. And where was Frank? He wouldn't let the others be locked up while he rode away free.

Then the truth dawned on Manfred. Frank didn't plan on leaving his men in jail. That's why he'd left the trail and probably why he'd been happy to have Edwin and Manfred join the group.

Whatever happened in the next hour or so would have a definite effect on whether or not the sheriff would believe his story. Manfred slumped to the second cot and leaned against the brick wall, his head down. If the Lord planned to get them out of this mess, Manfred preferred it be done now and not later.

A sigh escaped as he closed his eyes and leaned his head on the wall. How he longed for his pack and his journal. He wanted to get that letter to Sallie finished and posted before they left Hanover. But for now he had to work on keeping his attitude in the right place and convince Edwin to keep his temper in check. Anger and harsh words would only serve to strengthen the accusations against them, not prove their innocence.

❧

St. Francisville, Louisiana

After reading one page three times, Sallie laid her book aside and gazed down at Hannah, who sat on the floor with her books. Even though she'd soon be thirteen, she was still too young to understand everything about the past five years. At least she hadn't seen all that had happened in Woodville. Now that the war had ended, Hannah could keep her mind on her games and toys and plan for a future.

Every time the prospect of returning to Woodville came to mind, fear entered right along with it. How would she feel when she went up the back stoop and into the house again? If blood or any other evidence of the battle remained, she wouldn't be able to stand it. She had never intended to kill anyone. Papa would have the house cleaned up and ready for them to live in again, but mental images could never be erased.

"Sallie, will you help me with this puzzle?" Her sister held up two pieces of the wood puzzle Papa had made for her.

Sallie shook herself. She must forget Woodville and all she had experienced there. The happy memories of her childhood must be the ones to dwell on now. She could continue to protect Hannah from ever knowing the truth.

Sallie knelt beside her sister on the floor under the window. "What seems to be the problem?"

For the next half hour the two sat head to head fitting pieces together and giggling when they didn't. At one point Sallie glanced up and spotted Grandma in the doorway.

What a sight the elderly woman presented with her hair barely peeking out from the little cap she wore when napping.

"Good afternoon, Grandma. We didn't disturb your rest, did we?"

"No, and don't let me interrupt you. The two of you make a beautiful picture sitting there, and I wanted to savor the moment." She waved her hand and headed back to her room.

"Goodness. Look at the shadows." Sallie stood and shook out her green cotton skirt and adjusted the collar of her dress. "We've been sitting quite a spell." And what a wonderful respite it had been. As long as she had her little sister around, peace would replace the turmoil in her heart.

Hannah hugged her knees to her chest. "It's almost finished. Thank you for helping me. I can do it myself now."

"I'm sure you can. I'm going down to see if I can find a glass of lemonade somewhere. Flora usually makes some this time of day. Want to come with me?"

"No, I'll stay here." Hannah gazed up at Sallie. A slight frown formed. "Sallie, you looked so sad awhile ago. That's why I asked you to help me. I want you to be happy all the time now." She stood and wrapped her arms around Sallie's waist.

Sallie smoothed back an errant curl of her sister's hair. They were but an inch or so from being eye-to-eye. "Oh, dear, sweet Hannah. I want to be happy too. Maybe the birthday party will help."

Hannah tilted her head and gazed at Sallie. "I'm glad I'm going to your party. Jeremiah Simpson isn't so bad, except when he pulls my curls or unties my ribbons."

"He does that to make you angry. I think he likes you." Sallie released the girl's hold and stood back to look at her. If the young men here or in Mississippi had any sense at all, they'd overlook her deformed leg and see the beauty in her face and heart.

"Oh, pooh. He does not. He even makes fun of my feet."

Hannah plopped back to the floor and stuck her uneven legs out from under her skirt.

"I see." She'd never expected to hear that about Jeremiah. She leaned over and hugged Hannah. "Sure you don't want to come with me?"

"No, I'll stay up here until supper." She concentrated on another puzzle piece.

Sallie found Mama in the parlor working on a cross-stitch sampler. "Come in and sit by me, dear. Flora is bringing in lemonade and tea cakes in a few minutes. Lettie's running errands for her."

Sallie shrugged and sat down. Talk with her friend would have to wait. She settled on the sofa and fingered her skirt then leaned her head against the back.

Mama laid aside her stitching and peered over her glasses. "Now, Sallie, what is bothering you?"

"I don't know, Mama. I'm restless, and I guess bored too. It's always so quiet after Papa and the boys leave." She clasped her hands together in her lap. Why couldn't she speak up and tell her mother what was going on inside? Mama would understand and have good advice. Still Sallie hesitated. Bringing everything out in the open might make it worse.

"Hmm, I see. The invitations have been sent, the party's all planned, and your dress is nearly ready for a fitting at Mrs. Tenney's. Not much else to do."

Flora entered carrying a silver tray laden with a pitcher of lemonade, glasses, and a platter of cookies. A knock sounded at the door as she set the tray on the table. She scurried to answer.

A few moments later Flora reappeared carrying a cream-colored vellum envelope. "The Elliots' coachman brought this to you, Miss Sallie."

Sallie searched the envelope but found only her name in

black script. When she opened the flap, a card printed in black fluttered out. Retrieving it, she began to read. Her eyes opened wide and she gasped. "It's an invitation to the Elliots for a celebration welcoming home Benjamin."

Mama reached for the paper. "How wonderful. Next week, Saturday the twenty-ninth. That's soon, and it's formal. What will you wear...?" Her voice trailed off, her fingers on her chin.

Sallie slumped onto the sofa. "With my new birthday dress, we don't need to order another one so soon." She couldn't put the burden of another dress on her parents with the repairs going on at their home. Their house was more important than some party. Besides, her spirits didn't feel up to attending such a grand party as the Elliots would have. She would have to turn down the invitation.

Mama tapped a cheek with her forefinger. "I think we can manage to find something. Let's go look at your wardrobe." She grasped Sallie's hand to pull her from the sofa. "My dear, don't look so forlorn. Just remember that if Ben Elliot is home, then Manfred will be home soon too."

Sallie's spirits brightened. Mama was right. Soldiers were coming home, and nothing would keep Manfred from doing the same no matter how long it took.

When she followed her mother into the bedroom, Hannah had moved to a chair by the window and worked on her new piece of embroidery. Mama addressed Hannah. "Sweetheart, Flora has lemonade and cookies in the parlor. Wouldn't you like to have some?"

The young girl gazed from Mama to Sallie. She opened her mouth to speak, but closed it again promptly. "Yes, Mama. I think I would." She laid aside her needlework and left the room, trying in vain to keep her heavy shoe from thumping on the floor. At the doorway she glanced back, shrugged her shoulders, and disappeared from view.

Sallie caressed a pale blue silk dress hanging in her wardrobe, one she'd brought here several months ago to have on hand for special occasions. Why didn't joy and excitement for Ben's homecoming fill her as it normally would have? Mrs. Elliot had reason to celebrate just as Manfred's family would on his return.

A cold chill passed through her body, and she turned to grab her mother. "Mama, something's happened to Manfred. He's in danger."

Mama gasped then wrapped her arms around Sallie's back. "Dear child, how can that be? The war is over."

"I don't know, but I do know something has happened. I can feel it. Oh, Mama, he's in terrible trouble. What are we going to do?"

"We're going to pray for him right now." Mama grabbed her hand and pulled Sallie down beside her on the bed.

CHAPTER 13

Hanover, Virginia

EDWIN PACED THE cell and continued to mutter, "We didn't do anything. We don't belong here. Why didn't you do something, Manfred?" He kicked his cot and heaved a slop bucket at the wall.

The pail banged against the brick then clattered to the floor. Manfred winced then reached out and grabbed Edwin's arm. "Get control of yourself. This'll get you nowhere." The same anger raging in Edwin roiled inside Manfred's own heart, but a few added years of maturity and common sense allowed him to contain the anger.

Manfred pushed the younger boy onto the cot and sat down beside him. "Soon as they see the paper from Mr. Grayson, they'll let us go. We were planning to spend the night here anyway, so let's rest and enjoy our meal. It should be here soon."

The outer door swung open and an elderly woman entered, followed by the jailer. They carried trays of food covered by large napkins. The plump little woman smiled and shoved the tray through the slot on the cell door. "Hello, boys. Brought your meal for you. Hope you like stew and cornbread."

Manfred grasped the sides of the tray and pulled it through to his side. "Thank you. We appreciate your taking care of us." The aroma of stew and cornbread reminded him of how long it'd been since their last meal. Then he shook his head. He'd gone much longer than this between good meals in the past few months. Gratitude for the Lord's provision filled his heart, even if the meal happened to be in another prison.

The woman waited while the jailer deposited the tray in the cell across the way. She tugged at the man's arm. "These two young'uns over here don't look like any horse thieves to me. Sheriff Dobson better let them go."

The jailer patted her hand. "I think he will, Miss Maude." He stopped and spoke to Manfred. "The sheriff'll be back soon. Then maybe we'll get this mess straightened out. I sure hope you boys are telling the truth."

"We are. The paper's in my pack. Thanks for the dinner." Manfred gripped the bars, his knuckles white. Why couldn't the man just look in the saddlebag and find the proof? Sometimes the ways of the law took forever to find the truth.

After the deputy departed, Manfred removed the cloth from the tray and sat down to enjoy the dinner. Edwin took his bowl and spoon and sat on the cot opposite Manfred, still mumbling about wanting to get out of the place.

When the door thumped closed, Clem leaned against the bars of his cell. "We don't plan to be here when that sheriff returns." He tipped his hat back on his head and peered across at Manfred and Edwin with a smirk on his face.

Edwin jumped to his feet. "Just how are you going to manage that?"

"Frank didn't hide in them trees for nothing. He'll be here to get us out soon. You two better come with us." Clem scratched the stubble on his chin.

Manfred grabbed Edwin's elbow and squeezed it. "I don't think so. They'll be hunting you for sure. We don't have time to be running from any lawmen."

Edwin glared at Manfred. "You really think that sheriff will let us go?"

"Yes, I do."

Jesse snorted. "Leave them be, Clem. If they're dumb enough to think they'll be free any time soon, then they can stay here and rot." He pulled a pack of playing cards from his pocket and hunkered down to play a game with Clem and Al.

Edwin gripped the cell bars. "You don't know anything about rotting in a jail. We've spent the last few months in a place that makes this jail look like a palace. Go ahead and play your games. We'll be just fine."

The brave comments sent pride soaring through Manfred. The boy's true spirit shone through when it counted most. "That's good, little brother. Keep your head on straight. Those boys are real trouble we don't need."

Edwin nodded. "I know." He returned to his dinner and grinned. "That jailer was right about one thing. Miss Maude is a great cook." He stuffed a hunk of cornbread into his mouth.

Manfred had to agree. He finished off his meal and set the tray by the door. The shadows through the high cell window indicated the sun would be setting soon. Where was that sheriff? He should have been back by now.

A commotion in the outer office brought every man in the cells to their feet. Jesse hollered, "It's Frank. Get ready to ride." The three prisoners across the way grabbed the bars of the cell. Jesse hollered, "Hey, Frank, we're waiting."

The door swung open and Frank charged through, tossing a set of keys to Jesse. While Jesse unlocked the cell, Frank handed guns to Clem and Al. "Got the horses out back saddled and ready." The men plucked their saddlebags from Frank's shoulder.

Jesse unlocked Manfred and Edwin's cell. "Come on with us. They won't get a posse together to come after us until we're long gone."

Manfred sensed Edwin moving beside him. He reached out to grab hold of Edwin's shirt. "No thanks, we'll take our chances here."

Jesse's evil laugh sent a tremor of fear through Manfred. The outlaw might not give him a choice, but then a sneer spread across Jesse's face. "Have it your way." He hurried after the others. In a few moments Manfred and Edwin heard the thunder of horses galloping away, then all became quiet.

A moan broke the silence. Manfred turned toward the noise. "Sounds like the jailer. He must be hurt. I'm going to see." He cautiously peered around the door and spotted the jailer on the floor by his desk. His gaze darted about the room as he tiptoed to the man and knelt beside him. Blood trickled from a large gash just above the man's temple. Manfred turned him over as the injured man moaned again.

His early training from his medical courses took over. A pitcher of water sat on the desk, so Manfred took the man's kerchief and dampened it with the water. He wiped the blood away, careful not to move the man's head, then poured a stream of water over the man.

The deputy shook his head then winced in pain. He scrambled to sit up and grabbed for a shotgun.

Manfred raised his hands and slowly stood. The outside door swung open, and the sheriff entered with another man and the other deputies. The lawman drew his gun. "What happened?"

The deputy tried to stand but swayed and sat back down with his hand on his head. "Got hit from behind and blacked out. Next thing I knew this here fellow was pouring water on me."

The sheriff glanced at Manfred before racing into the cell area. "They're gone!" He swung around and yelled. "Who let them go?"

Manfred remained standing with his hands up. "Their partner, Frank, came in and took them. Said he had horses waiting out back."

The sheriff stared at Manfred then over at Edwin. "Why didn't you go with them?" He shoved his gun back into its holster.

Manfred shrugged. "Didn't see a need to." He nodded toward his brother. "We tried to tell you we weren't with those men in the first place. We've done nothing wrong."

The man accompanying the sheriff said, "He's right. These boys weren't with the others when they stole my horses. Besides, only three of those horses in the stable are mine. I have just one of mine missing now, remember?"

"Yes, I do, Hank, but where did they find more?" The sheriff wiped dust from his face with a handkerchief and removed his hat. He shrugged. "I suppose that's a foolish question. If he could steal once, he'd have no problem doing it again."

He turned to Manfred. "Now, young man, you said you had proof you own the horses. Let's see it."

Manfred scurried over to his pack. He dug around inside it for a minute then brought out the paper with a triumphant wave of his hand. Sheriff Dobson reached for it and read the document. "Manfred and Edwin Whiteman. You say you were prisoners in Maryland, and Mr. Grayson gave you these horses in return for labor."

"Yes, sir, he did." Manfred wiped his hands on his pants.

Sheriff Dobson refolded the paper and handed it to Manfred. "Looks in order to me. Get your gear. I'm sorry about the delay, but we can't be too careful. You're free to go."

Edwin slapped Manfred on the back and whooped, "Yes, sir. Let's get out of here." He grabbed up his pack and pushed his hat onto his head and headed out the door.

Manfred shouldered his load but lingered behind. "Anywhere we could spend the night in this town?"

"My wife, Mattie, is in charge down at the inn. Miss Maude is her cook. Check with her. She may have a room for you." Sheriff Dobson stacked a few papers on his desk.

"Aren't you going after those men?" Manfred raised an eyebrow.

The sheriff picked up a pen and handed a paper to Hank. "If Mr. Carswell here wants to send a posse after his missing horse, I will. Right now I need your signature for the ones we found." He shoved his hat back on his head and shrugged. "If those boys are riding horses from around here, I'll find out about it and go after them again. Other than that, not much else I can do except maybe put out a few wanted posters around the territory in hopes some other lawmen in other towns will take care of them."

Manfred shook his head. "Seems to me they're getting off mighty easy."

"Maybe so, but their kind are all around now the war's over. Always wanting something for nothing."

Hank Carswell slapped on his hat. "My boys and I will go on after them. If we catch them, we'll bring them back here."

The sheriff nodded. "Be careful, Hank. I have a bad feeling about those thieves." Then his eyes changed as though he'd made a decision. He turned to one of his deputies. "Go with them. I'll catch up to you soon as I get these boys situated."

Heading out the door with the deputy, Mr. Carswell called to his men to saddle up. Manfred walked out with the sheriff and found Edwin waiting on the street holding the reins of their horses. "How did you get the horses?"

"I left while you were talking with the sheriff. Figured I could save us some time and went on over to the stables and got them." He pointed down the street. "I see the sign for the inn down yonder."

Manfred shook the sheriff's hand. "You go catch those thieves. We'll be all right at the inn."

The sheriff nodded. "I wouldn't be going after them at all, but I can't let Mr. Carswell handle this on his own. You boys take care now." He headed for his own horse, mounted it, and then took off after Carswell and his men.

Manfred swung up onto his saddle and turned toward the inn. It was another delay in their journey, but at least they'd be sleeping as free men again tonight, and a hearty meal had given them the strength they'd need for tomorrow.

God did indeed take care of His children. After Manfred told the innkeeper about their lack of money and a need for a place to sleep, she said she'd give them one night free because she'd heard about their ordeal at the jail.

Once again they would sleep between clean sheets. As they settled down for the night, Edwin leaned on his elbow. "I won't question your judgment anymore, Manfred. You know what's best for us."

Manfred blew out the oil lamp and chuckled. They'd have to wait and see about that. Edwin meant well, but more often than not he let his mouth get ahead of his brain. At least this adventure turned out well. Mrs. Dobson had even offered to add breakfast and food for the road along with a room for the night. With only a few coins in hand that Mrs. Grayson had slipped into their knapsack, he appreciated every gesture like the good innkeeper's.

They hadn't covered as many miles as he'd hoped in the time they'd been gone, but having the horses would help in making up the time lost by their stop in Virginia. If things continued in the fashion of the past week, this wouldn't be the last delay or adventure before getting to Louisiana.

He reached for his journal to record the day's happenings and crept over to the window to write in moonlight streaming through. After writing a few pages, he stowed it away and opened the Bible he carried in his backpack. God's Word and the hope of seeing Sallie in a few weeks brought peace to his heart.

CHAPTER 14

A FTER SALLIE HAD prayed with Mama, cold and fear for Manfred plagued Sallie all night, making for a restless sleep. Would God listen to Mama's pleas? Sallie couldn't trust God to answer her own.

Now in the light of day the fear and dread disappeared. After dressing for breakfast with Lettie's help, Sallie drifted down to the dining room for breakfast, where Mama and Grandma sat discussing the day's duties. "Where's Grandpa?" Sallie asked.

Grandma adjusted her round, wire-frame spectacles. "He went into town very early this morning. Your mother and I have decided we don't need heavy meals at noontime with your father and brothers gone. We were planning what we might have instead."

Sallie made no comment but ladled oatmeal into a bowl. Lettie would bring her eggs and ham if asked, but a big breakfast held no appeal this morning. Flora did bring in a glass of milk and a bowl of early strawberries from the patch in back of the house. Mama and Grandma left to take care of their duties.

After sitting alone for a few minutes, Sallie shoved her half-eaten bowl away, drained her milk glass, and pushed back from the table. She had plenty of time now to read and write in her journal, but the hours dragged by.

By late afternoon she'd tired of writing and even reading her latest novel. She entered the parlor and ran her fingers over the keys of the piano. Grandma had given her a new piece to practice, but Sallie had forgotten all about it.

Maybe she could play a few minutes and concentrate on the beauty of the music rather than the ugliness of the past. But before she touched the keys, Grandpa entered the room accompanied by Benjamin Elliot.

When had Grandpa come home, and when had Benjamin Elliot arrived? Neither of them had made their presence known before this minute. Sallie clasped her hands in her lap and smiled. "Good afternoon, Grandpa, I didn't realize you'd come back from town. It's nice to see you, Mr. Elliot." She hadn't seen him in two years, but she had no trouble remembering him. How handsome he looked in his deep gray coat and pants and white shirt.

He bowed and said, "I came to speak to your grandfather since your father is not here."

Grandpa nodded. "Yes. I told him your father would be back the end of the week, but it seems he is anxious to take care of this matter as quickly as possible. Mr. Elliot has come to ask our permission to be your escort for his party on Saturday. I told him you'd be honored to join him."

Sallie gasped and pressed her fingers against her lips. The invitation had come only yesterday, and she hadn't even decided whether she'd go to the party or not, much less be escorted by Benjamin Elliot. How could Grandpa even think of accepting an invitation like that?

"Now, Sallie, I know you're surprised, but this is a chance for you to attend the celebration and give him a charming companion too."

Pushing back the disappointment rising in her, Sallie bowed her head and gave in to the respect she held for Grandpa. "Yes, Grandpa. I understand." She didn't, but this was not the time for disagreement. She stood and curtsied and held out her hand to Mr. Elliot. "I'd be honored to accompany you."

The young man grasped her hand in his. "To be sure, it will be my pleasure to be your escort on Saturday evening, Miss Sallie." He bowed again, released her hand, and turned to Grandpa. "Thank you, sir. I will speak to Mr. Dyer about the other matter when he returns."

"Of course, my boy. He'll be more than happy to talk with you."

Grandpa's words squeezed all joy from her heart. She fought back the tears as Grandpa walked with Benjamin Elliot out to the porch. When the door closed behind them, Sallie raced up the stairs and flung herself on her bed. She pounded the thick down comforter with her fist and muttered, "Oh, Grandpa. You don't understand. I don't want to go anywhere with Benjamin."

Hannah jumped up on the bed and put her arms around Sallie. "What's wrong, Sallie? Why are you so upset? Is it Manfred?"

"No, it's…it's…oh, Grandpa." Her muffled words caused Hannah to jump down and run from the room. Sallie heard her call for Mama to come.

A few moments later footsteps and voices told her of their entrance.

Mama sat on the bed and tapped Sallie on the shoulder. "My dear, what's the matter? I thought something had happened to you when Hannah came running to my room telling me to come see you."

Sallie sat up and brushed the tears from her cheeks. "Grandpa gave Benjamin Elliot permission to be my escort for his party. I don't want to go with anyone, but Grandpa gave his word."

"Why, that's wonderful, my dear, you should feel honored.

I can fix up that blue dress for you. It'll be perfect." She jumped up and headed to the wardrobe in the corner.

"Please wait, Mama." Sallie blinked her eyes and held out a hand to her mother.

She sat back on the bed and cradled Sallie in her arms. "What is it, dear?"

"Why did Grandpa do this? Do I have to go with Benjamin?"

"He's only doing what he thinks is best for you. He believes the party and going with Benjamin will help get your mind off Manfred, and time will pass more quickly." She laid her cheek on Sallie's head. "Sometimes men don't understand. Until Manfred is home and asks Papa about courting you, this is the way it has to be."

"I don't want to go against Grandpa. I love him very much, but I want to wait for Manfred." Sallie sat back and searched Mama's face for understanding. Why did Benjamin need her to be on his arm for the evening anyway?

"Of course you want to wait for him, but it wouldn't be proper for you to turn down such a nice invitation from Benjamin. You know Grandpa won't go back on his word either. Besides, you also have to face facts. It's been months since you heard from Manfred. Until you do, you'll have to be sociable with the other young men returning from war. To do otherwise would be impolite." Mama grasped both Sallie's hands in hers.

Disappointment clogged Sallie's throat. Why couldn't any of them understand? Maybe she could feign illness and not go to the party at all.

Grandma entered and sat on the other side of Sallie and hugged her. "I'm so sorry, my dear. Grandpa means well. I don't believe he realizes how much you love Manfred or what it means for him to make decisions for you."

"Well, I don't think it's fair. I'm almost nineteen and

145

perfectly capable of making decisions for myself. Why do we always have to do what the men think we should? I do have a brain."

Mama sighed. "Oh, my sweet child, the Bible tells me I must love and honor my husband, and you must do the same for your parents and grandparents. It's our way of showing respect."

"I understand, but I love Manfred, and in my heart I know he's coming home." Sallie sat up and squared her shoulders. Too much had happened for him not to come back.

Mama stood. "Remember, one party doesn't tie you to Benjamin. You can go and have a grand time. Perhaps it will help you remember the good times we had before the war."

She and Grandma left the room. Hannah tiptoed to the bed and put her arms around her sister's waist. "Oh, Sallie. You gave me such a scare. I thought something had happened to Grandpa."

Sallie pulled Hannah close. "I'm sorry, sweetie. He upset me, and I guess I was angry with him. It's all right now."

Amanda rushed down the stairs to find her father in his study. She stopped and smoothed down her skirt before knocking on the doorframe.

When he bade her to enter, she stepped through the door and composed her face to hide the concern welling in her heart. "I just spoke with Sallie. She tells me you gave permission for Benjamin Elliot to escort her to his party."

A wide grin creased her father's face. "I did, and when Thomas returns, the young man will be asking to court Sallie all proper like."

Amanda's heart plummeted to her stomach. "I've come from Sallie's room, and she's quite distraught."

Her father raised his eyebrows but gave no comment.

"I know it isn't necessary, but under the circumstances it might have been better to ask her first."

"And what circumstances are those, my dear Amanda?"

How to explain to him the thinking of a young woman's mind would not be easy, but she must try. She searched for the right words again. At least he knew Manfred and liked the boy. It wasn't as though she talked about a stranger.

"It's Manfred. Sallie is in love with him. Her only thoughts have been of him."

Her father frowned slightly. "I see, but we don't even know where the boy is or if he's even alive."

"I know, but he is important to her. So much has happened to her in the past few months that I fear for her future happiness."

Her father wrapped his arm about her shoulder. "I understand. You've all been under a great strain these past weeks after the ordeal of fleeing your home. That is precisely why I gave my consent. Sallie needs this party to take her mind off what happened in Woodville. If young Manfred comes home anytime soon, I'm sure Thomas can explain the circumstances to Benjamin."

Amanda said nothing. Her father had no idea of the delicacy of a young woman's heart, and it would be fruitless to discuss it further.

Someone pounded the brass knocker on the door. Her father rushed to open it before Flora could appear. A young man stood on the threshold, twisting his hat in his hands.

"What is it, young man? It's rather late to be calling."

"We've had awful news, sir. President Lincoln was shot and killed. Someone shot him at a theater in Washington."

Amanda's knees buckled, and she grabbed the stair railing for support. Lincoln dead? How could that be? She pressed her hand to her chest, praying it would halt the racing of her heart.

"This is most certainly disturbing news. When did it happen?"

"Good Friday. He was shot at a theater in Washington and died Saturday morning. That's all I know, sir."

The young man squashed his hat back on his head and ran up the sidewalk toward the road. Her father closed the door and leaned against it. Her mother stood near Flora in the entryway. "What is this going to mean now with the war over?"

"I don't know, but it can't bode well. I may not have agreed with some of his policies, but to kill the man is unthinkable."

Amanda closed her eyes against the tears forming there. Even with the war over, violence still reared its ugly head. Would sanity and safety ever return to her beloved country?

CHAPTER 15

DESPITE THE TRAGIC news of Lincoln's death, Amanda decided that planning for Sallie's birthday party should continue without interruption. He had been president, and her family would properly mourn for him, but life would go on as usual here in Louisiana. So she gladly accepted her sister's invitation to lunch at Magnolia Hall, followed by an afternoon of planning for the party.

After a light luncheon of cold meats and salad, Amanda followed her sister through the spacious Bradford home as her sister explained plans for the party. Abigail spread her hands. "Now here in the foyer I plan to have urns and vases of fresh spring flowers, and the balustrade will have garlands of flowers and ivy also."

"It will look lovely. You're so fortunate to have your beautiful home restored to such beauty as before the war." Only a little damage remained on the stately home nestled among the beautiful creamy white magnolia trees that gave the home its name.

Abigail linked arms with her. "I'm so sorry for the damage to your beautiful house in Woodville. All of us in St. Francisville are thankful the fighting came no closer than Port Hudson and the little skirmish down on the river. If those renegades hadn't set fire to our home, we wouldn't have had any damage at all. I'm thankful our men were able to extinguish it before really major destruction occurred."

Amanda patted her sister's hand. "Don't worry about our home. It will be restored. Things that were in it don't count.

Our lives are more important." She turned to gaze straight at Sallie, who noticeably shuddered under scrutiny. She had to do everything possible to help her daughter forget that dreadful day.

Peggy leaned toward Sallie. "She'll have it looking more like a funeral than a birthday. I'll add other decorations and things."

Sallie nodded and started to say something in return, but Amanda shot a warning glance in that direction. She would not have her daughter be critical of such generosity. The house would be lovely despite Peggy's comments.

Amanda followed Abigail into the dining room. Her sister continued the spiel. "Refreshment tables will be set up here in the dining room, but we'll have the musicians in the adjoining parlor. We'll line the chairs up around the wall and have plenty of room for dancing." She directed her lace fan toward a large room on the other side of the dining area.

"How many musicians are you planning to have, Mama?" Peggy winked at Sallie.

Abigail tapped her cheek with her folded ivory fan. "I think two violins, a cello, and a piano will suffice. Mrs. Wolfe from our church will take care of putting together an ensemble."

Peggy raised her eyebrows. "What? No orchestra with horns and reeds and drums?"

"Oh, Peggy, my dear. Be practical. We've just come out of a war. No need to be ostentatious." She strode from the room.

Peggy collapsed into a chair and stifled her giggles. "Sometimes I wonder if Mama really knows what's going on." She shook her head.

Amanda smiled. Her sister did seem to have her head in the clouds about the war, but at other times she gave the impression of being quite aware of it all. Perhaps this was her sister's way of banishing all the demons of war, once and for all. Abigail's voice called from another room. "Come along, girls, Amanda. There's more."

Sallie grabbed Peggy's arm and pulled her along. Amanda followed them. What her sister referred to as the "music conservatory" was a rectangular space with a piano at one end and chairs arranged in small groupings for conversation or listening to a musical program. Landscape paintings and still-life pictures adorned the walls. Oriental carpets covered the gleaming hardwood floors. Yes, it would be perfect for the number of people expected.

After another half hour of touring and planning, Abigail brought them back to the front porch. They'd decided on a simple menu because some foods were still too scarce. Even what they had seemed too elaborate to Amanda, but she wouldn't question her sister's generosity.

After their good-byes and promises to visit again soon, Amanda climbed into the carriage beside Sallie, who took the reins for the ride home. She rested her hand on Sallie's arm. "Your aunt Abigail means well, my dear. She wasn't as close to things as we were. The Colonel had already sent her away before the attack on their home. Forget what's happened in the past few months, and think about the lovely party you'll be having in a few weeks."

Sallie nodded, but Amanda noted the sadness still lingering in her daughter's eyes. So easy to ask, but so hard for her sweet daughter to do. To distract her, Amanda said brightly, "Do you remember the time the war stopped for the day? News didn't reach us in Woodville until days after Port Hudson fell."

"Isn't that the battle where Manfred's brother was captured?" Sallie asked.

Amanda nodded. When Manfred came to see Sallie and rest of the Dyer family last summer, he had talked about his officer brother being taken prisoner, but they had no idea where Charles had been sent. Manfred had been lucky enough to be one of the soldiers sent away from Port Hudson before the siege began.

"If I remember correctly, a naval officer in the Union fell ill and died. As he was a Mason, a Masonic funeral was requested by his fellow seamen. The Masons in St. Francisville went down to the docks and escorted his body back up to Grace Church, where a proper Masonic burial was held. All fighting stopped that day in memory of the officer. Then the next day everything went back to the way it was and the war continued."

Sallie furrowed her brow. "If they stopped the fighting for one day, why couldn't they just quit then? Why do men have to fight about everything?"

Amanda pulled her close. "Some things are beyond our understanding, Sallie. We just have to trust that God can use even the great evil of war to bring about His greater good."

Sallie didn't reply, and Amanda noted her silence. Perhaps the death of that Union soldier had taken more of a toll on Sallie than she had let on. Maybe she should talk to her daughter about that terrible day.

But remembering the awful scene, she dismissed the thought. The war was over. Better to keep their gaze to the future and not dwell on the tragedies of the past.

Virginia

The farther south Manfred and Edwin rode past Richmond and down to Powhatan, the closer they came to Tennessee, but that was still days away. Memories of Nashville and the horrors of the war there raced through Manfred's mind. He stiffened his back and shoulders. No need to dwell on that. He reined in his horse and dismounted.

"This seems as good a place as any to stop for a rest and some food." He tethered his horse to a tree and untied his pack.

Edwin did the same and opened his pack. He sat down beside Manfred. "When we get back to Tennessee, do we have to go back by Nashville? I don't think I ever want to go there again."

"I know I don't either. We'll head on down toward Alabama and cross over into Mississippi from there." No matter if it took a few more days, that part of Tennessee had no attraction now and wouldn't for a long time to come.

He figured at least several more weeks of travel before crossing into Mississippi and making their way westward. What would they find there and in Louisiana? He prayed Ma and Pa were all right and that they hadn't lost the shipping company. He wanted the Dyer family to be safe, but stories of damage along the river in Mississippi and Louisiana after the loss of Port Hudson continued to cloud his thoughts. How he longed to gaze into Sallie's eyes and caress her red gold curls.

They ate in silence, then Edwin banged his cup against a tree to empty it. "I'm glad this war is over," he admitted.

"Hmm. A little different feeling than you had a week or so ago." Manfred eyed his brother and tipped his hat back. Edwin had grown stronger and had matured in the days since their release.

"We've been very fortunate to have met people so willing to help us. This is the last of the food Mrs. Dobson gave us before we left Hanover."

Edwin drew his knees up to his chest. "That was an

experience I'll never forget. I wonder what happened to those men?"

"Don't know, but I hope we don't meet up with them again." He lifted his canteen to his lips and gulped down the water then brushed his sleeve across his mouth. "Water's getting low too." There had to be a river or stream in the mountains they planned to travel in the next few days.

"How far to the next town?" Edwin downed the last of his biscuit and dried fruit.

"Not sure, but according to the map we came through Goochland and we should be in Powhatan in another hour. If we don't find a stream or creek before then, we'll have to ration water until we do." Manfred stretched his legs out straight and contemplated the dusty toes of his boots. "We both could use a little cleaning up too."

Although they had gone months without good hygiene in prison, he wanted more regular baths and chances to clean up now they were free. Perhaps a hotel in Powhatan would offer baths for a small fee. By sleeping outdoors, they had managed to save the few coins from Mrs. Grayson. Even now her generosity touched his soul.

The saddlebag contained one day more of provisions. Tomorrow they needed to stock up for the next week with those few coins.

When they reached Powhatan, Manfred once again counted their money. He frowned and stopped. "Let's camp outside of town and save what little money we have for food tomorrow."

"Yeah, doesn't look like we could find a place here."

A few minutes later they set up camp thirty or forty yards from the road.

Edwin arranged his pack into a makeshift pillow. "Think I'll call it a night." He settled himself on the ground and pulled his hat down over his face. In a few minutes his gentle snores joined the chorus of crickets and other night insects.

A full belly and gentle night breezes lulled Manfred into drowsiness. Morning couldn't come soon enough.

CHAPTER 16

THE FIRST RAYS of sunlight awakened Manfred. He shook his head to clear it and sat up. Then he reached over and pulled a folded piece of paper from his pack. Reading his letter to Sallie again would help him wake up. He opened the missive and reread the words written a few nights ago. In all the excitement and turmoil of the past few weeks, he had yet to find stamps and post it.

Thanks to their horses they had made good time and would soon be in Marion. Since leaving Powhatan eight days ago they'd traveled about twenty miles a day and had even been able to ride by train to Wytheville. They still had about twenty to go until Marion. Most of the towns they'd come through had seen little damage since most of the big battles had been farther north or down south in the Carolinas, Georgia, and Mississippi.

Edwin stretched and stood up from his bedroll. "I'm sure glad those folks back in Hillsville told us to come up this way to go through the mountains."

Manfred put away his letter and opened his pack to pull out a few cold biscuits and hardtack. "I am too. I hadn't thought about trying to get over these mountains, and when that man at Hillsville said to come north by train to Wytheville and down through the pass to Marion, I thought it crazy at first until he explained."

"Whatever it took, I'm glad we're here now." Edwin reached for a biscuit. "Let's eat and be on our way. We're close to Tennessee, and that's one state closer to home."

156

That day proved to be uneventful. The haze over the mountains did have the look of smoke, hence their name. The mountains rose on either side and grew taller as they rode toward Marion in the foothills. Occasionally Edwin whistled or hummed a few bars to a song, and Manfred joined in.

Later Manfred spotted a stream flowing through rocks of a full creek bed and jumped down to fill his canteen. As he drank, he gazed around appreciatively. "This is beautiful country around here with the mountains. From the green of the plants and trees, they must have had some good rains this spring."

That was one thing Manfred enjoyed about traveling on horseback. He had a chance to really see the country and drink in its many features.

Once again on horseback they continued south as the sun dropped low to the west. They rode into the town of Marion in late afternoon. Here there was a little more evidence that a war had been fought, with bullet holes riddling a local covered bridge.

In the livery stable's side yard a blacksmith worked at his anvil. His muscles rippled as he pounded a horseshoe. He paused in his hammering when he glanced up to see Manfred and Edwin. "What can I do for you fellas?"

Manfred tipped his hat. "We're looking for a place to rest our heads and get a good meal. Don't have much money left."

"We have an inn, but not sure it has any room available now." He laid down his tool and wiped the sweat from his brow with a rag. "Stable's clean, and I only have one horse to care for now. You boys can stay there tonight with your horses. It'll cost you both a dime."

Manfred nodded. "That sounds all right to me. How about you, Edwin?"

"Fine with me." He swung down from his saddle and

scanned the street. "Sleeping on hay will be much more comfortable then the hard ground of the past few nights." He glanced around the area. "Looks like you might have had a battle around here."

The smithy tossed the rag aside. "We did a few months ago just before Christmas. Our town paid the price for being the location of the communication lines for the South. Most of the fighting took place at the east end of town for two days. The North wanted to destroy the covered bridge across the Middle Fork Holston River."

Manfred shook his head. "We know what that's like. We fought at the battle of Nashville and were taken prisoner there last fall."

The smithy stroked his black beard. "I'm not sure people will ever understand how much was lost in these past four years. We're doing what we can to survive, but it's been hard. Where you boys headed?"

Manfred dismounted and ambled over to the blacksmith. "Louisiana. I'm Manfred Whiteman, and this here's my brother Edwin." He offered his hand, and the burly man grasped it firmly.

"Bart Jensen. Welcome to the town of Marion."

Manfred scanned the street then asked, "Anywhere to get a good meal around here?"

The smithy's gaze went from Manfred to Edwin then back to Manfred. "We have a tavern, but my missus is fixing supper. You can put your horses in a stall and join us."

Manfred removed his hat. "That's kind of you. Are you sure she won't mind?"

"Not my Amy. She'll be happy to see you. Let me finish this shoe, and we'll mosey on over to the house." He pointed to a wood and stone structure across the way. "You can stash your stuff in the vacant stalls in the back of the stable."

While Manfred and Edwin tended their horses, Bart headed to his house then returned a few minutes later. "Amy said that would be fine, but I need to finish shoeing this sorrel first. You can wash up over yonder. I keep a basin and soap to clean up before going to the house."

When satisfied with the job, he slapped the horse on the rump and waved to Manfred and Edwin, who had just finished washing up.

"Come on, boys. Time to eat."

A petite, dark-haired woman stirred a pot over a fireplace. When she turned, her advanced state of approaching motherhood became evident.

Bart stepped to her side and put an arm around her shoulders. "Amy, these boys here are Manfred and Edwin. They're the ones I invited to share supper with us."

Amy's smile welcomed them even before her words. "Hello, Manfred and Edwin. We're not having much, but you're welcome to what we have." She reached into a cabinet for a large bowl. "Go on and have a seat. I'll be dishing up rabbit stew in a few minutes."

After supper Manfred and Edwin joined Bart and Amy in the corner of the room serving as both kitchen and parlor. Amy eased into the ladder-back rocking chair. "Wish we had another room for you boys to spend the night."

Manfred shook his head. "Don't worry about that. We'll be fine in the stable with our horses."

Bart stood next to the rocker where Amy sat. "You said at dinner you're from Louisiana. Amy is from North Carolina. She and her mother came here to live with relatives over three years ago. We met, fell in love, and married a little over a year ago."

"I pray your family back home is all right, Mrs. Jensen," Manfred said.

"Thank you, Manfred, they are, but Papa advised Mama to wait awhile before returning. My two younger brothers are here with her."

Bart caressed his wife's hair with his free hand. "Like I said earlier, the Yankees did come through this area and did some damage. We thought they'd burn the courthouse the way things were going, but it survived. Some of the outlying farms didn't fare so well. If it hadn't been for Susan Allen out at one of those farms, the bridge would have been burned, but she kept putting out the fires the Yankees set."

Manfred glanced toward Edwin then back to Bart. "Is there any way we can help for a few days?"

Bart stroked his beard then furrowed his brow. "I think there is. We're sending a group of men out to the Hilton farm to clean it up and do a few repairs. Most of the work here in town is about finished."

Although they were anxious to be home, the obligation to help those whose lives had been disrupted by battle took more importance. With Edwin being agreeable to staying, Manfred stood and said, "We'd be proud to help. Just tell us what we can do."

Bart reached out to shake Edwin's then Manfred's hand. "We can get right on it Monday morning. We'd be honored to have you attend church services with us in the morning. You're not the first soldiers to come through wanting to help, and we appreciate it."

Manfred picked up his hat. "Thank you, Mrs. Jensen, for your hospitality." He turned to Bart. "We'll go on out and settle down in the barn." Warmth filled his heart at the thought of helping out. It was worth the delay. Besides, the horses and they needed their Sabbath rest.

❦

St. Francisville, Louisiana

Lettie slipped a final hairpin into Sallie's curls and stood back to survey the results. "Miss Sallie, you look elegant. Mr. Elliott is a lucky young man."

Grandma kissed Sallie's cheek. "Yes, my dear, you look lovely."

Sallie turned in front of the mirror, and a young woman she hardly recognized stared back. Mama had done wonders with her blue silk dress. The added lace, ribbons, and flowers gave the garment a completely new look, feminine but not fussy. "It looks like new! Thank you, Mama."

The mirror reflected Mama's smile as she fluffed the lace around the neck. "It turned out to be easy to alter. I'm glad you like the results."

Hannah burst into the room. "Mr. Elliot is downstairs waiting for you. He looks so handsome in his uniform. I wish I was eighteen."

Sallie laughed. "And this is the little girl who didn't want to go to my party with Jeremiah Simpson?"

"Humph. He's a boy, not a man like Mr. Elliot." Hannah planted her hands on her hips. "Besides, Jeremiah is always teasing me."

Mama embraced Hannah, "Oh, my little one, how wonderful it is to have you around to brighten my day." She peered over at Sallie. "Mother and I will go down first to greet Mr. Elliot, but I think you'd best be going downstairs before Papa comes for you himself. "

Sallie counted to twenty after they left. She breathed deeply and tossed a light shawl across her arm. Tonight would be one of fun and gaiety. The war had ended, and that was cause enough to celebrate. Although she'd rather attend the party with Manfred, Benjamin Elliot would be a good escort. She grinned one last time at her reflection. Yes, she would have a good time this evening.

The voices of Papa and Grandpa chatting with Benjamin Elliot floated up the stairway as she descended. His profile came into view, and she had to admit he did look dashing in the dress officer's uniform. His raven hair gleamed in the light of the brass candle chandelier in the foyer. His gaze lifted to meet hers as she approached.

His smile broadened, and he stood as though at attention before another officer. "Good evening, Mr. Elliot." She extended her hand.

He grasped her hand lightly in his. "Miss Dyer, I shall be the envy of all men at this evening's gala." He placed her hand on his arm and cupped his hand over hers. "Good evening, Mr. and Mrs. Woodruff. Mr. and Mrs. Dyer, I shall take great care of your daughter. And thank you for your consideration."

A look passed between the two men that alarmed Sallie, and a knot formed in her throat. Had Benjamin already spoken with her father about courting her? Despite the fear rising in her heart, Sallie smiled at her escort. "I'm ready, Mr. Elliot."

The sound of movement and rustling of fabric drew Sallie's attention upward. Hannah sat near the top hugging the railing. She grinned and wiggled her fingers in good-bye. Sallie smothered a laugh and only nodded slightly in return. Hannah would want to hear all about the evening later, and Sallie vowed to bring back a glowing report.

Benjamin escorted her to his carriage, and they rode the few miles to his home chatting. Sallie answered his questions, but he said nothing of any real importance. Surely he knew more than the weather and church activities. She longed to know more about what went on outside the limits of St. Francisville, but bringing up other subjects may be construed as being unladylike.

As charming as Benjamin turned out to be, he lacked Manfred's sense of humor. She bit her lip. Such thoughts must stop. Mr. Elliot deserved her full attention.

The carriage rolled onto the grounds of the Elliot home, where other vehicles of all sizes and types filled the drive of the Elliot's plantation. They must have guests from as far as Baton Rouge if the number arriving were any indication. Excitement rose in Sallie's spirit. She would enjoy this evening first and worry about Benjamin's intentions later.

This home sat closer to Port Hudson and had sustained damage when the Union troops had traveled this road. Boarded-up windows on one side gave evidence of that attack. How long would it take to repair all the damage this war had wrought?

As if he read her thoughts, Benjamin whispered, "Mother's done an excellent job of hiding the damage. The left part of the house still needs repair, but we have plenty of room."

Sallie observed the windows stripped of draperies but decorated with urns of fresh flowers. Many of the home's elegant furnishings had disappeared, but the luxury it once held could not be mistaken.

Mr. and Mrs. Elliot greeted her in the expansive entry hall. "My dear, you look lovely. So glad you were able to come." Mrs. Elliot brushed her cheek against Sallie's.

Sallie returned the greeting. "It's a pleasure to be in your home. Thank you for inviting me." She then allowed Benjamin to guide her to a table burdened down with delicacies of all types. Pastries and cakes lent color and delightful aroma next to a bowl of fruit punch.

Benjamin hastened to explain. "It's not like the abundance we had before the war, but Mr. Brady did have staples." He filled her plate with butter pound cake and a pecan tart.

"This is quite wonderful. I love pastries." Sallie took the offered plate and glided over to a chair. Benjamin joined her. As they ate, she observed every detail of dress and decoration to relate to Hannah later. A group of musicians provided a background of music that lent a lively air to the occasion. Soon the area cleared, and the music became a waltz.

The evening passed in a flurry of dances with several other young men. Sallie relaxed and allowed herself to be caught up in the festivities. Young women outnumbered the men, but they tried to make sure all the ladies had ample opportunity on the dance floor.

Sallie glanced at her card and noticed Benjamin claimed the last two spots. Soon enough he was whirling her around the floor in time to the music. "You are quite agile on your feet, Mr. Elliot."

"Thank you. It is only because of the lightness and beauty of my partner." He smiled at her, and the look in his eyes sent shivers of delight through her heart. Her heart belonged to Manfred, but having another man interested delighted her. Still, she chided herself, such fickleness was most undesirable.

The memory of the look that had passed between Benjamin and Papa sent a chill through her bones. Benjamin likely had spoken to Papa about calling on her while he waited for her to come downstairs. Papa knew her feelings for Manfred, but he, like Grandpa, would think a young man actually here would be more suitable than one whose whereabouts were unknown. Having Benjamin for an escort would be an advantage sure to create envy, but it was also misleading and unfair to Benjamin to give him hope when her heart belonged to another.

Once again the war intruded into her life. If not for the war, she wouldn't be in this dilemma. To deny that Benjamin's attention charmed her would be a lie, but it also spoke of betrayal toward Manfred.

After the last round she and Benjamin bade his parents a good night. The warmth of the late April evening surrounded them as they climbed aboard the carriage for the ride back to her home.

Neither of them spoke on the short trip. Several times Benjamin seemed on the verge of saying something to her, but each time he cleared his throat instead. Finally he reined the horse and stopped in the Woodruff driveway.

He didn't make any movement toward leaving the carriage but turned to her instead. "Miss Sallie, I took the liberty of asking your father permission to call on you next week, and he agreed to my request."

Sallie swallowed hard, her heart lurching with regret. Papa had spoken, but Benjamin must be told the truth. Not telling him would be most rude and misleading. "I...I don't know what to say."

Benjamin frowned. "You're not spoken for, are you?"

Sallie twisted her hands in her lap. Finally she raised her head and met his eyes with hers. "No. No one has spoken for me as yet, but you must know that I promised to wait for Manfred Whiteman."

"I see." Benjamin seemed to ponder this, a muscle twitching near his mouth. Then he asked, "When was the last time you heard from him?"

Sallie bowed her head. "I had a letter just before he was to leave for Nashville."

Benjamin grasped her hands in his then dropped them when she flinched. "I'm sorry, I didn't mean to startle you. But Sallie, you've heard how fierce the battle at Nashville was.

The Yankees whipped us, and any left alive were herded up to prison camps. From what I've heard of those camps..." His voice trailed off.

"I've heard the stories too, yet I know Manfred will be home." She peered at his face, hoping he understood her.

His lips formed a grim line. He stepped down from the carriage and came to her side. As he lifted her and set her on the ground, he said, "Miss Dyer, until Manfred is home and claims you for his own, I plan to call on you, as your father permitted me to do so."

Sallie's heart thundered in her chest. Papa's wishes must be followed, and a part of her took pleasure in the idea of being courted by Benjamin. How could her heart be so divided?

Benjamin escorted her to the door, and Sallie paused before entering. "Thank you for this evening. I did have a grand time." She extended her hand to his.

He grasped her hand lightly and brushed his lips across it. "Thank you for your company tonight." He lifted his gaze and grinned. "You haven't seen the last of me, Miss Sallie Dyer."

Before she could think of a reply, he hurried back to the carriage, clicked the reins, and drove into the night.

Sallie leaned against the closed doorway, the brass handle cold against her arm. "Oh, Papa, what have you done? Why didn't you talk with me first?" Tears burned in her eyes as she opened the door and lifted her crinoline to race up the stairs and into her room.

CHAPTER 17

THE NEXT MORNING Manfred joined Bart in the stables as he hitched a horse to his wagon. "We have two churches here in town. Both were damaged by fire but have been repaired and are back in use."

"I'm not surprised. Mama wrote that our own church was damaged during the battle on the river by Port Hudson. I sure hope they repair it soon like they're doing here."

Bart led the wagon from the stable and up to the house, with Manfred and Edwin following with their horses. Amy met them in the yard. From his studies of medicine, her date for birthing was very close. She should probably stay home and not take the bumpy wagon ride to church, but then he wasn't a doctor as yet, so he remained silent. One thing about her, with her rosy cheeks and bright eyes, she certainly looked to be in good health.

Five minutes later Bart drove the wagon into the church-yard. The white clapboard church with its steeple looked nothing like Grace Church in St. Francisville, but it held a charm and beauty of its own that beckoned people to come and worship.

Many members stopped to say hello as Manfred made his way into the church with Bart and Amy. Several spoke to Amy and inquired about her health. Inside, the simple beauty of the sanctuary carried an aura of peace and calm that filled Manfred's heart with praise for the God who walked with them every day of their journey.

A small choir led the congregation in hymns, and

Manfred joined in the singing with joy that filled up his soul and spilled over, leaving behind peace and contentment. The elderly minister stood at the podium and welcomed the young men who were visiting and passing through town.

Manfred gazed about the room and spotted a number of other young men in clothing that spoke of their involvement in the war. He stopped when he came to one young man whose empty left sleeve was folded and pinned up just above the elbow. Something about the man looked familiar, but Manfred couldn't quite put his finger on where he might have seen the soldier before.

He'd seen so many men in the months he'd served, and he couldn't remember them all. His attention turned back to the preacher and the message for the morning. The minister spoke of the hope they had in Jesus Christ, and how He'd protected them and provided for them in the past few years.

Manfred prayed for all those who'd lost loved ones in the four years of conflict on both sides. It didn't matter whether the uniform had been dark blue or gray, men had defended their rights and stood for their country. He prayed the Confederate States would be reunited with her sister states so that all could be one nation once again.

The minister then mentioned the death of Lincoln and urged his congregants to pray for the new leader, Andrew Johnson. Manfred knew little about the man, but many from the South looked upon him as a traitor to his native land. Still, he was president of the United States, and that commanded respect, even as Manfred's uncertainty of his own beliefs about the man surfaced.

The one thing needed for certain was a man who would lead to unite the states and not drive them apart even more than they already were. Only the grace of God and His great mercies could heal the hearts of men and bind them together again, and Manfred prayed that would be so.

At the end of the service Manfred searched for the young man without an arm, but he was not to be found. Manfred shrugged off the idea that he had known the young soldier somewhere and accepted Amy's invitation to dinner.

"Only if it's not trouble for you, ma'am."

"Oh, it isn't. I prepared most of it in advance, and Bart did the rest of the work this morning. It'll be ready in just a few minutes."

Manfred and Edwin followed the couple back to their home. After a meal of roasted chicken and potatoes, the two returned to the barn to rest for the afternoon.

"How many days do you think we can stay here and help?" Edwin bunched up a pile of hay and covered it with a blanket.

"I'm not sure. Maybe two, but we need to get back on the road. No telling how many more stops we might have to make like this one." Despite his desire to get home, the vow he'd made to help people along the way was just as important. He hated to accept help from any man or woman he couldn't repay in some way.

Tomorrow would be a busy day and one that most likely would need all their strength. Best to rest easy this afternoon and be ready to begin early in the morning.

⤳

St. Francisville, Louisiana

Sunday afternoons in the Woodruff household meant a quiet time of rest and reflection on the past week. Sallie sat at the window and noted the gray skies of the day that reflected her own dismal attitude. As much as she wanted to please her

father, she didn't desire to lead Benjamin Elliot into believing he may have a chance at winning her affections.

How could God do such things to her? He had left her alone to defend herself, and that ended in the death of another person. Now He had abandoned her and left her to cope with her father and Benjamin. He had answered none of her prayers for peace of mind and had given her no hope for Manfred's return. Each day she drifted farther away from her trust and faith in her heavenly Father.

Even her church attendance had become one of social opportunity and not one of worship. She enjoyed seeing her cousin and Miriam Tenney, since they didn't see much of each other during the week. This morning she had tuned out the sermon and service to concentrate on her problem of what she was going to do about her attraction to Benjamin. It couldn't take the place of her love for Manfred.

Mama and Grandma would be mortified at her behavior and attitude toward God, and Papa would be sorely disappointed if she didn't consent to see Benjamin. She had little use for God in her life right now, and Benjamin only complicated the affairs of her heart. Keeping up a front before her parents would be difficult, but she'd manage it.

A pebble hit the windowsill. She leaned over and found Will and Tom in the yard beckoning to her. What on earth did they want? Will nodded his head toward the side door and waved his hand. Usually her brothers had little to say except to tease, so this must be important.

She gathered up her skirts and tiptoed from the room so as not to disturb Hannah napping on the bed. Silence greeted her when she stepped into the hallway. The downstairs foyer and rooms sat empty and quiet. The only noise came from the pantry area where Flora and Lettie must be preparing for the usual light Sunday supper.

The side door to where her brothers waited was at the end of the dining room and opened onto the side portion of the house's porch that wrapped around that side. With as little sound as possible, she eased open the door and out onto the porch.

Will greeted her with a finger to his lips. "Let's go out to the barn. Don't want our talking to disturb anyone."

He led her out to the barn where Tom now sat on a bale of hay. Sallie stood with her hands on her hips. "What in the world is so important that you had to bring me out here?"

"We want to talk to you about what happened in Woodville a few weeks ago." Will hitched his foot to prop it on the bale where Tom sat.

"What are you talking about?" They couldn't mean her shooting at the soldiers. They weren't even in the house when it happened, and her family had never discussed it.

"Come on, Sal, you know what I mean. I was there."

Sallie's heart lodged in her throat. Why did he have to spoil a beautiful Sunday afternoon with a reminder of that awful day? She clenched her fists and narrowed her eyes at Will. "I don't want to talk about it, and don't call me Sal. Sounds like you're talking to a mule."

"Sometimes I think I am when you're so stubborn." He reached for her hand. "Look, I've seen the sadness in your eyes when you think no one is paying attention. I know it has to do with what happened. I thought maybe you might want to know what we did afterward."

"Papa sent us here and then stayed behind to fight with you and the others. That's all I need to know." Then her curiosity took hold. "What did you do?"

"Papa and I went up to the house after you and Mama left in the carriage. That's when we found the dead man. You dropped the gun, and it was lying on the floor not far from the body. Papa figured out what must have happened. Since Mama won't handle a gun, we knew it had to be you who shot him. We carried the body out to the barn, but then so much started happening that we just left it there."

Bile rose in Sallie's throat. Will had helped carry a dead body out to their barn. How awful for him, and for that poor boy. "He...he...wasn't much older than I am." Tears misted her eyes. "What happened to him then?"

Will squeezed her hand. "I know." He breathed in deeply before glancing at Tom then back to her. "Papa found him still in the barn when he went back up to check the damage to the house. The Yanks must not have known he was out there, or they would have taken him with them. Papa buried him out back."

The tears flooded her eyes and streamed down her cheeks. "Oh, no. That's so sad. Somewhere, somebody's wondering where he is. His poor mama."

A sob escaped her throat. What if that had been Manfred shot and buried in an unknown plot? God punished her yet again with this news.

Tom stood and wrapped his arms about her waist. "I'm sorry it happened too, Sallie, but he could just as well have shot you and then the rest of us as not."

"But he wasn't aiming to shoot. He had a loaf of bread, not a gun. I acted foolishly in haste when I should have asked him why he was there."

"I was out in the barn hitching up the horses when I heard the first shot," Tom said. "I came running just in time to see that other guy you shot in the arm. He had a gun. I saw it when he ran from the house, and he might have killed you if you hadn't surprised him and shot first."

Sallie sniffed and swallowed hard to control her breathing.

That could have happened, but she hadn't considered it until this minute. In war everything turned upside down.

Tom went on to tell what else had happened in those frenzied moments. "Papa and Will were out by the road when they saw that other soldier with the wounded arm and guessed where he'd been. That's why Papa sent you away so quickly. He saw that the fighting was getting too close and that hungry soldiers were likely to start looting."

Will nodded. "You did the right thing, Sallie. Even Papa said so. He doesn't talk to you about it because he doesn't want to upset you, but we thought you should know."

"Thank you for telling me." But the new information certainly didn't help her. Now even more worry filled her heart. Somewhere a mother, sister, and possibly a girlfriend waited for a young man who would never return. She'd never forgive herself for causing such grief to a family.

She pulled away. "I must go back inside now."

Will touched her arm with his fingers. "I'm sorry, Sallie. I didn't know it would upset you this much. I thought you'd want to know that he wasn't left lying in our kitchen with nobody to look after him. Maybe Papa should have left him for the others to find. I don't know."

Sallie nodded mutely. Leaving her brothers behind, she ran back to the house. Tears once again streamed down her cheeks, and drops of rain fell as though the skies mourned a loss with her. The entire tragedy of that afternoon returned to haunt her heart and soul. If only she hadn't been so scared. This awful war hadn't ended soon enough to keep her from committing the greatest of sins against another person. God would never forgive her for murdering that young, hungry soldier, but right now she didn't care. She couldn't even forgive herself.

CHAPTER 18

Marion, Virginia, Monday, May 1, 1865

THE NEXT MORNING Bart met Manfred and Edwin in the livery stable. "First we'll find the man in charge of the repairs, and he can tell you what you need to do." As they walked into town, the evidence of repair and moving to the future struck Manfred's soul. Life after war had begun, but for some the recovery would never erase the past.

When they reached the center of town, Bart directed them toward the building over which hung a mercantile sign. Inside the store a man handed out orders to men and sent them out to the wagon.

Bart approached the man. "Mr. Nelson, here are two more young men who want to help out at the Hilton farm."

Manfred extended his hand to the man. "My name is Manfred Whiteman, and this is my brother Edwin. Just tell us what to do."

"Come with me. We're about ready to leave." Nelson picked up a sack of supplies and headed out the door.

Manfred and Edwin followed Nelson to his wagon and helped him secure the load. Four other men sat in the wagon bed with the supplies. Manfred mounted his horse. "Was there much damage to the farmhouse?"

Henry climbed aboard the wagon. "Not as much as some. Won't take long to repair, but we wanted to get the house livable. Your help out there will greatly appreciated. Several of the ladies from town are preparing food for the noonday meal. We'll come back here for supper." He clicked the reins and rolled away. "Come on and follow me."

Shortly the trio rode into the yard of the Hilton home. Manfred and Edwin dismounted and helped Henry unload the wagon. Several others came out to lend their assistance.

Manfred handed Edwin a crate and picked up a box to follow Nelson inside. There several other men worked at repairing holes in the walls and broken bricks in the fireplace. This was work he knew how to do. He rolled up his sleeves. "Where do you want us to begin?"

Henry called out to several others by the fireplace. "Show these two what to do."

Manfred listened and watched as the men demonstrated how to remove the damaged bricks and replace them with good ones. In a few minutes Manfred and Edwin began the job on their own.

After a half hour or so Manfred glanced up to see a young man in gray pants with his left shirtsleeve folded and pinned below the elbow. Manfred recognized the pants as Army issue and the young man as the one he'd seen in church.

"Manfred Whiteman here. We're on our way home. Didn't I see you in church yesterday?"

"Yes, I was there. Name's Matt Grayson, and I'm headed for Virginia."

Manfred jumped up from the floor and grasped the man's right hand. "Matt Grayson? Your family…but…are you Eli Grayson's son?"

Matt nodded. "Yes, but how would you know that?"

"We spent time with them a fortnight ago. They think you're dead." Manfred wrapped his arm around Matt's shoulder. "Rachel is going to be so happy."

Puzzled, Matt stepped back and asked, "What do you know about my Rachel?"

"Only that she's been mourning for you," Edwin said.

175

"Mark came back with his injuries, and Luke was in prison with us. What happened to you?"

Matt glanced at his arm then shook his head. "Guess you might say I was dead. My name got on the casualty list. Somehow I ended up in a hospital without my arm. I didn't know who I was or where I was for several months. They released me a few weeks ago, and now I'm trying to get home. I sent a letter to Rachel, but I have no idea if she'll get it. I don't want her to be in shock when I arrive."

Manfred grinned. "That'll be cause for celebration. Luke came home just before we left. Your pa got the spring planting started and helped us when we set out for our home." His heart rejoiced at the discovery of the young man believed to be a casualty of the war now standing before him, alive. One family's mourning would be turned to joy with Matt's arrival home.

"I'm overwhelmed to think you were with my family such a short time ago." Matt picked up a brick. "Here, let me help with this. We can talk more as we work. I want to hear all about Rachel and my son."

The three returned to the task of replacing broken bricks, and Manfred relayed what he knew of Rachel and the baby. God had certainly been working overtime to bring about this chance meeting. If his trust wasn't completely in the Lord before, it would definitely be there now.

Matt stirred the mortar. "I haven't seen my son since a week or so after his birth. Tell me more."

Edwin sat back on his haunches. "He's good-looking boy and very friendly. Don't think we ever heard him really cry."

"That's right," Manfred added. "Rachel's done a fine job with him." Manfred still marveled at this miracle. How thrilled Rachel would be to see Matt again. How many others would make it home to families who supposed their loved ones to be gone? He remembered the letter to Sallie. He must get it posted that day. What if Sallie thought him to be dead since she hadn't heard from him in so long a time? If that be the case, Mr. Dyer may have found someone else for Sallie.

A stout, gray-haired woman appeared in the door and called out, "A pot of soup waits for you in the yard. Come and get it."

Men swarmed down from the second floor and joined Manfred, Edwin, and Matt in heading outdoors where a table with a kettle of bubbly soup and a large platter of biscuits sat waiting. The men ahead of Manfred in line addressed the woman as Mrs. Hilton. She must be the Widow Hilton who owned this home.

One worker held up his hands for quiet then gave thanks for the food prepared by the widow. Manfred's heart filled with thanksgiving at the turn of events that morning. He must come up with a way to help Matt return home more quickly. While his journey may take a month or more, Matt could be home in days.

Manfred grabbed a bowl and waited while Mrs. Hilton filled others from the steaming pot. When he held his bowl out, the hostess said, "Sorry it's not more, but it's hearty and should fill you up."

Manfred nodded. "Thank you, Mrs. Hilton. Soup and biscuits are one of my favorites."

The rotund woman laughed heartily and poured a full ladle for him. "Having you young men around helps me believe we're going to recover from all that happened."

If women like Amy and Mrs. Hilton represented the spirit of the women of the South, the future looked brighter. The widow's sense of humor and friendliness spilled over onto all the young men as they came through the line. How good to see so many smiles and happy faces after months of sadness and deprivation. Stops like this energized Manfred's heart and gave him even greater incentive to spend his life helping others.

Finding Matt here among the other volunteers had been an extra serendipity as God showed His love and protection yet once again. No wonder Matt had seemed so familiar yesterday. He looked so much like his brothers. What a wonderful surprise for Rachel and the Grayson family. Manfred almost wished he could be there when the reunion took place.

The rest of the day went as the morning had, and everything but painting and moving things back into the house had been accomplished. Manfred's muscles ached, but the soreness didn't bother him because of how he'd obtained the aches.

Manfred fell into step with Matt en route to where the wagon and horses were waiting. "Where are you staying?"

"At the boarding house. In return for work I get a few days bed and board and a little pay. My three days are up, so I plan to leave tomorrow."

Edwin from behind them snorted. "We're at the livery stable. We're sleeping on hay."

Manfred shook his head. "It's better than nothing, and certainly better than what we had in prison. We'll stay another day if they need us, then be on our way to Louisiana. We wish you Godspeed on the rest of your journey."

They reached the wagon, and Matt climbed aboard. Manfred and Edwin mounted their horses, the very ones Matt's father had given them weeks before. An idea formulated, but he'd have to discuss it with Edwin first. The plan would affect his brother as much as it did Manfred.

They rode on ahead of the wagon into town. "I'm thinking that Matt has a long journey just as we do, but with the loss of his arm, he might have a harder time. What do you say to the idea that we give Matt one of the horses his pa gave us?"

Awe and disbelief swept across Edwin's face before a broad grin split his face. "That's exactly what I was thinking and wondering how to ask you about it."

"We can take turns riding and possibly ride double some of the time. It might slow us down some, but it'll help Matt get home quicker, and that's what counts. Just think about it. His pa gave us two horses to make our journey easier, so now we have one to give back to his son."

"God does work in mysterious and wondrous ways. We still have Lady, and that's still one horse more than we started out with."

Instead of going straight to Bart's livery, Manfred followed the wagon to the boarding house. When Matt jumped down from the wagon, he waved to Manfred. "Thought you were going to the livery."

Manfred dismounted and held out the reins of the horse. "I am, but first I want you to have this horse for the rest of your journey. Your pa gave us two horses and saddles when we left the farm as payment for our work. You'll make quicker time with a horse."

Matt peered at the brand on the horse. "Why, this is old Mr. Whitney's mare, and this is my old saddle." He ran his hand across the smooth leather.

"Didn't know it was your saddle, but I'm glad it is. You'll be even more comfortable. And you're right about the horse. According to your pa, Whitney abandoned his farm and went to live with his daughter, but he gave what was left of his stock to your pa."

Matt took the reins from Manfred and shook his hand. "I'm much obliged. Sure you can get by with just one mount?"

"We'll be fine. You get on back to Rachel and your little

boy." Manfred slapped him on the back and gripped the young man's shoulder. "We're mighty grateful for your folks and how they took us in. Tell them we're doing well, and we'll be leaving tomorrow or the next day. Let me get my things from the saddle, and I'll be on my way."

After removing his personal items, Manfred hefted his pack over his shoulder and reached for Matt's right hand. "You take care now. Maybe we'll meet again one day."

He sauntered off and headed back to the stable. He and Edwin would have to figure out how to share Lady, but that shouldn't be too difficult. It just meant they couldn't travel as fast. Getting Matt home to Rachel and their son meant more to Manfred then having a little inconvenience. His suffering had no comparison to that of Matt and so many more like him.

After supper with Bart and Amy, Manfred and Edwin again bedded down in the stable.

In the dim light of the lamp he wrote in his journal of meeting Matt and working on the Hilton place. He'd given his letter to Sallie to Amy Jensen at dinner, and she'd promised to post it the next day along with Edwin's letters to his parents and to Peggy. As soon as it arrived, Sallie would know he was on his way home. One more day of hard work, and they'd be on their way again with a few provisions Amy promised.

After a night of sound sleep, the next day passed much the same as the one before, but without meeting anyone new. This time he and Edwin helped with clearing out one of the buildings in town and getting it ready for a business to move back in.

That evening, when they arrived back at the livery, they decided to eat at the boardinghouse to give Amy a rest. Manfred enjoyed the camaraderie of the men at the table who told and retold stories of battles and skirmishes of the past four years.

At the stables after dinner, Manfred's muscles ached from lifting and toting lumber all day. He stretched his arms and legs to ease the tension. A wide yawn brought a chuckle from Edwin.

"I see you're as tired as I am. Let's get some sleep for our trek tomorrow."

Manfred nodded and settled on his mat. He skipped writing in his journal and closed his eyes. Sometime later during the night a commotion out in the streets awakened him, but weariness kept him from investigating. It was none of his business anyway.

The next morning Manfred arose and took care of packing his belongings for the next leg of his journey. Strange, but Bart had not yet come into the smithy shop. He had come in yesterday before Manfred and Edwin awakened.

Manfred headed to the house to say good-bye, and Bart greeted him at the door with a grin as wide as the outdoors. "Come in. Come in. Want you to meet someone." Edwin stepped into the room behind Manfred.

A slender woman with salt and pepper hair stood at the fireplace stirring a pot. Bart placed an arm around her shoulders. "This is Ma Carson, Amy's mother. She's here to help us with the newest member of our family."

Bart rapped on the door to the bedroom and opened it. "Amy, Manfred and Edwin are here to say good-bye. They're off for Louisiana this morning." He turned and motioned for the boys to follow him.

Manfred and Edwin tiptoed into the room. Amy lay in the bed with her ash brown hair cascading down her shoulders. She held a tiny, blanket-wrapped bundle in her arms.

Bart slid his hands beneath the baby and lifted it. He

turned to Manfred and Edwin. "Meet Mercy Elizabeth Jensen, born at two this morning."

The baby's rosebud mouth twitched then opened in a wide yawn. Manfred reached out to touch her velvet soft cheek. "She's beautiful." Seeing new life filled him with fresh hope.

Bart nodded and handed Mercy back to her mother. He extended his hand to Manfred. "Thank you both for stopping here in Marion. You helped us, and if we helped you, then it's even better."

The three returned to the larger room. Mrs. Carson handed Manfred a basket covered with a checked cloth. "Take this with you. It's cornbread, dried apples, carrots, dried ham, and cookies. Not much, but enough to get by a day or so."

"Thank you, Mrs. Carson. We're much obliged. Come on, Edwin, it's time to head out." They shook hands again with Bart and left the house.

"God's blessings on you. And thank you for your help," Bart called.

Manfred and Edwin waved and headed for the next leg of their journey to home and family. Manfred turned to his brother. "You see, Edwin, every time we stop to help someone else, we come away blessed ourselves. We just can't give more than God gives us. He's way too generous."

Manfred lifted his eyes toward heaven. Springtime had come to the mountains with fresh air, flowers, and green leaves everywhere. Each step took them closer to their destination. What other great adventure did God have in store for them on down the road?

CHAPTER 19

St. Francisville, Louisiana, Wednesday, May 3, 1865

S ALLIE READ ANOTHER page of *Emma* before dropping it in her lap. She glanced over at Hannah, who had gone to bed early, citing a headache. Restless, Sallie tiptoed to the window and knelt with her arms leaning against the sill. She spent so much time these days sitting here and thinking about Manfred and the future.

When she returned from her meeting Sunday afternoon with Will and Tom, Papa had stopped her in the front hallway. He tried to explain his reasons behind giving Benjamin Elliot permission to call on her. When she told him she wanted to wait for Manfred, his answer put an end to the discussion.

With his hands on her shoulders, Papa had said, "Sallie, I gave my word to Benjamin Elliot, and a Dyer never goes back on his word. Until Manfred Whiteman returns to St. Francisville and asks for your hand properly, Benjamin has my permission to come calling on you. I'm sorry, my dear, but that's the way it has to be." He had then kissed the top of her head and retreated to the parlor.

Disobedience wasn't an option, and by no means could Sallie argue with his reasoning. It would not be honoring him as the head of the family and her father. If only Benjamin were unkind or rude, rejection would be easier, but his courtesy and good looks attracted her. What if the unthinkable happened and Benjamin asked for her hand in marriage before Manfred returned? No, she simply couldn't let that happen.

Fighting her attraction to Benjamin could be difficult. All

her patience as well as resistance to temptation would be tested in the days ahead.

She had started to ask Papa about what Will and Tom had told her, but then decided that it wasn't a good time after his speech about Benjamin. She stared up at the clouds, now light and silvered with moon glow. The clouds may have changed, but her spirits hung as low and dismal as they had on Sunday.

Her head jerked up when a carriage turned toward the house. The carriage looked like theirs, but Papa was supposed to be in Woodville for the week. Why would he be home so soon?

Sallie scurried across the room and down the stairs. She pulled open the door and found her father supporting a young woman and assisting her up the porch steps. Sallie shouted over her shoulder for Mama and Grandma to come quick. She reached out to the girl then gasped.

"Jenny? Oh, Papa, what happened to her?" Sallie put her arm around her one-time neighbor and friend, Jenny Harper, who barely had the strength to acknowledge her.

"Help me get her into the parlor, Sallie."

After they had her situated on the sofa, Mama hurried in giving orders to those behind her. "Lettie, bring me cool water and a cloth. Flora, we may need that ointment for these wounds. See what we have." She knelt beside Jenny and arranged a pillow under her head. Sallie stood to the side staring at her best friend from Woodville. Jenny's eyes were closed, and she seemed unconscious to the world around her.

"Thomas, what is Jenny doing here? Where is her family?" Mama's questions echoed those of Sallie's thoughts.

Papa removed his hat and slumped down in a chair. "On the day we were attacked, the Harper plantation was almost completely destroyed. The family had to flee."

Lettie set a bowl of water on the floor beside Mama and handed her a cloth. Mama dipped it into the water and washed dirt from Jenny's pale face. She peered up at Papa. "Where are Mr. and Mrs. Harper?"

Papa shook his head. "It's a long, sad story. Mr. Harper died while they were trying to defend their home, and Jenny and her mother took his body with them and traveled to Mrs. Harper's sister's home, Greenwood Manor. But Union officers had commandeered it for use as a command headquarters."

Mama shook her head and dipped the cloth again in the water. "So where did they go?"

"Union soldiers took them prisoner and put them to work taking care of the officers living in the home. That's all I know right now. Maybe Jenny can tell us more later. I left Millie Harper with the Chambers family in Woodville. I thought Jenny would be better off here with us."

Sallie sat on the floor and held Jenny's hand. "Jenny, oh, Jenny. I'm so sorry." Her own experience paled in comparison to what Jenny and her mother had endured.

Mama patted Sallie's shoulder then went to stand by Papa. They whispered briefly, and Mama covered her mouth with her hand and shook her head. Then Mama laid her head against Papa's chest and wept. Things must be much worse than Papa had first said, but how could they have been any worse than they were?

Without a word Grandma took over the duty of nurse and finished washing Jenny's face. She smoothed back the girl's hair then stepped around Sallie to remove Jenny's slippers. Instead of shoes, she found rags tied around the girl's feet. Grandma unwrapped the dirty cloth, her hands careful and gentle as though handling a newborn infant.

When the final rag fell to the floor, Sallie gagged. Never

had she seen feet so bloody and covered with blisters. Grandma sucked in her breath.

She motioned to Papa. "Run out and fetch Dr. Andrews and bring him quickly. We must tend to Jenny." Then she told Sallie, "Go up to your room and stay with Hannah. I don't want her to wake up and see this."

She didn't like leaving her friend, but the wisdom of Grandma's order compelled Sallie to go shield her sister from this tragedy. Lettie met her in the hallway, arms laden with more water and bandages for Grandma to treat Jenny. "Papa has gone for the doctor," Sallie told her.

Gathering up her skirts, Sallie raced up the stairs and into the room she shared with her sister. Hannah still slept soundly in the middle of the bed. Sallie sank down onto the feather mattress beside her sister, biting her knuckles to keep from sobbing and awakening Hannah from sleep. Tears streamed down Sallie's face, and all the nightmares of the past weeks flashed through her mind like a kaleidoscope of color and stabbing pain.

Technically the war was over, but would it ever be over for Jenny or for her? She had no idea what had happened to Jenny, but from the looks of her, it had been bad. Her feet testified to the severity of her journey to come home.

Once again God had failed to protect one of His children. How could God have been so cruel as to allow Jenny and her mother to suffer so?

Sallie bit her lip. She and Jenny had shared so many happy times in Woodville. Mrs. Harper loved giving parties, and their home had been the site of many balls and cotillions through the years. As young girls Sallie and Jenny often sat at the top of the stairs and watched the festivities below. The war intervened before they had a chance to attend as eligible young women. Sallie shuddered to think of the Harper home in ruins.

Hannah began to stir and suddenly sat up in bed. "Sallie, what are you doing here? Why don't you have your night-gown on?"

"Oh, I thought I'd go to bed in my dress." She grabbed her sister and hugged her tightly.

Hannah pushed against Sallie. "What's the matter with you? You're squeezing me to death."

"I'm sorry. I love you so, dear sister Hannah." Sallie released her hold. She'd do anything to protect her sister from the bloody realities of what waited downstairs.

The door squeaked, and Mama stepped into the room. "You can go in to see Jenny now, and your father wishes to speak with you. I'll sit with Hannah and explain." Mama stepped over to the bed.

"Jenny's here? I want to see her." Hannah jumped from the bed, but Mama grabbed her gown and pulled her back.

"Later. I want you to stay and talk to me." She gestured for Sallie to go. "Jenny's in my room for now."

Jenny lay still and quiet in Mama and Papa's bed. Across the room Dr. Andrews talked with Papa.

When Papa saw her, he said, "Come in, my dear. Jenny asked for you."

Sallie sat beside the bed and stroked Jenny's hand. The girl's eyelids fluttered, and a hint of a smile curved the corner of her mouth when she saw Sallie.

"Jenny, I'm here." She felt a slight answering pressure on her hand. "If there's anything you need or want, tell me." Sallie bent close to her friend.

Jenny's blue-violet eyes glistened with tears. "Oh, Sallie."

Sallie smoothed stray locks of hair back from Jenny's

forehead. "I'm so sorry for your loss." She tried to stem the flood of tears in her own eyes.

Jenny's dark lashes curled against her cheeks. She murmured, "I've lived a thousand years in the past few weeks. Father is dead, and so is Andrew. What are we to do?"

"Andrew is dead?" Sallie squeezed her eyes shut. Jenny's brother, always the life of the party with his pranks and winsome smile. He and Manfred were the same age.

"Yes, we received word just before the attack, and I think that's what killed Papa, not the fighting. I…I…oh, Sallie, it was awful."

Sallie fought back her own grief to comfort her friend. "Shh, don't talk now. I'm going to stay right here beside you. I promise not to leave." She lifted an imploring gaze to Papa, who nodded and pressed his lips into a grim line.

Dr. Andrews snapped his bag shut and shook Papa's hand. "I'll leave you now. She'll recover more quickly here with you and Sallie. Get some of Flora's good soup down her, and make sure you change her dressings frequently."

"We thank you for coming. I'll see you out." Papa came over and placed a hand on Sallie's shoulder. "Jenny has been through a terrible ordeal. If she wants to talk about it, let her, but don't force her to tell you what happened. I'll be back up shortly. I have something I must tell you."

"Yes, Papa, I understand."

The room grew silent after their departure, with Jenny dropping off into a deep sleep. Sallie gazed at her friend, filled with sorrow at the pain in her friend's life.

A few minutes later Papa returned and beckoned for Sallie to join him in the hallway. Jenny slept peacefully now, so Sallie joined her father.

He wrapped his arm around her shoulder. "Jenny didn't come back with just her mother. A young Yankee came with them to protect them, but he also had a mission here." His voice choked for a moment.

Sallie's eyes grew wide. Why would a Yankee soldier come to Mississippi? He should be going north to home.

"I know what you had to do the day you fled Woodville. I found the body of the young man and buried it behind the barn. Now it seems the Yankee who came with the Harpers was looking for his brother, because the unit he'd been with said the last time they'd seen him was around Woodville."

Sallie jerked back. "He's looking for his brother?" Sorrow rolled over her soul in waves. "How sad for him." Then the full implication of her father's words sank in. "Oh, Papa, did I kill his brother?"

At Papa's nod Sallie burst into sobs and buried her face in her father's chest. "I'm so sorry. I'm so sorry."

He patted her head and spoke with tears choking his own voice. "I know you are. I showed him where I buried the body, and he's going to make arrangements for it to be taken to his home in Pennsylvania. He'd come a long way to find him."

Sallie's heart broke into shattering pieces, but some comfort softened the blow. Now the boy would go home, and his family could give him a proper burial. She couldn't undo what she had done that afternoon, but at least now she'd have some peace in knowing his family would no longer have to worry and wonder about their son.

When her sobs ceased, Papa sent her back to sit with Jenny. The war was over, and nothing would ever be the same. Today a small piece of the burden Sallie carried had been lifted, but the weight of the remainder still buried itself deep into her heart.

After a night of rest under Amanda's attentive care, Jenny's color returned. Amanda stood aside as Sallie offered Jenny some broth, and the young woman took a few sips at a time. Once again Jenny said nothing, and her eyes closed in sleep after she finished. Sallie had said she planned to stay by her friend's side in case Jenny awoke and wanted to talk.

Still, Sallie must know the truth. Amanda decided the time had come. She motioned for Sallie to follow her into the hallway because she didn't want Jenny to wake up and hear their talk.

"What's the matter, Mama?"

"I haven't had time to talk to you about Jenny. Let's go into your room. Hannah is downstairs with her lessons, so we can talk."

Sallie followed her mother into the room where they seated themselves by the window. Amanda leaned over and held Sallie's hands in hers.

"Last night Jenny awakened for a while and told me the story of what they endured since leaving Woodville. We had terrible things happen to us, my dear, but nothing like what happened to Jenny and her mother." Tears welled in her eyes, but she fought them back. Sallie had to understand the gravity of the situation.

"Young Andrew died in battle away from home, but Jenny and her mother watched Mr. Harper die in their arms." When Sallie gasped, Mama squeezed her hands. "It happened when they escaped from their home after the Yankees set it afire. I think Mr. Harper's heart couldn't take seeing his home destroyed. He had a heart attack and died on their flight away."

Sallie's gaze locked with Mama's. "What else happened?"

Amanda took a deep breath and looked down at her lap. "They continued on to Millie's sister's home up at Natchez with Mr. Harper's body in the wagon. When they arrived at the house, they found it overrun with Yankees too. Before they could get away, some soldiers caught them and forced them to work there for a time." She paused, shook her head, and stood. With her hand to her mouth, she paced the floor.

Sallie grasped Mama's arm. "Tell me, Mama. Tell me what happened. What did the soldiers do to Jenny? Did they…" Her voice trailed off, unable to utter the words.

"No, Jenny said that a young lieutenant stopped two soldiers who accosted her, and rescued her. He was quite kind to her and her mother."

Sallie wrapped her arms around her and sobbed. "That's terrible. I'm so worried about Jenny."

Amanda patted Sallie's back. "We all are, my dear. What we can do is to love her and take care of her."

Sorrow for her friend's ordeal wrapped around Sallie's heart. "Why didn't they stay in Natchez when they knew that their home in Woodville was gone?"

Amanda frowned. "After what the soldiers tried to do to Jenny, Millie no longer felt safe there. They fled the house with only the clothes they wore, not much food, and no one to help them."

Tears glistened in Sallie's eyes. "Then how did they get home?"

"They walked. Luckily they met up with a young Yankee soldier who was also headed for Woodville, and he traveled with them to protect them as best he could. Jenny had no shoes and attempted to cover her feet with rags, but you saw the results. Mrs. Harper asked Papa to bring Jenny here because she felt you could help her."

"Papa told me about the soldier. I'm glad he helped Jenny

and her mother, and I'm glad he found his brother. I only wish…" Her voice trailed off and Mama grasped her hands.

"It's all right, dear. It's over, and our concern now is Jenny."

Sallie wiped the tears from her cheeks with her fingers. "I'm going back to her now. Tell Lettie to bring my meal up with Jenny's. I'll eat there. I don't want to leave her."

Amanda kissed Sallie's cheek. "Yes, dear, I understand. I want you to also think about what could have happened to us if you had not been brave and protected us. I have not spoken to you about it till now because I thought we should put it behind us. But I see now I was wrong. You need to know that what you did was brave and right in that situation."

"Oh, Mama. I wasn't brave. I was scared out of my wits, and what I did was horrible."

"I know. It was a terrible tragedy, but you did what you had to do." She pushed a stray strand of hair off Sallie's forehead. "You go to Jenny now. She's going to need you."

Sallie hastened from the room and back to the bedside of her friend. Kneeling on the floor, she pressed her face against Jenny's hand and stroked the sleeping girl's arm. "Oh, Jenny, I don't know what to say. You and I have experienced and done things we would never have done in ordinary times."

All through the morning and into the afternoon Sallie sat by Jenny's side. She talked to her friend and even read a few pages from *Emma*. Still, Sallie could see no improvement except that Jenny's face wasn't as ashen as it had been earlier.

Lettie and Mama came in to bring food and to check Jenny's wounds, leaving behind the odor of antiseptics and alcohol. Sallie awakened Jenny long enough for a few more sips of chicken broth and a little water. Most of the time Sallie simply watched her friend sleep.

The room grew dark. Sallie glanced out the window and noted the sun had gone down and darkness covered the earth. Mama tiptoed into the room. "I've come to stay the night. You must get some rest yourself, or I'll have two patients to tend."

"But, Mama, I want to stay here with her. She might wake up, and I promised to be here." How could she leave Jenny's side and go sleep in her own bed? She had to stay right where she was.

"I know, my dear, but you need to stay strong and healthy yourself in order to help Jenny. You go on to your room and get some sleep." Mama helped her from the floor and shooed her out the door. "I'll come get you if she awakens and asks for you."

Sallie obeyed, but sleep wouldn't come. Her mind was wound tighter than a clock and refused to slow down. She again sat by the window and gazed at the star-studded sky. Half of the waxing moon hung among the glittering jewels in the velvet darkness. What a spring this had been. So much had happened in the past few weeks that Sallie couldn't control.

Images of soldiers, guns, fires, and death flashed through Sallie's mind. She squeezed her eyes shut and pressed her palms against her temples. She had to forget. When would peace return to her soul?

The next morning Sallie dressed and hurried to Jenny's room. Grandma stood by the bed, brushing Jenny's hair. Smooth, dark waves spread out over the pillow, replacing the tangles and snarls of yesterday.

When Sallie covered Jenny's hand with hers, the girl opened her eyes. "Sallie, you are here. I haven't been dreaming."

"No, I wouldn't leave you." She sank down to her knees by the bedside.

Grandma patted Jenny's shoulder. "The only time she left your side was to sleep. I'll leave you in good hands. Lettie will be up with your breakfast shortly." She laid the brush on the dressing table and left.

Sallie pulled a footstool over and perched on it. "You look so much better today. We've been so worried."

Jenny reached up to touch her hair then her face. "I must have been a fright. I vaguely remember your father bringing me in a buggy, and your mother and grandmother washing me."

"Yes, we all tended to you. Now you're getting well."

Jenny pulled Sallie's hand to her cheek. "I remember your mother saying something about God taking care of us. If I had not believed that with all my heart, I would not be here today. I fought hard to stay alive for Mother's sake, and I knew God would help me."

Sallie said nothing. Some care God had taken of Jenny. Her father and brother were both dead, her house ruined, and her mother ill. If that was God's care, she didn't want to even think about His punishment for her own behavior.

"Oh, Sallie, it was so awful." Jenny turned her ahead away. "Our house, Father…"

Sallie whispered, "I'm so sorry, Jenny." She covered Jenny's hand with hers.

Lettie entered with breakfast, tea and toast with jam. Sallie poured the tea and stirred in milk while Jenny eased up on the pillows. In silence they shared a meal. Too much had happened to both of them, too much to tell, much less grasp. Now Sallie understood how fragile and precious life was, and how lives could come undone in an instant.

CHAPTER 20

Alabama, Monday, May 15, 1865

A FTER LEAVING MARION, Virginia, Manfred and Edwin traveled ten days across Tennessee, with stops in Knoxville and Chattanooga, as well as other smaller towns along the way. Sunday the fourteenth of May was spent in the far northwest corner of Georgia, attending church in Trenton and resting. On Monday Manfred and Edwin entered Alabama, which meant only one state to cross and then they'd be in Mississippi and closer to home.

A breeze ruffled through the leaves of the trees in the grove where Manfred decided to stop for a break. His feet ached and his back hurt from walking all morning. Edwin had done the walking the day before, and they had even ridden double part of the way, but both of them in the saddle would be too much for Lady all the time. They'd made it down through the mountains and now faced farmlands as they headed across Alabama. He studied the crude map he'd picked up in Chattanooga. They should get to Fort Payne in less than an hour and from there head on down to Birmingham.

Manfred lifted his gaze toward the sky where thick gray clouds rolled across and blotted out the sun. "I smell rain." Manfred lifted a finger in the wind. "Coming from the northwest. This time of year means thunderstorms." As if on cue, lightning split the heavens and thunder rolled across the meadow.

Edwin jumped, as did the mare. He grabbed the bridle

of the prancing horse and brushed his hand down her neck. "Easy, easy. It's gone now, Lady."

Manfred stood and surveyed the area. "If my counting is right, I'd say that was about ten miles away. The wind's picking up, and the rain'll be here in a few minutes. Let's keep heading to the west. We don't want to be under trees with the lightning like it is. Maybe we'll find shelter." He picked up his gear and started walking toward open ground, his aching feet forgotten.

"This is tornado country, and that's the last thing I want to see right now. Get on, and we'll ride double for a ways." Edwin held the reins while Manfred swung into the saddle.

The sky grew darker and more ominous as they traveled. Manfred kept his eyes trained on the field, searching for a gully or culvert in case of strong winds and lightning. Another bolt creased the clouds. This time Manfred counted to six. "Getting closer. Looks like we're in for a soaking."

Edwin pointed ahead. "Do you see that? Looks like a farm."

Manfred peered in that direction and saw the faint outline of a roof in the distance. "Think so. Maybe we can make it there. See if anyone's at home."

By the time they drew close enough to see a house and a barn, the wind stirred up dust and debris in their path. The clouds had turned an eerie green, and rain began to pelt their heads.

"Come on, let's get to the house. I don't like the look of those clouds." Manfred slapped the reins against the horse's flank, and they raced for the house.

Both jumped down from Lady and ran up the porch. No one answered their fierce knocking and yelling. Manfred turned and looked around the yard. "They must be in a shelter. Let's see if we can find it."

In the back yard of the house they spotted a barn. The

wind began to pick up, and the rain increased. Manfred and Edwin ran for the barn, horse in tow. After they tied up Lady in an empty stall, Manfred surveyed the grounds of the farm and spotted a cellar. He gauged the distance of the dark clouds from the house and made a decision. "Let's get to that cellar." Edwin nodded.

With the wind buffeting them, they raced to the storm shelter and pounded on the door. It opened a crack, and a man in work clothes motioned for them to come inside. The rain now fell in sheets and the wind grew fiercer. All three men pulled on the wooden door until they were finally able to secure it.

Manfred offered a dripping hand. "Mighty grateful to you for letting us in."

A slender woman with graying hair handed Manfred and Edwin blankets. "Here, these'll warm you up some."

The burly farmer dried himself with a towel. "I thought maybe it was just the wind pounding before I heard you yelling for help. Glad you got here in time."

He handed the towel back to his wife and held up a lantern. "I see you boys are wearing the colors of the Confederacy. Where y'all from?"

Manfred removed his rain-soaked hat and rubbed his head with a corner of the blanket. "Louisiana. We're headed home from the war. That was a close call. Wasn't sure anybody was here."

"Mattie here saw the storm a'comin' and shooed everyone from the house." The man wrapped his arm around the woman by his side.

The storm raged overhead, but a noise in the corner of the dimly lit space drew Manfred's attention. He gazed at three children huddled there.

The oldest of the three stepped forward. "My name's Billy.

You said you were in the war? I was planning on joining up come this summer, but it's too late."

Manfred lightly grasped the boy's shoulder. "Be glad, Billy. The war was no fun. Too much killing and heartbreak for both sides. Your ma and pa need you more than the army."

Mattie clasped her hands against her chest. "Thank you. The war's all he's been talking about. I was scared he'd run off and try to join up."

The farmer offered a hand to Manfred. "Here I'm forgetting my manners. Name's Zeke Jordan. This is Mattie, Billy, and over there's Betsy and Davey." He gestured toward the two children still in the corner.

Edwin sauntered over to them. "Hello. My name's Edwin, and that there is my brother Manfred. Looks like you have a good safe place here in the cellar." He sat down beside the boy.

Betsy bobbed her head. "Lightning can't get us down here. I'm six years old. How old are you?" Edwin's laughter echoed in the small space; he had made a new friend. How easily he talked with strangers, especially children. Manfred spoke to Mr. Jordan. "Sir, I tied up our horse in your barn. I didn't know what else to do with her."

Zeke nodded. "Let's pray the barn is still standing when this is over." He looked toward the ceiling. "Speaking of storms, sounds like the worst may be over. Tornados sure don't take long to do their damage. All I hear now is rain."

After a few minutes Zeke shoved his straw hat onto his head and pushed against the slatted door. The smell of fresh air and rain drifted into the cellar as he exited.

In a few moments the door squeaked. "Come on out. The rain's slower now."

The occupants of the cellar trooped up the stairway and

through the opening. Manfred gazed skyward. "At least the clouds are breaking up."

Zeke picked up a few pieces of debris. "Yeah, and we're mighty lucky. Only damage I see is to the fence and trees out in the pasture. Barn and house look intact. Think we only lost a few shingles." He embraced his wife.

Manfred headed toward the barn. "Better check on the animals."

He found their mare safe and dry, although she pranced and pawed the ground when Manfred approached. "Whoa, there, Lady. You're fine now. Storm's all gone."

Manfred's words soothed the horse, and he removed the saddle. Zeke sauntered in. "Glad to see she's all right. Ma will have supper ready soon if you'd like to stay and join us."

"Thanks, long as it's not any trouble for Mrs. Jordan." Manfred dropped the saddle in a corner then removed the blanket and folded it.

After making sure the horse was brushed and fed, Manfred and Edwin joined the Jordan family for their evening meal. After a prayer of thanks for safety during the storm, the two young men enjoyed a hearty supper of fried chicken and potatoes. The crispy coating of the chicken brought back fond memories of Bessie's cooking.

Manfred flicked a small piece of breading from his mouth with his napkin. "This is the best chicken I've had in a long time."

Mattie Jordan beamed. "Thank you. One thing we have right now is plenty of chickens." She plopped another drumstick onto Manfred's plate. "Now, tell me about yourselves and where you're going. Are you going to Birmingham?"

Manfred ladled gravy over his potatoes. "Yes, but I thought we'd stop at Fort Payne to see if we could get a few supplies there. From there we'll head on across to Mississippi and then to Louisiana."

Zeke shook his head. "No need to go to Fort Payne. Nothing much there."

Manfred furrowed his brow. "We're about out of rations. Any suggestions as to where we can get any?"

"Oh, I can take care of that for you boys." Mattie rose and grinned at her guests. "Anyone have room for dessert?"

The children and Manfred all nodded and answered "Yes" with one voice. After everyone enjoyed a slice of pecan pie, Zeke pushed his empty plate aside and turned to Manfred. "On your way to Louisiana, you say. Whereabouts? We have kin down there."

"Our pa has a shipping business at the landing in Bayou Sara."

Mattie's eyes lit up like a Christmas tree full of candles. "I can't believe it. My oldest sister married and moved to Louisiana. She and her husband have a store in St. Francisville. Their name is Brady."

Manfred gulped. "Brady? Why, we know them. Their son Nathan is a good friend. We do business with the store all the time."

Mattie's hands covered her mouth, and tears welled in her eyes. "When was the last time you saw them?"

"Almost a year now. In the summer of sixty-four. Our town depends on them for supplies, and they depend on our business to bring in their merchandise."

Mattie rested her arms on the table. "It's been over a year since we heard from them. Was the town invaded?"

Manfred shook his head. "Port Hudson went down, but the Yankees stayed on the river and went on to New Orleans. Everything in St. Francisville survived intact except for some damage to the church and a few homes." At first he'd been angry to have been sent away from the battle at Port Hudson, but then he realized the commanding officer didn't want to risk all of the regiment. He'd been fully confident that the men he kept with him would be enough to defeat the enemy.

"Oh, that's wonderful." Mattie jumped from the table and scurried to a chest in the corner. A pungent odor of cedar wafted through the room. From its depths she removed a large, patchwork pieced length of fabric.

Mattie held the quilt close to her chest and returned to the table. "I made this from the scraps of dresses we wore growing up, and I wanted my sister to have it. With the war and all, we haven't been to visit."

Manfred fingered the soft cotton fabric. "It's a beautiful quilt, Mattie. The stitches are so tiny and neat, like my grandmother's quilts. Do you plan to take it to her?"

Mattie's lip quivered. "I don't see how we can. We must have a good crop this year or . . . " Her voice trailed off.

Zeke wrapped his arm around his wife's shoulder. "You know what it's been like the past few years. Without the money from a decent harvest, we won't be able to make it."

Manfred stroked his chin. He cut his eyes toward Edwin and saw the slight nod of his head. Manfred nodded back at his brother then said, "Edwin and I would be honored to take such a gift to the Brady family."

Mattie's eyes now glowed with hope. "You would? Thank you. I'll write a letter to go with it." She grasped her husband's hand in hers. "Wouldn't it be wonderful if Rebecca could come here for a visit?"

Zeke smiled and placed his hand on his wife's cheek. "It'd be a more than that. We'll pray and let God take care of it."

Mattie leaned over to kiss her husband then rushed out to find a proper wrapping for her gift.

The farmer sighed and sat back in his rocker. "I feel bad

because Mattie hasn't seen Rebecca in over five years. They corresponded regularly until a few years ago when the mail delivery became so sporadic. She truly misses her older sister."

"Then I'm more than happy we can help her keep in touch. Edwin and I have two brothers we haven't seen in several years, and another brother we saw last summer."

Edwin leaned forward, hands resting on his knees. "I especially miss our little brother Theo. He's about the same age as your Davey and was too young for the military when we left to join up."

"The war separated so many families. It's been only a month, but we've already had men from the north down here buying up land and property in town." Zeke rocked and drummed his fingers on the arm of the chair. "We're not looking to sell. We believe the Lord will take care of us if we work hard and follow His will."

Mattie returned with the quilt folded and wrapped into a neat package. Betsy peeked from behind her mother's skirts. "Mama says you're going to take the quilt to Aunt Rebecca. Do you know my cousins too?"

Edwin knelt beside the young girl. "Yes, we do. Your cousin Caroline has blonde curls just like yours."

The young girl smiled and tentatively stepped toward Edwin. "She does? I don't remember her. Our grandmother gave us dolls one Christmas." She held a cloth doll for Edwin to examine. "It's this one."

Manfred grinned. Edwin still had a way with the ladies, no matter their age. He grasped the paper-wrapped parcel in his hands. "We'll take good care of this and make sure it gets to Brady's store and your sister."

Zeke stood and sauntered to the door. "I'm going out to check on the animals. They may still be skittish after the storm. Davey, you come with me." He clamped a straw hat onto his head. "You're welcome to come, too, Manfred, Edwin."

After seeing to the horses, Manfred and Edwin returned to the house for an evening of quiet reading and some reminiscing. After the Jordan family retired, Manfred settled himself on the floor near the fireplace. The fire burned low, the embers sending their warmth into the room.

Edwin removed his outer shirt and sat down. "I'm glad you offered to take that quilt to the Bradys. They'll be glad to know the Jordans are all right."

"That's what I thought. I'm thankful Mr. Jordan said he didn't really need us to stay and help. Much as I would have been willing, I'm anxious to get on to Mississippi and see about Sallie and then home to Louisiana." Manfred tucked the blanket under his arms and closed his eyes.

Edwin snickered, "Can't wait to see a pretty little redhead. Hmm, I'd like to see her cousin myself."

Looked like both of them had reason to get home. Peggy would be a good match for Edwin. Both had similar free spirits. Life would be different because of the war, but love could make up for the changes.

Mattie served a hearty breakfast of fresh eggs and biscuits with grits. Much as Manfred liked grits, he'd had enough of the dish to last a while. Then he remembered the days when he had nothing to eat and decided he could eat grits every day.

Mattie produced a checkered cloth bundle. "Here are a few things to eat along the way. This should get you through to Birmingham."

Manfred clutched the package. "Thank you, Mattie. You and Zeke have been more than generous."

Billy and Betsy stood on either side of Edwin. "We wish you didn't have to go this morning. Can't you stay a while longer?" Betsy pleaded. Billy nodded in agreement.

Mattie knelt and cuddled the two youngsters in her arms. "Manfred and Edwin want to get home to their own families. Their mother must miss them terribly."

Betsy seemed to ponder this a moment then smiled. "Do you have brothers and sisters?"

Edwin knelt to her level. "I have three more brothers. I'm going home to see them."

Mattie stood and spoke to Manfred. "I'm sorry. I know you're in a hurry. Betsy does like to talk once she gets started."

"No apology necessary, Mrs. Jordan." He touched Edwin's shoulder. "Come on, little brother. It's time to be going."

Outside, Manfred shook hands with Zeke then tipped his hat to Mattie. "Thank you for your hospitality, ma'am. I'll get your gift to Mrs. Brady soon as we get home." He settled his hat on his head and swung up behind Edwin on Lady.

Manfred glanced back at the family. They waved again, and Manfred raised his hand in a salute before turning his gaze back to the road leading to their next destination, Mississippi.

Later that day they stopped for a noon meal. Manfred counted the remaining money in his pack while Edwin napped in the shade of an ancient oak tree. They had traveled all morning since spending the night with the Jordan family. The next stop would be somewhere near an old Creek Indian campsite listed on the map. It was now just a settlement, but they could spend the night there.

Edwin stirred then opened his eyes. He shoved his hat back on his head and peered at Manfred. "How we doing with the money?"

"It'll last a few more days." Manfred dropped the coins into a leather pouch and pulled the drawstrings tight. Sleeping in the open and making do with less food had allowed the small amount they had earned to last longer.

"Figure we'll head straight down to Birmingham tomorrow. Should get there by Friday. From there we go across to Tuscaloosa." He spread a map on the ground and traced the route with his finger.

Edwin shook his head. "That's a lot of miles still to go. I had hoped with the horses we'd get home sooner, but it looks like we won't make it home until June after all."

Manfred folded the paper and stuffed it into his pocket. "That's about the size of it. Takes longer than we figured because we lost a horse and some of the roads have been lousy. Still, I figure we should be able to walk for ten hours a day and make it home in a few more weeks."

"At least we're getting closer. I hope Mama gets that letter we sent from Marion." Edwin stood and slapped his thighs to remove dirt and twigs from his pants.

Manfred swung his pack to his shoulder. "I'm sure she will, and I'm going to post another one to Sallie when we reach Birmingham. With two letters from me, she'll be more than assured of our arrival by June." He glanced up at the sky. "With the days getting longer, we might get there sooner. That is, if you can hold up for an extra hour or two." Manfred cut his gaze to his brother.

Laughter erupted from Edwin, and he handed Lady's reins to Manfred. "We'll see who has to stop for rest. I'm even letting you ride first."

"You're on, little brother, and it won't be me begging to stop for the night." He mounted Lady and snapped the reins. As he rode, he dreamed of Sallie and her sparking green eyes. *It won't be long, dear Sallie. I'll see you soon.*

CHAPTER 21

GOOD DAY, MR. Brady. Grandma sent me for sugar. She's planning on baking her buttermilk pound cake." Sallie greeted the proprietor and plopped a basket on the counter.

"Wouldn't mind having a piece of that myself." Mr. Brady turned to a barrel across the aisle and picked up a scoop.

"How's Miss Jenny doing?" He filled a paper cone with sugar.

"Much better now. Flora's cooking and Grandma's nursing have put the color back in her face."

"Your grandmother's a special lady. I remember how she helped my Rebecca when our Nathan was born." He folded in the top of the cone and set it on the scale to weigh it.

"He's on our invitation list for my birthday. I do hope he will come to my party on Saturday."

"Sure he will. How thankful we are the war ended before he had to be involved in any more battles." He pulled a paper from a drawer and wrote a number on it. "Anything else you need?"

"Not now. Mama and Lettie will be in later this week to buy more." Sallie reached for the basket handle then eyed the sparkling candy jars.

"As much as I like peppermint, I think I want cinnamon candies today." She dug into the reticule dangling from her wrist and removed a few coins.

"In honor of your Manfred, I presume." Mr. Brady removed

some of the red candies from a container and placed them in a small bag then handed it to Sallie.

"Yes, sir, I feel he's really getting closer to home. I believe I'll hear from him any day now." She plunked the pennies on the counter and hooked her arm through the basket. "Thank you, Mr. Brady." She popped a cinnamon ball into her mouth and puckered her lips at its spicy flavor. She couldn't understand why Manfred loved them so. She bade the storekeeper good-bye and hurried back home.

Sallie found Jenny in the parlor when she returned. The young woman's cheeks glowed and her hair fell loosely on her shoulders. She truly had made remarkable progress since she arrived over two weeks ago.

"It's so good to see you out and about. How are your feet?" She looped her bonnet on the hall tree peg and handed her purchase to Lettie.

"Much better. I can wear slippers and walk on them now." Jenny lifted her skirt to reveal her cotton-slipper-clad feet.

Sallie picked up her embroidery basket and joined Jenny on the sofa. "Grandma's baking her special buttermilk pound cake, so we'll have a good dessert at supper tonight."

"Oh, I remember eating it at a party at your house. I look forward to having it again."

A knock sounded on the front door. Sallie jumped up, but Lettie reached the foyer first. Sallie sat back, but straining her ears and stretching her neck to see who may be coming to call this time of day.

Lettie appeared. "Miss Sallie, Miss Jenny, Mr. Elliot is here to visit." She stepped back, and Benjamin Elliot entered the room. She'd managed to avoid him while tending to Jenny over the past few weeks, but evidently that excuse had worn itself out.

He held his hat in the crook of his arm and bowed. "Good afternoon, Miss Dyer, Miss Harper."

Sallie remained seated, but glanced sideways at Jenny. "Mr. Elliot. Nice of you to call on us."

"I stopped in to see if you would be interested in a ride before dinner." Benjamin nodded to Sallie.

"Thank you, Mr. Elliott, but I can't leave Jenny behind." Sallie grasped her friend's hand.

"Of course not. I'd be honored to have Miss Harper accompany us. I have the carriage out front with room for you both."

Sallie turned her pleading gaze to Jenny. "Oh, do come, Jenny. Being out in the fresh air will be good for you."

Jenny patted Sallie's hand and smiled at Benjamin. "Thank you for including me, Mr. Elliot. I'd love to have a ride."

Sallie breathed a sigh of relief. She didn't really trust herself to be alone with Benjamin. As much as she thought she cared about Manfred, the attention of a man in person did tempt her.

Then she remembered Jenny's injured feet. "Oh, dear, Jenny has on slippers. Could you assist her, Mr. Elliot?"

"Of course." He held out his hand to Jenny. At her grimace on standing, Benjamin said, "If I may be so bold, may I carry you?"

At Jenny's nod, he gathered her in his arms and strode outside. After seating Jenny, Benjamin stood back and assisted Sallie, who chose to sit beside Jenny. She noted Benjamin's disappointment when he sat across from them.

After several minutes of exchanging pleasantries, Benjamin addressed Jenny. "I understand your home in Mississippi was heavily damaged."

Sallie felt Jenny tense as she lowered her gaze to the floor and answered, "Yes, it was."

"I'm so sorry about that. Our home suffered in the conflict but is livable for us. My condolences on the loss of your father and brother too."

Benjamin's quiet, even words seemed to have a soothing effect on Jenny, and Sallie sensed the young woman relaxing in her seat. Benjamin Elliot was a true Southern gentleman through and through, and that impressed Sallie even more than his good looks.

"Thank you, Mr. Elliot. The war has affected so many families and changed our own lives forever." Jenny raised her eyes to meet his in a steady gaze.

Sallie beamed and listened to them speak of their families. Benjamin couldn't know all of what had happened to Jenny, but he treated her with kindness and sympathy now.

Sallie noted Jenny's heightened color and lovely eyes with long lashes framing them. Jealousy reared its head, but only for a moment as Sallie realized how good of a distraction Jenny had proven to be. If Benjamin could become interested in Jenny, that left Sallie free to think only of Manfred. She had no right to meddle, but how nice it would be if Benjamin were to decide to court Jenny instead.

Jenny laughed, and it floated in the air like music. "Are you daydreaming again, Sallie?"

"What? Oh, I apologize for being inattentive. What were you saying?" Sallie fussed with her handkerchief.

"Miss Dyer, I feel you left us there for a few minutes. I asked how the plans were progressing for your party."

Embarrassment at her lack of attention sent heat waves to Sallie's face. "Aunt Abigail assures us everything is ready, and Jenny is going too. She's getting stronger every day."

Benjamin's steel blue eyes narrowed as he peered at Jenny. "I can see she is. I must be sure my name is on your dance card, Miss Harper."

Jenny lowered her head then peered back up at Benjamin. "Thank you, Mr. Elliot. I'd be pleased to have your name there."

The remainder of the ride Sallie let Benjamin carry the conversation and returned his questions with brief answers. When he escorted them to the door, Jenny excused herself and left Sallie with Benjamin.

Benjamin held the brim of his ivory-colored hat in hand and smiled, his eyes twinkling. "A most delightful afternoon ride, Miss Dyer. I thank you for your company and that of your friend."

"We thank you, Mr. Elliot, for inviting us. If you'll excuse me, I must prepare for dinner."

"Of course, and until I see you again, have a pleasant evening." He bowed then sauntered down the steps to his carriage.

If only she'd have word from Manfred, she could put an end to Benjamin's courting. He'd be perfect for Jenny. Just perfect.

Sallie sat up in bed, hands over her ears to drown out the sounds of anger. Her eyes adjusted to the dark, and she realized the noise came from her dreams. She glanced at Jenny now sleeping peacefully beside her and Hannah's soft snores filling the night air. A chill skittered down her spine. She lay back against her pillow and shut her eyes. The dream had been so real with shouts of anger and fear, but from where or whom she didn't know. In a few minutes calm returned, and she drifted back to sleep.

Later in the morning Sallie shared her dream with Jenny in the privacy of the bedroom. "I kept hearing voices in the dark. Men were shouting and yelling in anger, but I couldn't hear what they were saying. It scared me so much I woke up."

Jenny reached out to embrace her friend. "Oh, Sallie, I once heard voices like that for real. It's frightening to know men can be so angry with each other."

"I was afraid something had happened to Manfred." Sallie returned Jenny's hug.

Jenny pushed back from Sallie and gazed at her. "Everything's going to be all right. How many times have you told me that?"

"Too many times to count, I guess. Oh, Jenny, you always find a way to make me smile." Having her friend here, even under the circumstances that had brought her, helped her deal with the somber moods that overtook her now and then.

Still, Jenny knew her too well, and soon her good friend was pressing her to tell her what really was wrong. Before she knew it, Sallie was spilling out her own story. Of the terror of that day. The horror of killing someone. The guilt that never left her.

Tears glistened in Jenny's eyes as she listened. "I'm so sorry, Sallie. We have both seen such awful things. But we have to remember that God has been so very good to us despite all the horrors and pain."

When Sallie didn't respond to her words, Jenny wrapped her arms around Sallie's shoulders. "Sallie," she said gently, "since I've been here, I've sensed that you have not been close to God, and now I know the reason. Things in our lives will never be the way they were before. We've seen and done things we should never have experienced, but because of them, I believe we'll be stronger women. God did not promise us we would never have trouble in this world, but

He did promise to strengthen our character and bring us hope even in the midst of our sufferings."

Could it be possible? Jenny spoke with such assurance that Sallie wanted to believe it could be true. Jenny possessed the same strength seen in Papa and Mama and her grandparents. Sallie would draw on that strength in the days ahead, and perhaps soon it could be her own.

CHAPTER 22

St. Francisville, Louisiana, Saturday, May 20, 1865

A FTER ANOTHER NIGHT of dreams about the past and of Manfred in a prisoner camp somewhere, Sallie awoke exhausted, every bone in her body aching for sleep. She pulled the covers over her head and turned on her side.

Moments later something pounced onto the bed beside her and began shaking her. "Wake up, Sallie. It's your birthday!"

Her sister's cheerful voice grated on her nerves, causing them to shred even more than they already were. "Go away, Hannah, I don't want to get up. I need to sleep."

"Let her sleep. She had a restless night again and didn't get much rest." Jenny's whispered comment must have appeased Hannah because the weight lifted from the mattress.

In a moment their footsteps padded to the hallway. Then the door closed and Sallie squeezed a pillow to her chest. Her eyelids, heavy as lead, drifted closed, and she returned to blessed sleep.

When she opened her eyes again, sunlight streamed through the window. Sallie threw back the covers and pushed her feet to the floor. What time was it? She hoped Lettie had saved her something for breakfast.

The nightgown she'd been wearing billowed at her feet as she dropped it to don her petticoats and camisole. As she tied the strings of her petticoat, the door opened and Lettie poked her head around the edge.

"Oh, you are up. I thought I heard you moving about." She scurried to Sallie and picked up the dress laid out across a chair. "Here, let me help you finish dressing. Your family finished breakfast hours ago, but my mammy saved you back a plate."

Sallie didn't resist Lettie's help. The restless night had left her listless and not caring one way or the other about getting dressed.

"Now, Miss Sallie, Miss Jenny said you didn't sleep well at all last night. I'm sorry to hear that, but with tonight being your birthday ball, you will need to rest again this afternoon so's you can look your best this evening."

Sallie gasped and stepped away from Lettie. How could she have forgotten today was her big party? All thoughts of celebration had vacated her mind in the aftermath of her dreams. Partying was the last thing on her mind and heart. "Oh, Lettie, I completely forgot about it."

"That's all right. We'll get you all prettied up for it, and Mr. Elliot will think you're the most beautiful girl there." She picked up a brush and motioned for Sallie to sit.

"I don't feel like a party, but Mama and Aunt Abigail have gone to so much trouble." Perhaps with a rest this afternoon she might be more inclined to look ahead to the evening with anticipation rather than dread. She sat still and allowed Lettie to use the brush on the tangles and snarls caused by tossing and turning during the night.

God certainly liked to play cruel jokes on people. He'd allowed her to have nightmares when she should awaken happy and ready for a fun-filled day. That wasn't the God of love who wanted only the best for His children like she'd been taught all her life. No, He was more of an enemy who haunted her nights with horrible memories.

Jenny burst into the room and caught Sallie's hands in hers. "It's your birthday, and we have much to do. Think of it. Benjamin Elliot will be here this evening to escort you to the ball, and he's a fine gentleman. You are so lucky." She whirled around, her skirts billowing out around her. "And look, I'm wearing shoes and there's barely any pain." She stopped to grasp Sallie's hands again.

Sallie yanked her hands away. "I'm too—" She clamped her mouth shut. No need to take her frustration and anger out on her dear friend. She reached for Jenny's arm.

"I'm sorry. I'm out of sorts this morning. I shouldn't take my foul mood out on you."

Jenny knelt beside Sallie. "I heard you last night, moaning in your sleep. It was those dreams again, wasn't it?"

Sallie nodded. Jenny understood the pain in Sallie's heart, but nothing could erase the memories or replace the images in her mind.

The door opened again, and Mama entered with a smile that outshone the sun. "Mrs. Whiteman is downstairs with a letter from Edwin she wants to share with you."

Sallie sprang up and brushed past Mama and Jenny. Edwin! A letter from Edwin would be almost as good as having one from Manfred. Maybe he would have news of his brother. She hurried downstairs.

Seated in the parlor, Mrs. Whiteman looked up when Sallie entered. Her blue eyes sparkling with joy, she removed a folded sheet of paper from her reticule and handed it to Sallie. "I think you will be pleased with what you read."

"Thank you, Mrs. Whiteman. Shall I read it aloud?" Sallie sat beside the older woman and unfolded the sheet of paper.

Mrs. Whiteman removed her lace gloves. "Just the part I indicated. I think it will be of greatest interest."

Sallie's gaze scanned the page then stopped when she spotted the star by a paragraph. She read the passage aloud. "'Manfred and I are in good spirits. Everywhere we've been, we've found good people who have taken care of us. Manfred is strong as he ever was, and I've completely recovered from my wounds. We're making good time, and Manfred figures we'll be home by early June. We're slowed down some because Manfred and I want to help people. Manfred said it was the least we could do to return the kindnesses shown us along the way. Manfred sends his love to all. Please tell Peggy I'm thinking about her and would like to see her upon my return.'"

Sallie laughed and clasped the paper to her chest before handing it back to Mrs. Whiteman. "Oh, Mrs. Whiteman, that is the best news I've heard in months. What a wonderful birthday present!"

Mrs. Whiteman smiled and patted her hand. "I knew I had to share it just as soon as I could."

Sallie beamed. The nightmares of last night disappeared as mist in the sun. Her birthday would be a wonderful day after all.

Her gaze caught her mother's, and she jumped up. "Mama, Manfred is coming home. I have to tell Papa." She raced from the room. Papa and her brothers had returned from their work in Woodville yesterday. He should be out in the stables.

At the back door Sallie tripped and stumbled. Lettie appeared from nowhere and reached out to catch her.

"Careful there, Miss Sallie. I know you is excited, but you don't want to meet Mr. Manfred with a broken leg."

"Oh, Lettie. Isn't it wonderful? They'll be home in a few weeks!" She wrapped her arms around her friend and twirled her around. "I have to find Papa. Is he in the stables?"

"He's…at…Magnolia Manor with your aunt and uncle." Lettie shoved on Sallie's arms. "Stop spinning…so's I can breathe."

Sallie stood still. "I'm sorry, Lettie. I'm so excited. You said Papa is at Magnolia Manor?"

"Yes, Miss Sallie. He's over helpin' your uncle get things ready for tonight."

Sallie chewed her lip and brushed a wayward wisp of hair from her eyes. Of course he would be, but she must talk to him now. "Then I'll ride over there and find him." She started in the direction of the stables to find George to take her to Magnolia Hall.

Lettie grabbed her hand. "Miss Sallie. Your party is tonight, and Mrs. Tenney will be here with your dresses. You can see your papa after he gets back. You must eat something now and then rest so you'll be ready when it's time to dress for your party."

"But Papa needs to know Manfred is coming home. I can't have Mr. Elliot escort me tonight."

Mama's piercing voice spoke from the doorway. "Yes, you will. You will not go back on your word. Now go in and speak with Mrs. Whiteman. You ran off and left our guest most rudely."

Mama's words sent a dagger into Sallie's heart. Didn't Mama see that everything had changed with that letter? The set of Mama's mouth and tightly drawn lips meant no arguing. "Yes, ma'am, I'm sorry. That was thoughtless of me." Her shoulders drooped as she headed back to the parlor.

Mrs. Whiteman stood in the entryway with Jenny and had been joined by her son Charles. After kindly accepting Sallie's apology, she said, "I'm sorry there hasn't been a letter from Manfred. Perhaps one will arrive in a day or so. The postal service has been so sporadic. I wouldn't be surprised if we saw the boys themselves before another letter reached us."

Sallie said nothing, her heart aching with desire to see or hear from Manfred himself. Until she did, she had no way of knowing if he still cared about her like he'd claimed last year. What if no letter meant his heart had changed?

Mama embraced Mrs. Whiteman. "Jenny will be ready this evening when Charles comes for her."

Come for Jenny? Sallie jerked her head around to find Jenny behind her with a smile on her face. When had that happened?

Mama closed the door behind Mrs. Whiteman and Charles. "Now, Sallie, you must have something to eat and have a bath before Mrs. Tenney arrives with the dresses."

Sallie bit her lip. "Yes, Mama." Her stomach rumbled from having missed breakfast.

"I will join you," Jenny said.

The two young women headed to the dining room. Lettie brought out tea for Jenny and eggs, bacon, and toast for Sallie. After eating a few bites, Sallie turned to Jenny.

"When did Charles become your escort for this evening?"

"Just now. He brought his mother up so you could read Edwin's letter and asked your mother about escorting me tonight since you would be going with Benjamin."

The reminder tightened like a rope around her heart. "Oh, Jenny, I haven't heard from Manfred. Edwin's letter says they're coming home, but why hasn't Manfred written me himself to tell me? Maybe he doesn't love me anymore."

Jenny set down her teacup and grabbed Sallie's hand. "Sarah Louise Dyer, why fret over the unknown? Enjoy the good news you've just received. Manfred is on his way home. Besides, you have a party tonight, and Benjamin is a good escort. Go and have a good time."

Easy for her to say. Jenny didn't love anyone with all her heart and soul like Sallie did Manfred. And what of Benjamin? "I don't want Benjamin to think I'm interested in him. I'll tell Papa tonight that I can't see him anymore."

Jenny said nothing but shook her head and returned to her tea. Joy and fear warred within Sallie. Manfred was coming home. But would he still love her after she told him what she'd done?

CHAPTER 23

St. Francisville, Louisiana, Saturday, May 20, 1865

A FTER HER LATE breakfast, first Sallie and then Jenny bathed and washed their hair in preparation for the party that evening. As their hair dried, they sat reading quietly in their room. Sallie tried to read, but her thoughts were in a turmoil. What would Papa say when she told him she did not want to see Benjamin anymore? How would she handle Benjamin tonight? What would she say when she first saw Manfred? How would she act?

A knock sounded at the door, interrupting her thoughts, and Mama entered along with Hannah. "Are you girls ready to dress for the party? The gowns are here from Mrs. Tenney."

Hannah ran to Sallie and grabbed her around the waist. "Please be happy, Sallie. This is a most wonderful day."

And it was for her sister. Sallie had to think of others and their joy and not let her own doubts and fears color the evening for them. This was her birthday, and she would not spoil it for others.

Lettie and Grandma walked through the door, followed by Mrs. Tenney and Miriam, each carrying a box. Grandma waved toward the bed. "Place them on the bed, and Lettie, please help Sallie with her garment. I'll take care of Hannah, and Miriam will assist Jenny." She opened the first box. "Now let's see how these look."

Mama retrieved a filmy dress from one box and laid it out on the bed. Sallie gasped at the beauty of the dress. "Oh, it looks even more beautiful than it did at the fitting."

Lettie helped Sallie remove her dress then secured the

crinoline about her waist. The frothy fabric of the dress now slipped over Sallie's head. She smoothed the skirt over her petticoats. Mrs. Tenney was a genius. It looked just like the dress in the Godey book.

The seamstress straightened the tiny puff sleeves. "You have such a lovely figure, it was a pleasure fitting you."

Miriam held a second box in her hands. "Mama has a knack for knowing just what details to add to a dress to make it special." She opened the box and held up a heap of lavender silk. "This is for you, Jenny."

Sallie held her breath as the seamstress spread the garment before Jenny. At the sound of Jenny's sharp intake of breath, Sallie relaxed.

"Oh my, I expected to see the peach one of yours we picked to alter. I don't know what to say." Jenny's eyes glistened with tears, and she fingered the delicate fabric.

Mama placed her arm across Jenny's shoulder. "It's our gift to you, my dear." Mama grinned and nodded at Miriam. "Time to see how it looks on her."

Sallie noted Jenny's shaking hands and reached over to hold them as Miriam fastened a crinoline petticoat around Jenny's waist. "Mama and I thought it would be a grand surprise for you. And many people had a part in it because we all love you." The pure joy radiating from Jenny's face was worth every minute they'd spent planning. To see it there now gave Sallie a new determination to make the evening as memorable as possible for everyone. After all the sorrow and suffering of the last few years, people needed a time to celebrate.

With Miriam's and Lettie's assistance, Jenny slipped the dress over her head. Sallie stood back and clasped her hands to her chest. "Oh, Jenny, it's perfect with your eyes. They look positively violet."

The mass of lavender fell to settle at the waist and hips. Jenny's hand went to one of the fabric rosettes at the neckline. Tears sparkled in her eyes. "It's gorgeous. I can't begin to thank you enough, Mrs. Dyer. You've been more than generous with me these past weeks."

Mama spread the skirt to get the full effect of the deep purple trim around the hem. "No need for a thank-you. All we want now is for you to have a grand time tonight."

Then it was time for Hannah's dress. When Mama had secured the sash and straightened the lace at the neck, she turned Hannah toward the mirror. "What do you think, my sweet girl?"

"I...I love it, Mama. Thank you." Hannah hugged her mother then twisted back and forth to get a better look at her reflection.

The smile on her sister's face brought joy to Sallie's heart. She pulled a box from under the bed. "And here's an extra surprise for you to wear with it."

When opened, the box revealed a pair of white shoes nestled in paper. "Grandpa had them made special for tonight."

Trembling hands gathered up the shoes, and Hannah held them to her chest. "They're beautiful, even with the extra inches on the sole." She plopped on a chair, her crinoline flying up. Hannah giggled. "I'll have to learn how to sit properly in these."

With Mama's help the shoes were in place in a matter of seconds. Hannah stood and took a few steps. "They're perfect. I feel like a princess."

Tears filled Sallie's eyes as she wrapped her arms about Hannah's shoulders. "You are a princess, and don't you forget it." Gone were all the doubts and fears about tonight. With family and friends around her, it would be a glorious time.

Once every hair lay in place and every bit of grooming

completed, Lettie left to go downstairs to greet Benjamin and Charles when they arrived. Hannah pirouetted in her blue frock. "Look at me. I hardly limp at all."

"I do believe Jeremiah will have a hard time keeping his eyes off you this evening." Sallie hugged her sister. "With your bouncy curls and ribbons, you'll outshine me."

Hannah beamed with pride. "Do you think Mr. Elliot might ask me for a dance?"

Jenny smoothed lace gloves over her fingers. "I wouldn't be surprised if he did. He's a gentleman and most certainly would pay attention to the guest of honor's sister."

Sallie's patience would be tested many times in the days ahead until she had a letter from Manfred in hand. Tonight she'd be courteous with Benjamin, but with news of Manfred's impending return, it was time to end the courtship. She'd have to tell Papa first of course, and she'd do that before the evening ended.

As the sun set and painted the clouds with hues of orange and purple, Sallie and Benjamin arrived at Magnolia Manor. Aunt Abigail and Colonel Bradford stood positioned in the front entry to greet the arriving guests.

Aunt Abigail kissed Sallie on each cheek. "You'll stand here with us until all the guests arrive. We want everyone to grant best wishes and to see how lovely you look."

"Yes, Aunt Abigail." Sallie whispered to Jenny, "Go ahead. I'll see you in a little while."

Jenny and Charles disappeared into the ballroom, but Benjamin stood by Sallie's side. Aunt Abigail held her fan to her mouth and whispered to Sallie.

"I must say Jenny Harper looks more ravishing than ever.

With all that happened to her, I would never…" Her voice trailed off as the first guest arrived.

Sallie shuddered. If her aunt knew about the disaster in Woodville, no telling what she might say about her own niece.

As the line progressed, the smile became pasted on her face and her jaws ached from being pleasant with each guest as they offered congratulations. Not only that, the new slippers pinched her toes. Who knew a reception line could be so long. How had that many people come to be invited? Finally the last of the guests greeted her, and Benjamin escorted her to the ballroom.

There she spotted Hannah seated against the wall drinking punch with Jeremiah. Jenny and Charles stood nearby deep in conversation. Sallie headed for the nearest chair and eased down with a sigh. How would she ever manage to dance this evening with her feet hurting so? She should have known better than to wear new shoes to a dance.

"May I bring you some refreshment, Miss Dyer?"

She glanced up at Benjamin. "Yes, Mr. Elliot. I'd most appreciate a cup of punch."

He departed, and from across the room Peggy waved before rushing over to Sallie, her eyes shining with joy. "A letter from Edwin Whiteman arrived today. He didn't say outright, but I think he's going to ask Father if he can call on me."

So Peggy had a letter from Edwin, but nothing had come from Manfred. Worry again reared its head. "I'm happy for you, Peggy. And according to one to his mother, Edwin said they should be here soon."

Peggy's mouth curved downward in a frown. "You didn't get one from Manfred?"

Sallie shook her head. "I'm...I'm so afraid he doesn't love me anymore, and that's why he hasn't written."

"Oh, fiddlesticks, I don't think that for a minute."

Papa appeared at her side at the same time Benjamin returned. "Good evening, Mr. Dyer." He handed Sallie a cup of pink liquid. "Here's your punch, Miss Dyer."

Sallie smiled and accepted the cup, but her father reached for her other hand. "If you don't mind, Mr. Elliot, I'd like the honor of the first dance with my beautiful daughter."

"Of course, Papa." She set her cup on the nearby table and followed her father to the dance floor as Colonel Bradford signaled the musicians to begin the festivities. Papa's love beamed from his eyes as they kept time to the music. He thought nothing less of her for killing that poor soldier, so why couldn't she forgive herself?

From the gossip Sallie overheard from conversations throughout the evening, many people believed more had happened to Jenny than she had told. What would they think if they knew Sallie herself had killed a man? A shudder ran through her. Then those sly looks and sneers would be directed at her, and they would be well deserved.

During a break Sallie beckoned Jenny to her side. From the glow on her face, Sallie could see the gossip had not affected Jenny's evening. "You do look like you're having a grand time."

Jenny clasped her ivory and lavender fan to her chest. "Oh, I am, I am. Your friends have been polite and so nice to me. And Charles Whiteman is a true gentleman."

Sallie slipped her arms around Jenny. "I'm so happy for you." She pulled back and grinned. "Look, I do believe Mr. Elliot is asking Hannah for the next dance."

Across the room the young girl gazed into the eyes of her

partner with pure rapture. "Look at her, Jenny. I do believe she has a crush on Benjamin."

Mama tapped her shoulder, a smile curving her mouth. "Sallie, did you ask Mr. Elliot to do that?"

Sallie tilted her head. "No, Mama. I think he did it on his own. Hannah does look quite grown up in the longer dress." And indeed she did. Her little sister was growing into a very pretty young lady. She had to give Benjamin credit. He knew how to charm women. Too bad his charms were wasted on her.

The festivities began to wind down, and soon guests said their good-nights and left. Sallie had completely forgotten her worries and aching feet in the fun of the evening. She searched for Papa and Mama, but Jenny told her they had left to take Hannah home. Jenny herself soon left on the arm of Charles.

Sallie bit her lip. She hadn't had the opportunity to say anything to Papa about not wanting to be courted by Benjamin any longer. Now she'd have to be polite for the remainder of the evening and keep quiet for another day.

By the time she and Benjamin left, all the other guests had also departed. On the ride home with Benjamin she tried to carry on intelligent conversation, but words stuck in her throat. Finally he said, "You don't need to talk. You've grown tired, so rest, and we'll be at your home in a few minutes."

Grateful for his consideration, she could only smile then turn her eyes straight ahead to her home coming into view. When the carriage rolled to a stop at the front steps, Benjamin hopped down then came around to help her alight. He held her hand and walked with her up the steps to the door.

He bent his head and kissed her hand then said, "Thank

you for another lovely evening, Miss Dyer. May this be the first of many birthdays we'll celebrate."

Sallie's mouth dropped open. What did he mean by that? Before she could reply, he had bowed and bounded down the steps to the carriage. Speaking to her father now became even more imperative.

When the door clicked shut behind her, voices floated from the parlor. Mama and Papa were still up. This would be the perfect time to talk with them about Manfred. She reached for the doorknob, but Papa's voice stayed her hand.

"Amanda, I say we can't wait around any longer. Benjamin Elliot has asked permission to seek Sallie's hand in marriage, and I have a mind to give it to him. He's been courting her a few weeks now and he's a fine young man. It's time for Sallie to face reality. Manfred may not be coming home to her."

Those words stabbed with a pain like none other she'd ever experienced. It went straight from her heart to every bone and muscle in her body. Hadn't Mama told him about the letter from Edwin? She pressed her fist against the sobs rising in her throat and raced up the stairs and into her room.

Tears streamed down her cheeks as she undressed. Leaving her clothes in a heap on the floor, she pulled on her nightgown and crawled into bed, being careful not to disturb Jenny. Sallie buried her face in her pillow and let it soak up her tears.

Moments later a hand reached over and touched her shoulder. Jenny's soft voice spoke close to Sallie's ear. "What happened? Are you hurt?"

How could she explain to Jenny the betrayal that permeated her soul? Papa had ruined everything.

CHAPTER 24

Alabama, Monday, May 22, 1865

SINCE LEAVING THE Jordan farm, Manfred and Edwin had traveled long and hard. The lure of home was upon them, and the closer they came, the faster and longer they traveled. On Friday they had arrived in Birmingham and stocked up with provisions. When the store owner saw they were returning prisoners of war, he didn't charge them for the food. To Manfred it was another example of the goodness of the people of the South and God's provision for their needs.

They had come through Tuscaloosa earlier today but had decided they had enough daylight for more miles west. Now they prepared to hunker down for the night. Tomorrow they'd be on their way to Meridian. If his calculations were correct, that would take about three days. Each night they collapsed exhausted but with more determination to press on the next morning.

Deep into the darkest hours of the night, Manfred awakened with a start, a hand squeezing his arm. "What?"

"Shh, listen. Hear that?" Edwin whispered.

Manfred lifted his head, but he heard only crickets at first, before picking up the sound of horses and riders nearby. The murmur of their voices penetrated, but no words came clear. He lay still with Edwin's hand still gripping his arm, warning him into silence.

The murmurs now became shouts laced with hatred and anger. A chill swept across Manfred, and his heart pounded. Sitting up, he gestured to Edwin to keep low. He crawled across the clearing on his belly and peered through the trees. He spotted a glow through the brush. Fire! Now the fear rose with a bitter taste of bile. That was no ordinary fire.

Edwin inched up behind him. "What's going on out there?"

"I don't know. Let's get a closer look." Manfred scooted along the ground with Edwin at his side. The voices became harsher, the emotion more intense.

Manfred parted the branches and discovered a group of men on horseback circling and yelling at a figure hunched in the dirt. Light flared from torches carried by men who wore white coverings over their head.

Manfred sucked in his breath. A young, colored boy, hands bound behind his back, tried to sit up. A whip cracked in the air and slithered like a snake across the boy's back.

Edwin jerked and stifled a cry beside him, and Manfred reached out his hand to still him. He let the branches fall back in place and wriggled back from the scene, pulling Edwin to come along.

When they returned to their gear, Edwin hissed, "We can't just leave that boy back there."

"I don't like it, but we have to. At least fifteen men are back there with guns and torches," Manfred whispered as he packed his belongings.

"They're gonna kill him. We gotta do something."

"There's nothing we can do without getting killed ourselves. Come on." His heart pounded harder, and sweat dropped from his brow. He scurried to Lady and untied her reins. "With all the shouting, they shouldn't hear us, but we'll walk a little ways before we ride."

Lady yanked at the reins, her head rearing back and then to the side. She must have seen the fire or smelled it. He turned her away from the noise and stroked the mare's forelock. "Shh, Lady, it's all right." He led her through the trees until the sounds of the angry mob grew dim. Then suddenly a roar went up from the group behind them.

Whatever happened back there was not good. Greater urgency surged through him. "C'mon, Edwin, we have to run." The moon offered enough light to see a thinning of the trees and then a road. He mounted Lady and pulled Edwin up behind him.

They raced down the path to escape the shouts. Manfred clung to the reins, his body bent forward, his face close to Lady's neck. *Dear Lord, forgive me for being such a coward. This wasn't like any battle we faced in the war. God, help them. Help us all.*

Manfred lay awake in the gray shadows of the creeping dawn a day later. After a frantic pace yesterday to get away from what they'd witnessed, they had crossed over into Mississippi. The image of what he had seen that night refused to go away. He choked back tears as the cries of the young black man rang in his ears. Nothing could be done to stop a mob like that. Men with hatred in their hearts would not be stopped by two unarmed young men. Great sorrow filled his heart at the idea of other scenes like that happening all over the South.

What evil had been born as the result of the past four years? Is this what the fighting had brought to the South? What was the use of so many dying if hatred flared up yet again, causing even more murder and mayhem? Manfred wanted only to see the good in everyone he met and take care of their illnesses and ailments. God willing, he'd do just that in the years ahead, but what could he do now?

Manfred stared heavenward as fingers of pink, lavender,

and orange stretched across the sky. He'd pray this morning, but sadness hung heavy over his soul. Edwin still slept, exhausted by the hard ride from Alabama and away from the violence they'd witnessed. Another week or two, and they would arrive in Woodville. That is what he must dwell on, not the horrors of the night.

A dip in a creek or spring headed the list of things he wanted to do in the days left. He had no desire to face Sallie dirty and smelling of the road. Even now the thought of seeing her soon renewed his strength.

When the sunlight finally peeked through the lacy branches overhead, Manfred sat up and stretched. Nearby Edwin began stirring too. A few pokes with a stick brought the glowing embers back to life. Manfred prepared coffee in an old pot given them by Mrs. Jordan.

When the aroma of the brew wafted through the air, Edwin sat up and sniffed. "Umm, smells good. Anything left to go with it?"

Manfred poured a cup and handed it to Edwin. "Just a few biscuits and a little hard tack from what we picked up in the last town yesterday. I have dried fruit left we can have for lunch."

Edwin scratched his face and took the cup from Manfred. He took a sip and smiled. "Going to be a good day today. We're almost home. What day is it?"

Manfred shook his head and opened the packet of biscuits. "If I kept track right, it's May 23. If we keep going like we have been, we'll be in Meridian by tomorrow."

The boys ate in silence for a few minutes. Manfred began a little mental calculation in his head. They left weeks ago early in April... Suddenly Manfred slapped his forehead. "Edwin, I clean forgot Sallie's birthday. With the days running together like they are, I never even thought of it."

Edwin laughed. "Well, I reckon your coming home will be about the best birthday present she ever got."

Manfred's brow furrowed. "I guess so, but it'd be nice to have a gift for her. I only pray her feelings haven't changed since last year."

Edwin swallowed the last bite of the slightly dry biscuit. "I'm sure they haven't. I'm hoping to call on her cousin Peggy when we get home. And speaking of home, let's get on the road. You ride first today."

For once Manfred didn't argue with him. His brother had slept soundly last night while sleep had been elusive for him. Nothing he'd seen in all the battles he'd faced had produced the nightmares of that one night in the woods. He'd never forget it, and for some reason he knew he *mustn't* forget it.

After a few hours of travel they stopped to rest. Edwin eased himself onto the grass, and Manfred swung down from Lady and plopped beside his brother. A cloud of trouble hovered in Edwin's eyes. "What's the problem, little brother?"

Edwin chewed a piece of grass. "I keep thinking about the other night. What were those men thinking by torturing and killing another man?"

"I don't know. I killed a few Yankees, but not with the anger and hate I saw in those men." They hadn't seen the men's faces, but their voices and bodies spoke of a hate that bore deep into a man's heart. Manfred stared at the toes of his dust-covered boots. He'd never have a satisfactory answer for what they'd witnessed.

"I heard tell of how many owners beat their slaves for no good reason." Edwin's voice trembled.

"I'm glad Papa didn't keep slaves. He always said no man should own another, but I got a gut feeling we're going to see and hear more like we saw last night." As much as it hurt, he spoke the truth. Losing the war would make some men bitter and turn them to persecuting others.

Edwin seemed to contemplate the idea. Finally he stood. "All I can say is that I hope I never witness anything like that again. And if I do, I pray I can do something to stop it."

Manfred rose and wrapped an arm about his brother's shoulders. "So do I. Let's get cleaned up and head for home." The sooner they got there, the sooner he could begin healing and helping others.

After another sleepless night of nightmares and thoughts of marriage to Benjamin, Sallie had feigned illness Sunday and stayed in her bed all day. Mama had come in a number of times to check on her, but Sallie always pretended to be asleep. The only one she talked to was Lettie, but even then she couldn't tell her what she'd overheard Papa say. She imagined many different scenes with her father as she tried to explain why she didn't want to marry Benjamin. Her love for Manfred should be enough for Papa to understand, but not if he had his mind set on Benjamin as her husband.

She hadn't even told Jenny what Papa said. If she spoke the words aloud, they may actually come true. As long as she kept silent and pretended to be too ill to see Benjamin, the proposal couldn't happen.

Mama had let her stay in bed this morning, but now she must go down and join her family for dinner. Voices from downstairs drifted up. Then her mother shouted, and footsteps thundered up the stairway.

"Sallie, oh, Sallie. The most wonderful thing." Mama burst through the door and waved a piece of paper in her hand. "A letter from Manfred. It's a letter from Manfred."

Sallie squealed and grasped the paper in her hand. "Where did it come from? How did you get it?" Her hands shook as she held the precious paper.

"It came just now." Mama wrung her hands. "Well, what does it say?"

Sallie scanned the page quickly then read again more slowly, savoring each word as she spoke them.

> *My dear Sallie,*
>
> *I pray this letter finds you and your family well and safe. Edwin and I are on our way home, but how long it will take, I do not know.*
>
> *My love for you has not abated in the least. It has rather increased and will do so until time shall be no more. This may not be in accordance with your feelings after these many months, but I pray it is so.*
>
> *Upon my return I will formally request of your father your hand in marriage. I have placed my abiding faith in the Ruler of the universe and know all will be well once I am again in your presence.*
>
> *Give my regards to your mother and father, and tell Hannah I think of her too. I pray you are both untouched by the horrors of this war and escaped the misery I have seen. Give my regards also to your brothers. I'm thankful they were too young for this conflict.*
>
> *You may not hear from me again because the posting of mail is uncertain in many of the places we may be. Be assured, I will be home.*
>
> *Lovingly and faithfully,*
> *Your own Manfred*

At the end she collapsed on the bed and held the letter in her lap. "Oh, Mama, he does love me." The aroma of the lilacs beneath her window drifted upward on the late spring air. She breathed deeply of the perfume scenting her room. They would forever be her favorite flower.

Mama grasped Sallie's hand and pulled her to stand. She embraced Sallie and whispered, "Oh, my child, I'm so happy for you."

Sallie laid her cheek against Mama's shoulder. "He said he's going to ask Papa properly if he may marry me." She pushed back and gazed at Mama.

Mama nodded. "Yes, that will be wonderful, but we mustn't make any other plans until Manfred speaks with Papa." Her hand flew to her mouth. "Oh, my, Benjamin Elliot. This will make a difference."

"Mama, Papa can't allow Mr. Elliot to ask me to marry him now. Manfred is coming home soon, and he's the one I want to marry." She paused a moment and worried her lip. "I'm sorry, Mama, but I overheard Papa and you talking when I arrived home from the party."

"I see, and that's why you've feigned illness these past few days." At Sallie's nod, she continued. "You didn't hear it all. I told him about the letter from Edwin. Papa then said that if you heard from Manfred in the next few days, he would deny Mr. Elliot the privilege of asking your hand in marriage."

New joy soared within Sallie. Papa had understood after all, and she'd made herself sick for nothing. She didn't care. Benjamin could find another girl to shower with love; her own love was coming home. "June will make a perfect month for a wedding."

Mama gasped. "Sallie, that's only a few weeks away." She shook her head. "No. June won't do. Maybe by July or August."

"Mama! It's too hot to have a wedding then. If we can't do it by the end of June, then..."

"Then you'll have to wait for October." Mama grinned.

"Oh, dear." Sallie chewed her lip then suddenly smiled

and hugged Mama. "Listen to me. You'd think Manfred was already home. I promise to be patient and wait until he's here before worrying about a wedding date."

"Now that sounds more reasonable." She hooked Sallie's elbow with her hand. "Let's go down to dinner. Mr. Elliot is downstairs with Jenny."

Sallie noticed the gleam in her mother's eye and the hint of a smile at the corner of her mouth. "Mama, you left Jenny to entertain Mr. Elliot? Now who's the matchmaker?"

"Not me, my dear. I'm letting nature take its course. Come, let's go down."

The murmur of their voices reached Sallie before she stepped into the hallway. She entered the parlor to find Jenny on the sofa with Benjamin perched on a chair across from her.

"Good afternoon, Mr. Elliot." Sallie extended a hand toward the young man.

Benjamin stood and clasped Sallie's hand between both of his. "Good afternoon, Miss Dyer. I understand you've had correspondence from Manfred Whiteman."

"Yes, I have. He's coming home and will be here soon." Sallie squared her shoulders. "I shall be waiting for him and…"

"And you'd rather I not come calling on you. Right?"

Sallie noted his arched eyebrow. "Yes. You needn't waste your time with me, but I do thank you for the time we spent together. Your presence did make my party much better." Not as good as Manfred's would have, but then she hadn't lied because she had enjoyed the party with Benjamin.

"It was my pleasure, Miss Dyer." He turned and bowed to Jenny. "And 'twas an extra pleasure to have you with us, Miss Harper." He straightened and extended a hand toward Mama.

"Thank you for your hospitality, Mrs. Dyer. I'll take my leave now and leave your family to make plans."

After Benjamin's departure, Jenny reached for Sallie's hand. "Come sit here and tell me all about Manfred's letter. Where is he, and how is he?"

Sallie sank onto the sofa and arranged her skirts to lie flat then reached over and grabbed her friend in a hug. "Oh, Jenny, he's all right, and he's coming home, and he still loves me."

She sat with her arms around her friend for a moment longer before sitting back. "The letter was posted several weeks ago. He and Edwin are well and making their way home. He said he'd ask Papa properly for my hand when he returns."

Jenny clapped her hands in delight. "Oh, that's wonderful. It's the best news I've heard in a long time."

"What's this news I'm hearing about?" Papa stepped into the room, his mouth set firm as though angry, but his eyes twinkled, revealing his true mood.

"It's a letter from Manfred, Papa. He says he loves me, and I love him with all my heart."

Papa nodded. "I see. Then I suppose when he asks for your hand, you want me to give my blessings?"

"Oh, Papa, I do, I do. He'll be home shortly, and…oh, Papa, I do love you." She leaned across and planted a kiss on his cheek.

Papa grunted, "Harrumph." Then he smiled. "Thank you."

Sallie's heart sang with joy and pictures of past miseries blurred, replaced with the images of what would lie ahead in the coming year.

CHAPTER 25

AFTER TWO WEEKS of hard travel from Tuscaloosa and stopping only to eat or rest for a few moments during the day, Manfred and Edwin had arrived in Mississippi near their destination. In another hour or so they'd be in Woodville. Now at dawn, Manfred scrambled from his bedroll to clean up for the day ahead.

He found the soap Mrs. Jordan had stashed in his saddlebag and headed for the creek. Edwin soon followed him. Manfred splashed the warm water on his face and longed for a razor to shave away the stubble on his chin. After washing his upper body, Manfred dried with the tablecloth that once held provisions then donned his threadbare shirt. Amazing what a little soap and water could do for a man's energy.

He handed Edwin the reins. "It's time for you to ride for awhile."

For the next hour they alternated riding Lady, but neither did much talking. The things Manfred had seen and done this past year shaped him into a new man, ready to fulfill his dream of becoming a doctor. No one could erase the past, but a future could be built on the hopes for a better world. The battles of Franklin and Nashville lay behind him, but the days ahead would write a new story for those who worked hard and followed their hearts.

His heart filled with emotion. "Edwin, I'm making a vow here and now. When I become a doctor, I'll never refuse treatment to any man, regardless of his color and station in life. I'll always remember the protection and care we've

239

received from perfect strangers and strive to do the same for those I meet in the future."

Edwin said nothing but nodded his head in agreement. He'd join his father in the shipping business and be a better man for his experiences.

In the next hour the terrain changed, and Manfred grimaced at the sight of the damaged and deserted buildings they now passed. Then he stopped in his tracks and grabbed Edwin's arm. "It's the Harper home."

Bile rose in his throat at the scene before him. The house lay in charred rubble, two chimneys standing as sentinels at either end as harsh reminders of how close the war had come to home.

Edwin gasped. "Oh, my, Manfred. What happened here?"

Fear coursed through Manfred's veins like ice water. Where were the Harpers? If this had happened to the Harpers, what would they find at Sallie's home? "I don't know, but pray the Harper family is safe. Pray they escaped before this happened. Come on, there's nothing for us to do here."

He turned away then quickened his pace toward the town. His heart pounded with dread for what they might find there.

Shortly the out buildings of Woodville came into view. Just before they reached the main center, Manfred turned south toward the Dyer home.

A few minutes later houses came into view. He broke into a trot. "Come on, Edwin, I see the Dyer place." As they drew closer, Manfred caught sight of three figures working in the yard. The damage to the structure now became apparent, and he couldn't see any evidence of the womenfolk nearby.

The taller of the three men raised his head from his sawing and watched their approach. Suddenly a smile split his face, and he waved his hat. Manfred recognized Mr. Dyer and signaled back.

Manfred broke into a trot then a dead run to meet the man running toward him. They wrapped their arms around each other. The older man pulled back and gazed into Manfred's eyes.

"I can't believe what I'm seeing. We've prayed and waited for this day so long." He shoved his hat back from his forehead.

Two boys raced up and grabbed at Manfred and Edwin.

"Hey, Will and Tom. My, how you've grown. You're not little boys anymore." Manfred started to ruffle Will's hair as he had in the past but stopped his hand in midair as he realized the boy stood as tall as he. He extended a hand to the boy instead.

Will grabbed the offered hand and squeezed it. "You're sure a sight for sore eyes. Ever since your letter, we've all been looking for you."

Manfred searched the grounds. "Speaking of which, where are your mother and sisters?"

Mr. Dyer rubbed his chin. "Sorry they're not here, but the house isn't quite livable yet. They're in St. Francisville with the Woodruffs."

Disappointment filled Manfred, but at least the women were safe. "We passed the Harper plantation earlier today. What happened there? Where are the Harpers?"

The boys became silent, and Mr. Dyer bowed his head then raised his eyes to lock with Manfred's gaze. "It's a long story. Mrs. Harper and Jenny are safe, but Mr. Harper and Andrew are dead."

Manfred sucked in his breath. "Where are the women now?" He followed Mr. Dyer back to the house.

"Mrs. Harper is with friends, and Jenny is in St. Francisville with Sallie." He expelled a heavy sigh. "We finished our breakfast, but there's coffee left. Come join me for a cup, and

I'll tell you about the family. Then you can go on down to St. Francisville."

What Manfred heard both chilled and warmed him. His family was safe, as were Sallie and her mother and sister. If they left within the next half hour, they could be in St. Francisville by late afternoon. In only a few short hours Sallie would know of his love for her and his desire to marry her as soon as possible.

St. Francisville, Louisiana

Sallie gazed across at Jenny. The girl's raven tresses cascaded from the ivory clip holding the mass at the crown of her head. They hid her face as she concentrated on working the tiny stitches of her sampler.

Jenny raised violet eyes to Sallie. "What are you thinking, dear friend?"

Sallie sighed. "About how beautiful you are, and you smile so much now that Benjamin Elliot is calling on you." In the two weeks since she'd received the letter from Manfred, Benjamin had called on Jenny four times.

Jenny's cheeks reddened, and she dropped the sampler to her lap. "He's been most kind to me. I so appreciate your father stepping in and taking Papa's place to give permission. I do enjoy his company despite..."

Sallie tossed aside her own stitching and grasped her friend's hand. "Of course. He's a gentleman."

A smile lit up Jenny's face, and she picked up her needle and sampler to resume stitching. "I know. He seems to sense my feelings and is so polite with me."

"You deserve good things in your life right now." Sallie

hugged her friend then sat back. She tapped a cheek with her index finger. "Mama thinks it's time for you to have more things of your own. She's arranged for Mrs. Tenney to make you a few simple garments. You and I aren't exactly the same size, and you're a bit taller too. You need something to fit like the lavender silk did."

"Oh, Sallie. I can't impose. You've already done so much for me." Jenny lowered her eyes and stared at her hands. "However, a simple skirt and blouse of my own would be nice. You must be tired of sharing."

Sallie reached across and lifted Jenny's chin. "I don't mind at all. What little I have is yours too. Understand?"

"Yes, I understand, but you and your family are too generous." Jenny laid aside her sampler once again and rose to walk to the window.

Sallie jumped up. "I know what. Let's go to Brady's store and look at pictures and find some material for a new garment."

Jenny spun around, her mouth agape. She gulped and said, "Right now?"

"I think that's a splendid idea. It's a lovely way to close this afternoon." Mama spoke from the doorway. "A walk in the fresh air will do us all good. I'll get my hat and join you."

Sallie tugged at Jenny's hand. "See, even Mama's excited about doing this for you too. Let's get our parasols."

In a few minutes the three women strolled down the street toward Brady's store. The few blocks of walking in fresh air raised Sallie's spirits. She lifted her eyes toward the brilliant blue sky where clouds floated like puffs of smoke from Papa's pipe. The only thing missing in her life was Manfred. When he arrived back home, her world would be complete.

The bell over the door tinkled, signaling their entrance.

Mr. Brady greeted them. "Good morning, Mrs. Dyer. 'Tis a beautiful day for shopping."

Sallie folded her parasol and stepped inside behind Mama. "Yes, it is, Mr. Brady. We've come for a look at your piece goods."

The balding man chuckled. "And I thought maybe you were here for more peppermints."

"Maybe later." Sallie hooked her arm through Jenny's. "Let's see what we can find back there." She led her friend to the shelves filled with bolts of rainbow-hued fabrics while Mama stayed in front and conversed with Mr. Brady.

The odor of dye in the fabrics caused Sallie to sneeze. "Eww, some of these need washing before they're sewn up." She covered her nose with a lace handkerchief.

"They do for a fact." Jenny agreed then pulled down a fold of dark blue cotton. "This would make a suitable skirt for general wear."

Sallie shrugged. "I suppose it's alright. A little plain. What about this calico or the red and yellow plaid." She held out the corners for Jenny's inspection.

"I like the design, but I'd rather have it in dark blue. Red and yellow plaid is your best color, not mine." She reached up and pulled out a piece of blue and white plaid with a touch of yellow.

Sallie smiled. "Of course. Blue is much more suitable with your coloring."

Jenny nodded then added white lawn to her stack. She headed for the Godey's books, and Sallie followed to peer over her shoulder as Jenny flipped through the pages.

"There. That's the one I like. What do you think?" Jenny pointed to a skirt topped with a mid-arm-length sleeve shirt-waist with a plain collar and buttons down the front.

"Hmm, yes, I do like that. Shouldn't take long for Mrs.

Tenney to make either." Sallie took the bundle of fabric from Jenny. "Don't you want one a little fancier too?"

"No, this will be quite nice for now. I have the lavender silk for special occasions." Jenny retrieved a slip of paper from her pocket and picked up a nearby pencil to note the page number to give to Mrs. Tenney.

Sallie eyed the braids and buttons on display and selected several. Jenny stopped by her side and added a length of blue braid to the stack of goods.

Sallie smiled. Seeing her friend enjoy her shopping warmed her heart. Once Jenny had access to anything and everything she could ever want, but now she had to rely on others for their generosity and kindness. She silently thanked Papa and Grandpa for being so generous.

They moved away from the dry goods and into the general merchandise area. Sallie breathed in the earthy aroma of fresh vegetables mingled with the scent of lamp oil. "I love coming into the store. So many different delights to tickle my nose." She moved toward the candy jars.

Jenny placed her selections on the counter, and Mama picked out a few staples. Sallie stood by the candy jars, enjoying the sparkling colors and delightful scents. She glanced up to see a broad grin spread across Mr. Brady's face and heard Jenny suck in her breath.

A voice behind her spoke up. "I still think the cinnamons are the best."

Sallie's heart skipped a beat, and joy rose in her throat. Could it be? She whirled around to face the voice of her dreams and whispered, "Manfred, oh, Manfred, it *is* you." She took one step toward Manfred then leaped into his arms. "You're here! You're home!"

Manfred held her tightly. "Yes, it's me. I'm here, Sallie. I'm really here."

Suddenly Sallie drew back, remembering her proper behavior. She smoothed her skirts, and heat flooded her cheeks. "Oh, my. Excuse me." How could she have been so forward in front of everyone in the store?

Manfred's eyes twinkled, and his mouth curved in a smile. "Still my beautiful, spontaneous Sallie. You haven't changed at all." He reached for her hand.

Sallie glanced over his shoulder and locked gazes with Mama. With a broad grin and tears on her cheeks, Mama nodded her approval.

This time Sallie let Manfred take her hand and pull her gently to his side. She heard murmurs and greetings all around her, but her eyes saw only Manfred. She gazed into his brown eyes, and her heart filled with the love reflected there. So many days, weeks, and months she had waited for this moment, and now he stood by her side. Her heart beat a wild tempo she had no desire to still.

"Pardon, Miss Dyer."

A hand rested on her shoulder, and she turned to find Edwin behind her.

"I'm so thankful we found you. I don't think this brother of mine could have stood looking for you much longer." He grinned and winked at Manfred.

Sallie squeezed Edwin's hand. "I'm grateful you both are safe."

Customers in the store crowded around, but Manfred didn't let go of her hand. Nathan Brady clasped Manfred's shoulder. "Hello, my friend."

The look passing between the two young men said what their words didn't. Sallie swallowed the lump in her throat and blinked back tears. Oh, what they must have endured in the months past. As if reading her thoughts, Manfred gripped her hand reassuringly and smiled down at her.

Nathan said, "I want to hear all about your journey."

"Speaking of which." Edwin laid a paper-wrapped bundle on the counter. "Mr. Brady, I've brought a gift from Mrs. Brady's sister in Alabama. They gave us shelter in a storm some days back."

Mr. Brady's hands trembled as he touched the parcel. "Nathan, run home and get Ma. We have a gift from Mattie."

The young man bolted through the door. Mr. Brady said, "This will mean so much to Ma. Thank you both."

Moments later Mrs. Brady rushed through the door. "You have something from Mattie?" She snatched up the package Mr. Brady held out to her.

She tore into the bundle and ripped away the paper. A moment later she shook out the brightly colored quilt for all to see. "Oh my, it's the quilt she made of pieces from clothes we wore as children." Her eyes glistened.

First she hugged Edwin then Manfred. "You two brought this? Oh, thank you, thank you."

Manfred tugged at a piece of paper in his pocket. "Here's a letter from her too."

Mattie's hand covered her mouth, and she reached for the paper. She read it and clasped it to her chest, joy filling her countenance.

Sallie blinked back her own tears of joy and thanksgiving. What a wonderful moment to savor and remember. Not even the shadow of her past could mar this moment beside Manfred.

Manfred gazed at Sallie with a crooked grin—the grin that had graced her dreams. He spoke to Mrs. Brady. "It has been a pleasure delivering this news to you, but Miss Dyer and I have some things to discuss." He led Sallie toward the door. "If you'll excuse us, ladies, I'll be walking her home."

Sallie glanced back to see Mama and Jenny and several others huddled around Mrs. Brady, admiring the quilt.

With the pressure of Manfred's hand clutching hers, Sallie wanted to skip, laugh, cry, and shout all at once. The sky shone a brighter blue with Manfred beside her. She matched his slow gait and contained her impulses, letting her insides do the rejoicing.

"How did you know where to find me?" Her heart danced with delight, and she couldn't take her eyes from his face lest he might disappear and she discovered this to be a dream.

"I spoke with your father in Woodville. He told me you were with the Woodruffs. Then when I arrived at the house, you were out, and Lettie told me to check at Mr. Brady's."

He stopped and turned to stand face-to-face with her. "Contrary to what Edwin said, if you had not been at the store, I would have torn St. Francisville apart to find you."

Sallie whispered, "Oh, Manfred, I love you and have worried so about you."

"I wish you could have been spared the agony of not knowing."

His grin captivated her again as it had so often in the past. "I always hoped you would return, and now here you are." The pressure of his hand on hers filled her with delight as they continued their walk to the Woodruff home.

Sallie glanced back and spotted Mama and Jenny following, both smiling like children on Christmas morning. To Sallie, this was Christmas, Easter, and her birthday all rolled into one glorious day.

At the house they sat in the wicker chairs on the wide veranda. Manfred said, "I remember the last time we were here. It's where I've pictured you so many times in the past months."

Suddenly the door swung open, and Grandma rushed

out, followed by Hannah, who grasped Manfred around the waist and hugged him. Grandma reached across and kissed Manfred on the cheek.

Manfred unwrapped Hannah's arms from his middle and stood back to peer at her. "Why, Miss Hannah. You're quite the young lady now. Growing up to be as pretty as your sister."

Hannah straightened her shoulders and stood tall, and her cheeks blossomed apple red. Sallie laughed. Manfred had not lost any of his charm.

Jenny and Mama joined them, and Sallie listened to their chatter with amusement and patience. As much as she wanted to be alone with him, she willingly shared his homecoming.

Mama clapped her hands. "Enough of this. Edwin told me you haven't been to your home yet. I know how anxious your mother is to see you. You'll be a wonderful surprise. I do offer an invitation for your family to join us here for dinner tomorrow evening. We'll have a joyous celebration."

Grandma placed her hands on Hannah's shoulders. "Let's go in and leave these two to say good-bye." The young girl trailed after Grandma and Mama, but looked back at Manfred and Sallie with longing in her eyes.

Alone again, Manfred grasped Sallie's hands and brought them to his lips. He stared at her, and his eyes bore straight to her soul.

His words were a whisper. "You are even more beautiful than I remember. When I return, I have an important matter to discuss. Until then, know my heart is completely yours." His head bent forward and his lips met hers. Breath caught in her throat, and for a moment she didn't respond. Then her arms went around his neck, and she returned the kiss with all the fervor she'd bottled up for so many months. Moments later they broke apart. With one last smile Manfred dropped a kiss on her fingers before he bounded down the porch steps. He stopped and pulled something from his pocket. "I almost forgot."

He returned to the porch and handed her a folded piece of paper. "This is a letter from a young woman we met at the beginning of our journey. She thought her husband was dead, but we met him on our journey, and he was on his way home to her. She asked me to give you this." With a last peck on her cheek, he trotted out to the road where Edwin had arrived with their horse.

Sallie collapsed into a chair and drew her hand to her lips. Such behavior would be frowned upon in ordinary circumstances, but these were anything but ordinary. She stared after the two figures until they disappeared down the hill leading down to Bayou Sara. The paper crackled in her hand. She unfolded it and read Rachel's praises for Manfred and Edwin and their help at the farm. Rachel then wished Sallie and Manfred a long and happy marriage. Sallie dropped the letter to her lap. The dark shadow of her past returned with a vengeance, and she sucked in her breath before exhaling. A shudder shook her shoulders, and her hands trembled against her mouth. What would Manfred think of her once he knew what she had done?

❧

Manfred whistled "Dixie" and quickened his pace as the landing came into view. Edwin slapped Lady's rump with his hat and let out a rebel yell. The horse galloped down the slope with the young man waving his arm and shouting. Manfred raced after him whooping and hollering.

Ma ran out the door wiping her hands on her apron with

Bessie close behind. Manfred watched her face light up like a full moon when she realized who came barreling toward her.

"Pa, come quick," she shouted as she scurried toward them.

Edwin slid off the horse and grabbed Ma. Pa rushed from the dock with Theo and Charles behind him. He enveloped Manfred in a bear hug. No words were needed. After a moment Pa released him, and Manfred turned to gather Ma into his arms.

With a boy on each side Ma cried, "My last two are home. Thank You, Lord, thank You."

Several workmen joined in the greeting. They bombarded Manfred with questions while Edwin talked with Pa. Finally, with his arm and Edwin's linked into hers, Ma led her returning sons into the house.

Home cooking had never smelled better. The aroma of chicken, potatoes, beans, and fresh-baked bread filled the house and set his stomach to growling. But just then he spotted a lone figure in the shadows of the parlor corner.

Henry, his brother, nodded. Manfred gasped. What had happened to Henry's hair? Once dark as the night, it now shone snow white, and his young countenance bore the signs of a man much older in age.

Manfred locked gazes with his brother, but Henry's eyes gazed back as empty as the windows Manfred had seen in deserted buildings. What had happened to rob Henry of his youth and zest for life? He stepped toward Henry, but his brother slipped away and closed a door behind him. Manfred would have to wait for any answers.

"Hmm, sorry, Ma, what did you say?"

"Did you stop by to see Sallie Dyer before coming here?"

Heat rose in his cheeks. "Yes, I did. I couldn't wait another minute to see her."

"I understand, son. True love must be fulfilled."

He hugged her. "Thank you for understanding. Oh, and Mrs. Dyer sent an invitation for us to come to dinner tomorrow evening. It's short notice, but I do hope you'll accept."

Ma's hands flew to her cheeks. "Oh, my. Dear Amanda. Of course we'll accept. But now I must be getting our supper ready." She took one last longing look at her boys before hurrying from the room.

Manfred left the conversations behind him and sought out Henry. He found his brother in a bedroom. "I wanted to let you know I understand why you may not want to be with the others, but I'd like to talk a bit."

Slumped in a chair near the window with his chin resting on his chest, Henry said nothing. Manfred leaned against the bedpost. "We've had a rough year, but can you tell me what happened to cause your sadness?"

When he gave no answer, Manfred knelt beside him. "I killed Yankees not much older than I am and watched my own comrades fall. Edwin and I survived months in a filthy prison, nearly starving in the process. But all the time I had faith God would take care of us."

Henry raised blank eyes to Manfred. "It was wrong. The whole thing was wrong. What we did…what they did…It was wrong."

Manfred said nothing. He could only imagine the horrors Henry must have witnessed. He squeezed his brother's hand. "You don't need to tell me now, but maybe someday…" Manfred grasped Henry's shoulder before leaving the room.

To avoid the group in the parlor, he slipped around to the front of the house. New lumber in the dock and shipping office building offered evidence of repairs. The river slapped against the wood of the pier and gently rocked a steamboat loaded with cotton and cane. Old, familiar sights and sounds soothed his mind. Tomorrow he'd ask Sallie to marry him, and together they would build a new life and a new South, one where men would be brothers in love and unity instead of brothers in arms.

CHAPTER 26

MANFRED HAD SENT word that he planned to rest and visit with his family for the day, so Sallie decided to spend the time helping Mama and Grandma with the dinner plans for the evening. Papa brought in a ham from the smokehouse, and Sallie helped Lettie prepare yams for Flora's sweet potato pie.

She rehearsed over and over again how she would tell Manfred about what had happened in Woodville. Nothing she said sounded right. Finally she blew out her breath in a huff. "Lettie, I can't figure out how to tell Manfred what I did in Woodville. I'm afraid he will be appalled and think less of me."

"Miss Sallie, he loves you with all his heart, so he'll understand. If he doesn't, then his love isn't worth a penny."

Her words sounded reassuring, but doubt still plagued Sallie's heart. Still, she'd tell the truth. Grandma always said truth was the way to tell anything that needed saying. Her knife scraped away the peel of a potato.

When the heat rose in the afternoon, Sallie retired to her room to rest, but she could not relax. Jenny sat on the edge of the bed with Sallie.

"I can see you're restless and disturbed, my friend. What troubles you?"

"What I'm to tell Manfred about what I did. I must do it tonight to keep us from starting a new phase of our relationship with secrets between us."

"Yes, you must, but don't worry. He'll forgive you because God has forgiven you."

When Sallie didn't raise her head, Jenny grabbed her shoulders. "Sallie, you do know you're forgiven by our heavenly Father? Look at how He's taken care of us and protected us during these dark days."

"Has He, Jenny? How is letting me kill a man, taking away your home and father and brother, and then allowing you to be treated as you were protecting us? I don't believe God really cares about us much, or none of that would have happened."

Jenny squeezed her shoulders. "Sallie, listen to me. He protected you by giving you the knowledge to use that gun. You could have been killed yourself. Yes, I realize it was a terrible thing to happen, but it got you safely out of the house and here with your grandparents. Then look how God sent that soldier to help me and then work it out so he was the dead soldier's brother and could claim him and take him back home."

The words bounced around in Sallie's head until they began to come together and make sense of her scrambled feelings. Manfred had come home safe and in good health, as had Edwin and Charles and Benjamin. Maybe God had been at work all that time, and she had been too blinded by the horror of the experience to see His loving hand at work in the midst of it.

The Lord still answered prayer, and He still loved those who had sinned, even her. A new realization hit her. If she didn't forgive herself, she was breaking the commandment to forgive as she had been forgiven.

"Sallie, are you listening to me?"

"Yes, I am, and it's all coming together. Instead of thanking God for His blessings, I've been blaming Him for all our bad times." She squeezed her eyes shut. "Oh, Lord, please forgive me for doubting You. I know I am Your child and You love me despite what I have done. Please help Manfred understand."

The first peace she'd felt in many months settled over her, and she could tell Manfred with the full knowledge that she was a forgiven child of God. She reached over and hugged her friend. "Thank you. Things are much clearer now. I can face Manfred without fear."

"Then let's get some rest so you'll be fresh and ready for what may prove to be a most memorable evening."

Later, as the dusk of evening fell, Sallie paced the floor in the foyer waiting for the clatter of carriage wheels or the pounding of horses' hooves against the ground. Finally the sounds she wanted to hear came from the drive. She yanked open the door and ran outside to find Manfred hitching his horse. She drew to a breathless halt at his side.

"I've been watching for you. I thought maybe you'd forgotten about this evening."

Manfred chuckled and finished looping the mare's reins around the hitching post. "Did you now?" He reached for her hand and drew it to his lips. "Your hands are like icicles on a winter morning. Were you really worried I wouldn't come back tonight?"

Sallie nodded then shifted her gaze downward. "Yes, even though your mother accepted Mama's invitation. I guess...oh, I don't know. I'm just glad you're here."

Drawing her to his side, he guided her up the steps to the chairs on the porch. "I came a little early to talk with you. My folks will be along shortly. My thoughts have been only on you all day."

Sallie's heart beat at staccato rhythm, and her hands trembled in Manfred's. The time had come to share her experience with him. She trusted God now to give her courage and the words to say.

"Something is troubling you. I see it in your eyes. If your feelings for me have changed and you're not sure of our relationship, I do understand."

"Oh, no, that hasn't changed at all." A stabbing pain pushed back the joy welling in her. She had to tell him what she had done.

Manfred squeezed her hand. "What is it, Sallie?"

She bit her lip then turned her gaze to his. "Oh, Manfred. I've done something so horrid. I must tell you, then if you feel the same…"

He gathered her into his arms and cradled her head against his shoulder. One hand held her close while the other stroked her hair. "You could do nothing to disappoint me. I love you with all my being. You don't need to tell me anything, but if you must, then I am here to listen, not to condemn."

The quiet words calmed the churning in her stomach but didn't release the fear in her heart. She pushed back from him and folded her hands in her lap. After a moment she moistened her lips. Manfred must understand the desperation of her act and the pain that filled her even now.

"Early in the spring, Yankee troops marched across Mississippi and into Woodville. On their way to the river they attacked and ransacked the Harper home." She paused with the words to the next part lodging in her throat. She squeezed her eyes shut, swallowed hard, and plunged ahead.

"Then they came into the town and attacked around the town square. Papa and our neighbors put up a fight, and the fighting and shooting came close to our house, so Papa sent all us women down to the cellar. He, Will, Tom, and the other men joined in defending our homes."

Manfred gasped and grabbed her hands. "You must have been terrified."

Her breathing sped up, and tears misted her eyes. "We were. Papa gave me his shotgun and a small handgun."

Images of that day in April tumbled into her mind one after the other. "I don't know how long we stayed downstairs. We had only a small glow from a lantern and were afraid to even move about in case someone heard. Mama whispered Bible verses to calm our fears."

The more she revealed, the easier the words came until the whole story tumbled forth. She sat back with her heart hammering in her chest and waited for Manfred's reaction.

Manfred's mouth worked from a pucker to a frown to a grimace. "How horrible for you. Killing someone is the hardest thing to face. I hated every time I pulled a trigger, but it's the only way we can survive at times." He pulled her close to his chest again.

Sallie wept and tears stained his jacket. "Oh, Manfred, he was just a young soldier, no older than I am. He had that loaf of bread, and..." A sob escaped her throat. "He was just a boy looking for food. Manfred, I killed a boy. And then another one came in with a gun pointed at us, and I fired again. This time I hit his shoulder and he ran back outside."

"I'm so sorry, Sallie. You should never have had to face such a situation." Manfred kissed her forehead and held her close. "You did what you had to do under the circumstances. I'm so sorry you had to see and experience such a horrible thing, but I'm thankful you and your family are now safe."

Sallie drew back and peered at Manfred's face in the shadows. "Can you still love me, knowing I killed one man and wounded another?"

He brushed a tear from her cheek. "Sallie, remember, I

too killed in this war. The only difference is I was expected to. What you did happened all over the country as men and women defended themselves."

"Killing is awful. To take another's life is sin. God said not to commit murder, and I did. I've prayed and prayed, and finally feel He has forgiven me, but can you?"

Manfred whispered, "Dear, sweet Sallie. If God has forgiven you, who am I not to do the same? I love you just as our Father loves you."

They sat in silence for a few moments, and peace once again filled Sallie's heart and soul.

"Sallie, I didn't intend to do this right now, but it may be the best time. I've already spoken with your father, and now I'm asking you. Will you marry me?"

The words she longed to hear for so many months now filled her heart to overflowing.

"I'm not the same innocent girl you left last year, but I love you, and yes, I will marry you."

He gathered her into his arms and held her close to his chest. "No, you're no longer a young girl. But you are a stronger woman because you defended your home in time of need. All of us have been deeply affected by what we experienced in the last few years. We can only pray that God will somehow use it for good."

His steady heartbeat and tight embrace brought peace to her tormented heart. "I pray so, Manfred. I pray so. Thank you for loving me and understanding me."

"How could I do less?" He paused then leaned away from her to gaze into her eyes. "You and I must do what we can to make a difference. The South will have to rebuild and be restored, and we must see it is done with love, hope, and faith in God."

Even in the twilight the beauty of Sallie's red hair, fair complexion, and the spattering of freckles shone brighter than the waning sun. The face he'd seen only in his dreams for many months had not changed, but she had become a woman who could face the uncertainty of the future by his side. No matter what her burdens, he'd help her bear them with his love.

He pulled her to her feet and bent his head to capture her lips in a kiss that sealed their love and their future together. As the kiss deepened, Manfred fought the longings that had built in his heart for so many months. Finally he broke away and stood back.

"It's up to those of us who survived to make sure our home is stronger and better than it was before, and we must do it without infringing on the rights of others."

Pure joy sparkled in Sallie's eyes, a joy springing from the depths of her soul. "You've always been so tender and kind, Manfred. I will be so proud to be your wife and work beside you. The things we have experienced have taught us to love life and live to do good for others."

"At least I can do my part in helping to rebuild and grow. Pa told us at dinner last night that your grandfather has kept my inheritance from Grandma Whiteman safe. That means I'll be able to finish my time with Doc and then set up my own practice when he retires."

Sallie hugged him. "I'm so proud of you. You'll be such a marvelous doctor."

"And you don't mind if we live here in St. Francisville? Won't you miss your home in Woodville?"

"Oh, Manfred, my home is wherever you are. I can't

imagine being anywhere else except by your side. I'd follow you wherever you want to go."

Manfred stood and drew her close, and the rapid beating of his heart matched hers. Oh, what a wonderful future they would have. He caressed Sallie's hair, his heart bursting with love. To think this beautiful young woman would be his wife. He didn't want to wait any longer to make it happen. He held Sallie by the shoulders and raised his head toward heaven with a whoop and holler. Then he took her hands and whirled her around, laughing and singing.

Her parents, grandparents, Hannah, Jenny, and his family all flew through the door and spilled onto the porch. Manfred stopped short. "How did you get here, Ma? Where have you been?" He kept hold of Sallie, and they stood hand in hand, beaming.

Ma smiled. "We drove up and saw you two up here in earnest conversation, so we went around to the back and went into the house from there. Jenny has been standing nearby to let us know what was going on."

Sallie grabbed Jenny. "Were you eavesdropping, my friend?"

Jenny laughed. "Not really. I simply checked for the right time for us all to make an appearance."

Hannah jumped up and down, clapping her hands. "We were beginning to think you'd never stop talking!"

Manfred bent and grabbed her around the waist and lifted her into the air. "Oh, you did, did you? How do you think you'll like being my little sister?"

He set her back down, and Hannah grinned. "I think it'll be grand. Sallie is so lucky."

Laughter bubbled forth, and he glanced over to see Sallie accepting hugs from her mother, grandmother, and Jenny. A hand grasped his shoulder.

"Congratulations, my boy. You'll be a welcome addition to this family." The elder Mr. Woodruff, with a firm grip, shook his hand.

"Thank you, Mr. Woodruff. And I must also thank you for watching over my inheritance. It means much to me to know I'll be able to continue with my plans to one day have my own medical practice." Without his grandmother's inheritance, his future as a doctor would have been almost impossible.

"It pleases me to know you'll use yours wisely. Your grandmother Whiteman was a generous, loving woman."

Manfred nodded. "She was, and I'm thankful she passed this life before seeing the ravages of war in her beloved Southland." His grandmother's love for people had instilled in him the desire to become a healer. He planned to make her proud.

Mrs. Dyer clasped her hands to her chest. "It's time to plan a wedding. We must make arrangements for a place and food, and... oh, goodness me... there's so much to do."

Manfred grabbed Sallie's hand. "Do you think it can be done in a few weeks?"

Sallie gasped then laughed. "Yes, the sooner the better, before the weather becomes too warm. I like the idea of June for our wedding."

Both mothers' mouths dropped open and their eyes widened. Mrs. Dyer then frowned. "I'm not sure we can do it that quickly." She glanced at Ma. "What do you think, Harriet? It will mean a lot of work."

Behind them Mrs. Woodruff waved a hand in the air. "We can do it. Abigail will help, as will her cook."

Sallie hugged her mother. "Oh, Mama, you'll have it all arranged and beautiful no matter when or where it is." She reached over and entwined her fingers with his. "All that matters is Manfred and I will be together for the rest of our lives."

"Then we'll make it the best wedding for you. Let's see, what date will you choose?"

Sallie glanced at him then back to her mother. "I think June fifteenth will be perfect."

Mrs. Dyer gasped then beckoned to her mother. "That's next week! Come, we have work to do."

She reached over and herded her children back into the house. "It's time for our young couple to make some plans of their own." Mrs. Dyer grinned and raised her eyebrows toward her husband and Mr. Woodruff.

Everyone reentered the house, but Ma went last with a word to them both. "Don't dawdle out here too long. Dinner is being served as I speak, and yours will get cold."

A cold dinner wouldn't bother him at all with the warmth of love flowing through him. All the words he'd stored inside for all these many months became lost in the joy of knowing Sallie would be his forever.

He grabbed her hands and pulled her to his chest. "The rest of our lives. Sounds pretty good to me."

"This is the happiest day of my life so far. The best one will be when we stand before the minister and say our vows."

"I want to give you a ring as a symbol of our love, but that may have to wait."

Sallie laid her head against his chest. "I don't need a ring. All I need is you."

He reached down to lift her chin and gaze into her eyes. "You're all I need too." Their lips came together to seal their love with a kiss that sent a flood of desire washing through his body once again. Sallie lifted her arms and wrapped them around his neck to deepen the kiss.

A minute or so later, she stepped back, breathless and

flushed. "Manfred Whiteman, I've dreamed of this moment for so long, and it's everything I dreamed it to be and more."

As much as he desired to stay here on the porch with her in his arms, that would not be the wisest thing to do for either of them at the moment. "I think we best join your family and have dinner before we…well, we should go in." He no longer trusted himself to be alone with her. He needed time to get his emotions under control.

Her eyes blinked and her throat worked itself in a deep swallow. "Yes, we should."

They grasped hands and headed for the door, but Manfred stopped short as an idea took form in his head. He remembered the gold coin his grandmother had given him on his sixteenth birthday. Perhaps it could be melted down for a ring. "Sallie, I just thought of something. I do have a way to get you a ring for our wedding. Charles and I will go down to Baton Rouge and take care of it. You won't be disappointed." He kissed her fingertips. "I love you with all my heart and soul, and I've waited so many months to tell you. Thoughts of you strengthened me and kept me alive, and finally brought me home."

She peered up at him with eyes so full of her love he could drown in them. His arms went around her and pulled her close. She lifted her head as he bent his and their lips met in another kiss that said everything he held in his heart. And in that moment the dreadful past fell away, and their future together appeared as bright and promising as the dawn of a new day.

AUTHOR'S NOTE

A NUMBER OF YEARS ago my father gave me a packet of letters belonging to my great-grandmother Sarah Louise Dyer Whiteman. Those letters sparked my interest in genealogy and led to this story. In my family research I found wills, marriage licenses, baptismal records, death records, and books with information about the Whiteman and Dyer family line. Other information about them came from my grandfather and great-aunt Alice's memories of their parents and from parts of a journal from that time. Although this story is loosely based on the love story of Sarah Louise Dyer and Manfred MacDaniel Whiteman, many incidents taken from letters and notes from journals have been expanded and fictionalized to complete the story. Real names have been used for many of the characters. And while this first book is based on the facts we have on our family at that time, we are still gleaning information for the following years. Therefore books 2 and 3 in this series are strictly fiction.

Sallie Dyer and Manfred Whiteman met in St. Francisville, Louisiana, when she visited her grandparents there. I am not sure of their ages at the time, but I do know it was before the war and that Manfred had shown affection for Sallie just prior to his leaving to join the Confederate Army in 1861. In a letter Manfred mentions seeing her before he left to rejoin his regiment in the summer of 1864. I used an excerpt of that letter in the story as the one he sends to Sallie to declare his love for her. The wedding ring Manfred had made from a twenty-dollar gold piece is still in the family. It was passed down to their youngest son, Thomas Dyer Whiteman, and has been used in several wedding ceremonies of family members since then.

Manfred's father, John Whiteman, owned a shipping company at Bayou Sara on the Mississippi River down the hill from St. Francisville, Louisiana. I've been down to the river that now covers the old settlement of Bayou Sara and found a map of the former town and the location of the company. Both black men and white men helped load the ships coming into the port at Bayou Sara, but none of the documents showed any slaves being owned by the shipping company.

Manfred came from a family of five boys. His brother Henry came home from the POW camp with snow-white hair and died a little over a year later. His story has been passed down through the generations. Although Manfred moved to Texas, his remaining three brothers stayed in the St. Francisville area, married, and had families. Most of them are buried at Grace Church in St. Francisville.

Sallie's father, Thomas Dyer, was a cotton merchant in Woodville, Mississippi, about twenty-five miles north of St. Francisville. As a businessman, Thomas Dyer used hired hands to handle the cotton sales. I found one of his letters to Sallie when she went to finishing school in New Orleans before the war; it reveals that he regarded women with high esteem and he wished her well in her endeavors to become whatever she chose in life. Sallie's maternal grandfather was known as Judge Woodruff, so I assumed he must have been a lawyer. None of Sallie's family owned slaves at the time of the war. Sallie's grandmother, Mary Woodruff, had two housekeepers, and from their ages I assumed they were sisters, but I made them mother and daughter in the story and put them in Sallie's household.

In this story I have included real towns and actual events

from the war, such as the attacks on Grace Episcopal Church during the battle of Port Hudson in 1863; the day the war stopped for a Masonic burial at that church on June 12, 1863; Susan Allen putting out fires to save the covered bridge in Marion, Virginia, in December 1864; and the deplorable conditions at the prisoner of war camp in Point Lookout, Maryland.

Manfred returned to St. Francisville from Point Lookout with his brother Edwin in June of 1865 and married Sallie that same June. He became a doctor and stayed in Louisiana until 1880, when he moved to Texas with his family to practice medicine in Victoria, Texas. That move became a part of the tree that formed the future and led to my being a fifth-generation Texan.

Coming in January 2014
from Martha Rogers...

Love Finds Faith

CHAPTER 1

WHERE WERE SALLIE and Manfred? They were supposed to meet her here at the station. Manfred she could understand, as doctors had emergencies arise all the time, but her sister, Sallie, didn't have such an excuse.

Hannah Dyer patted her damp brow with a handkerchief and tapped her good foot on the wooden platform where moments before she had stepped down from the afternoon train. She breathed in and then exhaled in a puff of air. The train whistle blew, and others now boarded the train. Waving away the soot in the air, she hobbled over to the luggage cart. Her baggage sat neatly stacked, ready to be picked up.

Mercy, the men had already unloaded the baggage car. Sallie should have been here by now. Resisting the urge to sit on her trunk, Hannah stood with her weight on her good left leg, resting the toe of her heavy, thick-soled boot on the platform. No matter how hard the cobbler tried when making her special shoes, her legs were never quite the same length, and the shoe for her shorter leg was always heavy and cumbersome. Even this new pair gave her an awkward gait as she walked.

Someone shouted her name, and Hannah shaded her eyes against the sun to find Sallie pulling up with a wagon. She hopped down, picked up her baby, and ran to Hannah.

"Oh, my, I'm so sorry. I couldn't get the children together, and Manfred is delivering Mrs. Fairchild's baby, and..." She

271

stopped to stare at the trunk and other bags. "Goodness, is all that yours? How will we ever get it into the wagon?"

"I'll be glad to help you with it, Mrs. Whiteman. That is, if you'll introduce me to the lovely young lady here."

Hannah turned her head to gaze into the warmest brown eyes she'd seen since leaving Mississippi. The speaker removed his light tan cowboy hat and grinned at her.

Sallie shifted her baby onto her hip. Her brow furrowed and she bit her lip. "Micah Gordon, I didn't know you had come home."

"Just got in. I was on the same train with this young lady."

"Oh, goodness me. Micah, this is my sister, Hannah Grace Dyer. She's come from Mississippi to help the doctor as his nurse. Hannah, this is Micah Gordon. His father has one of the larger horse ranches around these parts. Um...he's...he's been gone awhile."

Hannah smiled at the cowboy. His boots, hat, tan shirt, and string tie fit him perfectly, and she had to raise her head to meet his gaze. Funny she didn't remember seeing him on the train. Certainly she would have noticed this handsome face. Heat rose in her cheeks. "It's very nice of you to offer to help with the baggage."

He picked up two of the valises. "I take it you want them in the wagon over there, Mrs. Whiteman."

"Yes, yes, of course." Sallie scurried back to the wagon and the two children there.

Six-year-old Clara said nothing but stared with clear blue eyes at the aunt she most likely didn't remember. On the other hand, eleven-year-old Molly stood with hands on her hips in the bed of the wagon. "Auntie Hannah, it's about time you got here. I've been waiting and waiting for you to come."

Even at a young age Molly showed signs of the beauty her mother possessed. Two stiff plaits held her red hair in check, but still strands and wisps escaped to frame Molly's heart-shaped face and blue-green eyes. Hannah crossed to the wagon trying to minimize the awkwardness of her gait so her heavy shoe didn't thump on the hardwood platform.

"I'm so glad I'm finally here too, Molly. You've grown so much since your last visit to Mississippi." She hadn't grown but an inch or so, but Hannah remembered how much she liked to hear such praise when she'd been Molly's age. Sure enough, a wide grin split Molly's face.

Hannah waved her hand toward the trunk. "I brought everyone gifts from Mama and Papa. They wanted to come, but Papa said it was too far right now. They'll try to come for Christmas." She cast her gaze to Micah, who handled the trunk with ease. Such broad shoulders he had. No wonder her bags and trunk presented no problem for him.

Micah stepped back and swiped his hands together. "There now, it looks like you're all set for the ride, Mrs. Whiteman."

"Thank you, Micah. I'm glad you decided to come home. Your ma and pa are going to be so happy to see you." She patted Hannah on the back. "You go ahead and climb up, then I'll hand Daniel up to you."

Hannah stared at the wagon wheel. How did one get up to the seat? Sallie had used the wheel to step down, but where was a foothold? She might balance on her heavier boot and step up with her good one, but what if she lost her balance? At home they'd always ridden in a carriage with a stepstool to help. She bit her lip as a hand landed on her arm.

"Here, let me assist you, Miss Dyer. If you're not used to wagons, they can be difficult to maneuver." Micah offered one hand for support and pointed to the wheel with the other one. "Put your foot right there, and I'll boost you up."

"Oh, dear Hannah," Sallie said. "I'm so sorry. I didn't even think how difficult it might be for you to climb up on a wagon. Thank you, Micah."

Hannah had no choice but to pick up her skirt with one hand and set her normal foot on the little projection that jutted out from the wheel. Once her foot hit the wheel, Micah's hands went around her waist to hoist her up to the seat. *Thunk!* Her heavy boot hit the side of the wagon and she almost lost her balance. She glanced down at Micah only to find him wide-eyed, staring at her feet.

His facial expression was no different than all the others when they first saw her ugly shoes. Her words wanted to stay lodged in her throat, but she forced them out. "Thank you, Mr. Gordon. I'm all right now."

He stepped back and shook his head, pity lacing his brown eyes that had been smiling and friendly only minutes earlier. Hannah bit her lip again. Why couldn't people just see her and who she was inside and not look only at her deformity? Stoney Creek would be no different than all the other places she'd been. She might as well have stayed in Mississippi with Mama and Papa or in Louisiana with Grandma Woodruff. At least there people knew of her disability and had stopped shaking their heads with pity over it.

Sallie handed baby Daniel up to Hannah then sprang up onto the wagon seat with little or no effort. Would Hannah ever be able to move like that? So far she hadn't, but maybe here she'd have more opportunity to exercise and be less of a cripple. She'd endured stares and ridicule for all of her twenty-four years of living, so she'd manage with them in Stoney Creek as well.

Sallie flicked the reins and the wagon moved away. Hannah so wanted one last look at Micah, but as much as she desired to see his handsome face, she had no desire to see pity there. "Micah seemed like a nice young man. You say he lives on a ranch?"

"Yes, Micah's been gone for the past five years. Told his pa he was tired of ranching and wanted to see what else life had to offer, from what I've heard. I do believe there was much more to it than that, but I didn't pry or listen to gossip. I hope he's come back to make amends with his pa. Both his parents grieved terribly when he left. Broke some young ladies' hearts too."

A prodigal and rogue. How intriguing. Of course he'd have the girls pursuing him with his handsome face and those penetrating eyes. Not likely she'd have a chance with him after he'd seen her foot. That sent most young men the opposite direction right away.

She moved her skirt a bit and stared down at the special shoe that helped her stand straight. The shoes she'd worn as long as she could remember now became a burden she didn't want to bear. If only she could be normal, she might attract a young man and marry and have a family like Sallie. Still, God had been good in not letting the problem keep her from pursuing her dream of becoming a nurse. She hugged little Daniel to her chest. Instead of feeling sorry for herself, her heart should be full of thanksgiving for this opportunity to help her family.

Her sister chattered on about the town and those who lived there, but Hannah only half listened. She'd come here for a purpose. Manfred needed help with his medical practice, and she'd be the best nurse he'd ever had. If God wanted to send along a young man for her, then He would. But it would certainly be nice if that young man happened to be as handsome as Micah Gordon.

Micah stood in the middle of the street to gaze after the wagon stirring up dust as it headed for the doctor's home. Such a beautiful young woman to be burdened with a deformity like that. Golden hair framed a face set off by eyes so blue they defied a color description. Not that it should matter, because courting a cripple didn't come into his plans for his future.

What that future might be remained his number one concern at the moment. Those who'd known him before would think he'd been up to no good after the way he'd left town, and they'd be right. He had spent too much time and money on women and fun in the past five years. After hitting rock bottom, he had no place to go but home, but to come home begging was not an option he had wanted to face.

He'd finally pulled himself out of the muck and mire a few months ago and found a job cleaning the livery stable in a small town. When the livery owner had trouble keeping track of his money and who had paid what, Micah discovered he had a good head for arithmetic and numbers and took on the bookkeeping for the livery. The man had upped Micah's wages but not changed his job. If Micah had to muck stalls, he could do that just as well at home. So once he had enough money saved up for the journey, he headed for home.

As much as he hated ranching, here he was back seeking forgiveness from his parents and a chance to prove himself useful on the ranch. Of course he'd never be in complete charge of it. That job belonged to Levi someday, not the prodigal returning home.

Micah headed for the hotel to get a room for the night. After he cleaned up, he could still make it out to the ranch in time for supper. A good shave wouldn't hurt either. A glance up and down the main street revealed not much had changed. The bank and general store still sat across from each other on opposite corners, and the hotel stood in the middle of the next block. A larger building across from the station bore a painted sign declaring the building to be Brunson's Livery and Black Smith. Old Willy Brunson must have hired a smithy since Willy didn't have the strength it took for that job. If his father didn't welcome him home, perhaps he could find work with Willy at the livery until something better came along.

A midsummer afternoon on a weekday drew few people into town. Most would be at home resting or escaping the heat. The few who walked along the boardwalk stared at Micah then nodded, but no one showed real signs of recognizing him. That didn't surprise him since he was taller and more filled out than he had been as a wayward son leaving home. At twenty-four, he had become a man.

When Micah opened the door to the hotel, the clerk looked up, and a grin spread across his face. "Well, now, if it ain't Micah Gordon. Good to see you. What's it been? Three or four years?"

Micah laughed and dropped his valise to the floor. "More like five, Charlie. Got a room for me?"

Charlie swung the register around for Micah to sign. "Sure do, but ain't you going out to see your folks?"

"I am later, but I want to be in town tonight." He picked up the pen and signed his name on the book. No need to tell Charlie the real reason for not going home first. Without knowing how his parents would greet him, he figured staying in town was the better option, but he only had funds for a few nights. After that, he'd be back out on the streets again.

"Sure thing, Micah. Here's your key. Your room's at the

head of the stairs, then the second door to the right. Looks out over the street. It's one of our nicest rooms."

Micah gripped the key in his hand and bent to pick up his bag. Next thing in order after a good bath and shave would be renting a horse. That would go over big what with his pa having some of the best horses money could buy to run his ranch, but Micah wasn't at the ranch and had no horse here in town.

Charlie continued to grin and shake his head. "Can't believe it's really you. Your folks are going to be mighty proud to see you." Then his grin turned to a smirk. "Know a few young ladies who'll be glad to hear you're back too."

Micah shrugged and headed for the stairs. He doubted Charlie's last statement. The girls he'd known must surely be married by now with families of their own. Pretty women didn't stay single in a town like Stoney Creek where there were more than enough men for them.

After a bath and clean clothes, Micah was ready to face his parents and whatever future may be out there for him. Pa would say his oldest son needed to settle down, take over the ranch, and marry a nice young girl, but rounding up cattle and breaking horses wasn't on Micah's short list of things he wanted to do with his life. It hadn't made the long list either. Not that he didn't love horses, but he didn't want to spend all of his time on the back of one. However, he'd do whatever it took now to regain Pa's trust and convince him that his oldest son's interests and talents lay in business, not cattle herding.

After one last glance at the mirror, Micah closed the bag with his few belongings in it. No need to unpack until he learned what kind of reception he'd receive at the ranch. He locked the door to his room and pocketed the key. May as well get the trip over with now.

Downstairs, Charlie greeted him again. "Hey, there, Micah, you clean up nice. Bet your sister will be happy to see you. Maggie, I mean Miss Margaret, is always talking about you when she comes into town."

"I'll be glad to see her too." So Margaret no longer wanted to be called Maggie. A smile creased his face. Just like his little sister to decide to use the longer version of her name. Maggie would be twenty now and been a young lady from the day of her birth, always helping Ma around the house.

His younger brother Levi loved the ranch and all that went with it. At twenty-two, Levi had more knowledge of the ranch than Micah would ever have. Levi should be the one inheriting everything, even though Micah was the oldest. Of course, Pa could have changed his will and given everything to Levi anyway. Micah shook his head. Here he was thinking on something that may not even be a problem anymore. Best concentrate on getting to see his family and nothing else.

He crossed the street to the livery, curious as to whom Willy had hired as blacksmith. He must be new in town because Micah didn't remember any boys with the strength of a smithy. Of course they could have grown up by now.

Willy greeted him with a huge grin splitting his face. "Why, if it ain't Micah Gordon. Didn't know you was coming home. Come on in, boy. You wantin' a horse? Where's Red Dawn?"

"Had to sell her, Willy, so now I need one to get out to the ranch." A clanging noise rang out from the back. "I see you've hired a smithy."

"Sure 'nuff have. Come on and meet him."

When Willy introduced the new smithy to Micah, his eyes opened wide, not at the size and strength of the man, but the color of his skin, dark as midnight. Micah stuck out his hand. "Good to meet you, Burt. This town sure needed a good blacksmith."

The man grinned, his white teeth in sharp contrast to the black surrounding them. "Good to meet you, Micah Gordon."

Willy led a horse to Micah. "Let me get this one saddled and you can ride out of here."

Burt grinned again. "He picked you out a good one. I put those shoes on him myself."

Micah grabbed the saddle and helped Willy finish up with getting the horse ready to ride. "Thanks, Willy. I'll have him back tomorrow if not tonight." Micah swung up into the saddle, tipped his hat, and turned his horse to the northwest and the road out of town.

The bank door across the street opened, and an older man and beautiful young woman stepped out. He recognized the man as Horace Swenson, the owner, but who was the young woman with him?

She turned toward him, and her smile froze on her lips. Her eyes opened wide and her hand grasped her throat.

Camilla Swenson. If not for that golden blonde hair and beautiful face, he'd never have recognized her, but she had recognized him right away. Camilla had grown up into a shapely young woman. Suddenly, returning to Stoney Creek became the best idea he'd ever had.

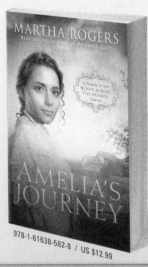

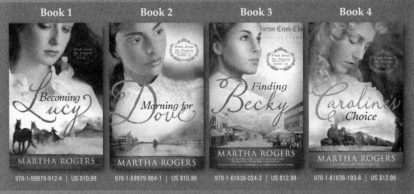

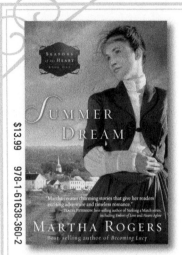
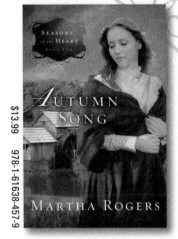

FREE NEWSLETTERS
TO HELP EMPOWER YOUR LIFE

Why subscribe today?

❑ **DELIVERED DIRECTLY TO YOU.** All you have to do is open your inbox and read.

❑ **EXCLUSIVE CONTENT.** We cover the news overlooked by the mainstream press.

❑ **STAY CURRENT.** Find the latest court rulings, revivals, and cultural trends.

❑ **UPDATE OTHERS.** Easy to forward to friends and family with the click of your mouse.

CHOOSE THE E-NEWSLETTER THAT INTERESTS YOU MOST:

- Christian news
- Daily devotionals
- Spiritual empowerment
- And much, much more

SIGN UP AT: **http://freenewsletters.charismamag.com**

8178